ULTIMATUM

LANDEG WHITE

INDEPENDENT INNOVATIVE INTERNATIONAL

Published by Cinnamon Press,
Meirion House
Tanygrisiau
Blaenau Ffestiniog
Gwynedd
LL41 3SU
www.cinnamonpress.com

The right of Landeg White to be identified as the author of this work has been asserted by him in accordance with the Copyright, Designs and Patent Act, 1988. © 2018 Landeg White.
ISBN 978-1-910836-91-0
British Library Cataloguing in Publication Data. A CIP record for this book can be obtained from the British Library.

Designed and typeset in Garamond by Cinnamon Press. Cover design by Adam Craig © Adam Craig.

Cinnamon Press is represented by Inpress and by the Welsh Books Council in Wales.

The publisher gratefully acknowledges the financial support of the The Welsh Books Council.

Printed in Poland.

Acknowledgements

Among a myriad of debts to the books and archival records of four countries, one is outstanding, both in respect of the facts and their interpretation, namely, Hugh Macmillan's meticulous analysis, 'The Origins and Development of the African Lakes Company, 1878-1908': Ph.D. thesis, University of Edinburgh, 1970.

To the two "Joãos", originally from Nazaré, captains of the molasses barges *Carla* and *Doddy* who, in July 1970, unaware of Portuguese colonial regulations, provided illegal but thrilling passage to Alice and myself up the Zambezi and Shire Rivers from Marromeu to Nchalo.

Ultimatum

Foreword

In January 1890, Britain threatened Portugal, her oldest ally, with an Ultimatum—infamous in Portugal, long forgotten in Britain. Abandon Africa, or at least the bits of south-east Africa the British coveted, or face a naval bombardment of Lisbon. The matter, declared Lord Salisbury, was non-negotiable. In dealing with lesser powers, the kindest course was to be brutal.

Over three centuries earlier, the poet Luís de Camões had described the region that was to be at issue:

> Behold the lake which is the Nile's source.
> And the green Zambezi, too, begins its course.

Camões was the poet who invented the idea of Portugal as a nation greater than its kings. Sentenced to exile as a common soldier, and coming from an Iberia where every town was walled and every substantial building had arrow-slit windows, what struck him most about southern Africa was the absence of fortifications:

> See how the Negroes' houses are like nests,
> Without doors, entirely confident
> Of royal justice and protection
> And the honesty of their neighbours.
>
> Look how their defence takes the novel form
> Of living without any defences.

These lines are from *The Lusíads*, his epic account of Vasco da Gama's pioneer voyage to India. To enter this region where 'love and humanity' prevailed in pastoral scenes such as are found in Virgil, Gama had sailed off the edge of the world. He had rounded the Cape of Storms, facing down Adamastor, the last of the ancient Titans, who warned him of multiple disasters to come, of whole fleets wrecked and their survivors murdered.

Adamastor neglected, however, to mention the Ultimatum.

The soldier poet Camões was no fool. He was well aware of different 'verdades', other sides to the story. Monomotapa's inland kingdom, with its walled capital at Great Zimbabwe, was one of those 'truths'. And he knew that Africa had other defences. Vasco da Gama describes losing half his crew at Quelimane in the Zambezi delta 'From a disease more cruel and loathsome / Than I ever before witnessed.' The symptoms described are those of scurvy.

Had Camões followed the great green river a little further upstream, halfway between the Portuguese settlements of Sena and Tete he would have encountered another delta, that of the Shire River where it joins the Zambezi. The Shire is a fast-flowing but mindlessly serpentine river. Ascending it is hard work. You can spend a whole day apparently travelling backwards, and end no further north than you began. A paddle steamer moves only marginally faster than a dugout canoe. Then over a hundred miles upstream as the fish eagle flies—it's three times that by boat—the mosquito-bitten traveller enters the vast swamp known to Europeans as Elephant Marsh and to Africans as Dambinyi.

It begins above Chiromo, a village at the junction of the Shire with its own tributary, the River Ruo. For three decades since David Livingstone's meanderings, the Ruo had marked, at least for the British, a *de facto* boundary between British and Portuguese spheres of influence. After Chiromo, the river divides into five channels. Three are as broad as the river you've been sailing on and they quickly lead into shallow watery wastes of pale blue lilies and purple hyacinths, where red-legged waders splash across floating palettes of leaves. Hippos surface with monstrous snuffles, yawning like pianos before submerging, leaving visible only their pink ears and nostrils.

You try again, taking one of the narrow channels with the plumed reeds slashing the upper deck on both sides. The muddy river runs fast and brown with tiny cabbages spinning in eddies. You are in a tunnel, the reeds bulky as sugar cane, grey spearheads closing above your head and overgrown with vines and creepers. The channel divides again, and the vegetation recedes. Suddenly, you can see for miles across a watery wilderness, from the Thyolo escarpment to the east to the Kirk range to the west, the bank only half a yard high, the muddy grass trampled with hippos' footprints. For the first time, you sense the scale of the maze you're lost in. Between November and April, when the Shire is replete with rain from the Highlands, the marsh covers some one-thousand-seven-hundred square miles, ending only at the small town of Chikwawa at the foot of the escarpment.

There are clumps of papyrus, their heads like enormous seed pods that have just exploded. There are monstrous baobabs, looking as though some Adamastor has ripped them up and replanted them upside down, their roots spreading in the heat. There are marabou storks, like coffins on stilts with beaks the size of pick axes. Every mud bank has a gang of crocodiles, their mouths gaping while tiny Egyptian plovers pick their teeth. A fever tree layered with the nests of fish eagles is eerily blanched with their guano. The air is thick with mosquitoes—as big as sparrows, as big as turkeys, as big as ostriches, said succeeding generations of travellers.

Out of nowhere, there's a group of five fishermen by a hut built of reeds, its roof covered with *chambo* or bream, slit open along their bellies, drying in the sun. Two dugout canoes are moored against the flat low bank. One of them contains fish traps, woven from reeds. Behind the hut is a clump of monkey bananas.

Minutes later, the scene has vanished behind another thick wall of reeds, and it seems impossible you really saw it. Where did the men come from? Do they really live there? The channel divides again and then again, disappearing completely as you enter a vast lake with no visible boundaries, the paddle-wheel churning up cabbage and hyacinth and the roots of water chestnuts. Every half hour, it becomes necessary to stop engines and clear the wheel slats. This is not a popular job. It involves wading in the swamp while two crewmen, leaning over the tap rail with their rifles, offer a feeble protection against crocodiles.

The pale sky is enormous, occupying seven-eighths of the waterscape, which seems crushed under its weight, sickening to sepia in the midday heat. The nearest horizon is a tousled fringe of swamp palms.

Could European powers have gone to war over such a wilderness?

It was this swamp that an army of one-thousand nine hundred African irregulars, along with six Portuguese officers, had captured when Lord Salisbury threatened to bombard Mozambique, Quelimane, Lourenço Marques and Lisbon if they didn't withdraw.

Part One

1. Mbewe

But Mbewe knew Elephant Marsh, as Chindevu used to say, 'like the back o' his ain hand.'

Mbewe and Chindevu of the African Lakes Company were about the same height but Chindevu's pith helmet, which he wore to avoid sunstroke, gave him a six-inch advantage. The pith helmet wouldn't have fitted on Mbewe's head, which was round as a cannon ball, with a close-clipped mat of curly black hair, but it was Mbewe who caught the eye. His build was slight but his arms were muscular, like one who had paddled canoes since childhood. By the same token, he was neat in all his movements, not one to rock the boat. When he smiled, which was often, his wide eyes lit up and he displayed a perfect set of white teeth. His only dress was a strip of white calico worn round his loins, and an amulet of black and red beans.

Mbewe wasn't his navel name, nor the name he was given on the day he was circumcised. But he used it in his childhood, and it was the name he asked the *azungu*, the white men, to call him by. Chindevu swore Mbewe was the only pilot he trusted on the River Shire, upstream or downstream. In fact, downstream was a bit easier, though he charged the same one rupee. Usually, he could allow the current to take him along, but sometimes it dived under the papyrus, and then he had to be careful. It could also run you aground where it turns a corner. That's what happened to the bishop, the one buried at Makhanga. His canoe overturned, and he lost all his quinine and died of fever. After that catastrophe, the *azungu* always took care to have someone like Mbewe to pilot them.

The marsh was never the same for two voyages in succession. It was not just that the water level varied from week to week, brown and sluggish in October, deep and fast in mid-December when the effect of November's rains in the highlands finally reached the lower Shire and the marsh widened to the nearest foothills. What also varied was the course the river preferred, switching its main channels on the slightest pretext because a tributary was swollen by a very localised rainstorm, or because drifting sud had lodged against a fallen fever tree, creating a huge dam overnight, or because water chestnuts had colonised a new mudflat in the process of creating a fresh island. Mbewe had to read these changes, anticipating an obstacle a hundred yards before he encountered it, from minute changes in the river's flow.

So he made a good living piloting the *azungu* through Dambinyi Marsh. It always puzzled him they called it Elephant Marsh. It wasn't a place for elephants, except at the very edges. They could have called it Crocodile Marsh or Hippo Marsh or Marsh of a Million Pythons, and that would have made better sense. Mbewe used to feel the *azungu* were living in a world of their own language, which didn't properly connect with his own.

Take the word 'slave', which was English for what he called *kaporo*. Chindevu of the Company always said he hated slavery and that he was here to put an end to the 'nasty business'. There was something called the 'three Cs', Christianity, Commerce and Civilisation. The Scottish missionaries up in the Highlands were telling people about the new religion. Then there was the Company attending to the commerce, starting with ivory, and then moving into oil seeds like sesame and millet. The third 'C' Mbewe hadn't quite figured out. It had something to do with wearing shoes and riding bicycles and drinking whisky, but quite how they linked up was a mystery.

Anyway, the English *azungu* were against slavery. It was why they were opposed to those other *azungu*, the Portuguese, who were the slavers. But here was another mystery, too complicated for Mbewe ever to explain, not even long after to his grandchildren. His mother's people, who were called Manganja, had always stopped the Portuguese coming up the river. Chief Tengani had blockaded the river as far as Dambinyi Marsh. Then Bwana Livingstone put the first steamer on the river and insisted on what he called 'freedom of navigation', and sailed through Tengani's blockade. After that, the Portuguese poured in and thousands of his mother's people were taken as slaves.

Mbewe knew these things could happen. What you intend isn't always what follows. And most of the Portuguese were only half Portuguese. Their other half was African like himself. But when Chindevu talked about the nasty business, there was something else he ignored. Or perhaps didn't know.

Mbewe himself was born a slave. That's what gave him the freedom to earn good money piloting the *azungu* through Elephant Marsh, and sometimes all way down to the Zambezi delta at Chinde. Three rupees *ganyão* for that trip, and there was usually a small party waiting to travel upriver to the highlands. That's how he paid *lobola* for his wife Masamanga, something his mother's people never did.

It started when he was small-small and his father sent him fishing in the marsh. He was *kaporo*, so he wasn't trusted to herd goats, which were too valuable. He was sent instead to weave fish traps and set them at the entrance to the inlets where the water lilies grew in the shallows. He wasn't alone. Mbiti his brother was with him, same father, different mother, and their neighbour Kashkinya who later was taken by a crocodile.

That was the worst day of his Mbewe's young life. Kashkinya was more than a neighbour. He and Mbewe had been circumcised together, in the same group of age-mates. They had received the same instruction in how to live like men. Kashkinya also played the *mbira* superbly, that little instrument the *azungu* called a hand piano, which you hold in your palms and play with your thumbs, making a plaintive, bubbling melody. He was so good he could compose his own tunes. He taught Mbewe how to play it, though Mbewe was never so good. He could play other people's tunes, but not make up his own.

The crocodile had come from nowhere, just a shallow inlet where you wouldn't have thought he could be hiding. There were always baby crocodiles around. When the boys arrived at their secret fishing creeks, Kashkinya would chase them down the mud bank, trying to stamp on their tails. Often, there would be big ones, basking in the sun with their jaws open, while little white birds picked their teeth. You kept well away from them because, although they looked completely immobile, that could change in a instant.

But the boys knew their bit of the marsh. They knew where the hippos gambolled and which were their favourite tracks. They boasted they could spot a python in the reeds before it spotted them. So the day Kashkinya was taken, when that terrible tail lashed and his age-mate was swept into the water, his left arm waving as the creature swept irresistibly down stream, was more than a terrible bereavement. Mbewe was forced to treat Dambinyi with a new respect as a place never to be mastered.

Next day, an ivory hunter shot a twelve-foot crocodile near Chiromo. They found Kashkinya's loincloth in the stomach, along with an amulet of black and red beans which Mbewe still wore in Kashkinya's memory.

Fishing's not like goat-herding. Nobody counts how many fish you're in charge of, and in Dambinyi there was always somewhere new to hide. Early on, he learned to deliver his catch to his father, but keep something back for his own use. At first, Mbiti and Kashkinya and he just made little feasts on fires of dried reeds. They ate *chambo* and mudfish and tiny *usipa* that flashed like silver rupees. It had been Kashkinya's idea to dry the fish on rafters, or smoke them over the same fires and sell them to women the other side of the marsh. They could even salt them, stealing from their father who did a big trade in salt. But that was dangerous because he kept his salt-pans well guarded.

Mbewe's father was Chipatula. He wasn't from the Shire valley. He came from Kololo far up the Zambezi beyond the rapids, like the other chiefs who settled there, like Ramakukan and Katunga and Moloka, sixteen of them altogether. They'd all been with Bwana Livingstone, guiding and protecting and cooking for him on his long journey, all the way to Luanda in Angola, and all the way back to Quelimane on the Mozambique coast. Sebituane, the chief of the Kololo, had hoped to open a trade route, to one coast or the other, so he could get guns in return for ivory and protect himself from the Boers. That's why he agreed to Bwana Livingstone's safari and told Mbewe's father and the other men to shield him with their lives. They weren't chiefs in those days, just Sebituane's slaves. But while they were away, the Zulu came and scattered Sebituane's people, so his father and the others had nowhere to go back home to.

Some of them stayed in Tete, the Portuguese side, but Mbewe's father and the others came to the River Shire. It was a time of famine, *magumanya* in his mother's language, 'heap upon heap'. But they had guns, and they'd seen the world, and they knew how to live. They settled right there in Dambinyi, Elephant Marsh, and made themselves chiefs. Katunga, Mululima and Moloka built villages to the north where the Shire river flows into the marsh. Ramakukan built a big stockade on the right bank, and Chipatula controlled the entrance to the marsh from the south. There were others, but these were the big ones, and they accepted his father Chipatula as paramount. Only Ramakukan was bigger than him.

They'd seen the world and they knew how to live. Even in the worst drought, even *magumanya*, the marsh always has water. They could lay fish traps, and make dry season gardens in the *dambo* lands on the fringe. They could hunt elephant and buffalo and kudu on the margins, because those animals had to come down to drink. There were lots of waterfowl, which his father had never seen before but became very fond of eating. There were reeds for house building, and in the surrounding forests there was plenty of fuel. For people who had travelled so far, further than Mbewe had ever done, to both African coasts, it was a paradise. They were nervous about taking canoes into the heart of the marsh though, with its pythons and crocodiles, so he was the only one who became a pilot.

Then there were the traders. When his mother was a girl it was just local. People would come from the highlands to buy millet in the dry season, or the new *mapiramanga* or 'foreign millet' which they used to call maize. It came in from the east coast and at first the ancestors didn't like it. If you were pouring a libation, it had to be millet beer because maize beer gave them headaches. But with maize it's easier to grow a surplus to sell to the people from the highlands, along with the cotton cloth they couldn't make for themselves. In return, they brought iron hoes made by their blacksmiths, or harpoons for the hippo traps. There'd never been any iron in Dambanyi.

So when the foreign traders began coming, after Livingstone breached the blockade, they already knew how to bargain. There was Chindevu of the Company, of course, the one who said Mbewe was the only pilot he trusted. Ndevu means 'big beard' and his was the biggest and hairiest anyone had ever seen. His English name was Mr Moir,. Mr Frederick Moir, to distinguish him from Chemandala, his brother, who was Mr John Moir. He was called Chemandala because of the way the sun shone on his spectacles. Chindevu gave Mbewe one rupee for each journey, upstream or downstream, so when the others came he used to say 'That's what Bwana Moir pays me' and that became his standard charge—even for the Indians who didn't have steamers and had to travel by canoe. He charged them one rupee for guiding them through Dambanyi where otherwise they would have got lost.

There were other Scotsmen, and some English, and two Jews, as well as *azungu* with strange accents who had paid their passage to travel on the Company steamers. He couldn't charge them for piloting, but he made them pay in other ways. It took five days to travel from Inhamissengo in the Zambezi delta to Katunga's at the head of the marsh. They would come to the prow when they thought no one was looking, and ask him where to buy ivory and sesame seeds and wild rubber.

'For ivory? Elephant Marsh', he would say, and they slipped him a penny for telling them what they already thought they knew.

'For rubber?' He always said 'Ramakukan's', because, unlike his father, Ramakukan rewarded him for sending traders to his village.

'For oil seeds?' He had to say 'Chipatula's' because his father was always more enterprising in these matters and had invested in a cotton gin.

As you see, he had a lot of freedom as a slave. He was becoming rich. Rich enough to pay *lobola* for his wife, Masamanga.

Suddenly, late one afternoon, everything fell apart.

He had guided a new gardener for the mission, a young Englishman in khaki shirt and shorts—a uniform that was new to him though it later became the fashion—as far as Katunga's where the road to the highlands begins, and was returning in his canoe through Dambanyi when, from a mud bank in the reeds, his wife Masamanga called out to him.

'Why are you here?' he demanded.

'There is war at Chipatula's. The warriors are looking for you.'

He took her into the canoe and paddled swiftly through backwaters he knew intimately, until they were safely downstream into Matakenya's territory, close to his late mother's village. He tied the canoe to a young baobab, and they walked home through the papyrus. She brought him a gourd of beer and some cold *nsima* with chicken relish. Only then did she tell the story.

'Chipatula is dead. Piri-Piri killed him. They had a quarrel over money, and Piri-Piri shot him.'

Piri-Piri was a *muzungu* called Mr Fenwick. They called him Piri-Piri because he was red-haired, red-faced and hot-tempered, like the hottest chilli pepper. First, he was with the missionaries. Then he quarrelled with them and worked with the Company. When Chemandala sacked him, he became a trader on his own account.

'What happened to Piri-Piri?'

'He is dead too. They chased him onto the island and speared him there. His head is on a pole.'

'Was he drunk?'

Masamanga spat derisively.

'Chipatula and Piri-Piri. They were both drunk like pigs.'

One of the things Piri-Piri traded was rum. Along with gunpowder. It was why he made money, though his bad temper made him unpopular. But Chipatula was a chief. Not as big as Ramakukan, but important. He must have thought even Piri-Piri would show respect.

'Chikusi is beating the war drums. He is angry with you.'

Chikusi was Mbewe's brother, same father, different mother, but the senior wife. Chikusi would now want to be chief.

'With me? Why?'

'He says you're the one who brought Piri-Piri. He says you are the friend of the *azungu* at Mandala, and he is going to destroy them.'

It was true he had piloted Piri-Piri, once to the edge of the marsh. He had promised payment, but after meeting Chipatula, he refused. Mbewe never had dealings with him after that.

He drank his beer, thinking hard. For the moment, he was safe where he was. If Chikusi was making war against the English, he wouldn't send his army to Matekenya's just to hunt for him.

But that was for the moment. Chipatula had already made war there. The last time was two years back when one of his wives ran away to Matekenya's. He attacked, and there was a big confusion. He didn't find his wife. He didn't find her because Mbewe had hidden her. She was his late mother.

So hiding there was not a solution. He could go to Ramakukan's. He was the senior Kololo chief, and it made no sense for him to be making war against the *azungu*. His people always boasted they were black Englishmen. That was what protected them from the Portuguese. Ramakukan would be keen to make peace quickly. So Mbewe would be safe with him.

Except that he wouldn't. He was just a slave. If handing him over to Chikusi was one of the conditions for making peace, Ramakukan wouldn't hesitate for a moment.

'You must go to *Sinyala* Maria's.'

That was Masamanga, as always reading his thoughts. He had paid *lobola* for her, but she was cleverer than him. Clever about people.

'You can stay at the *Sinyala's*.'

Senhora Maria was an ancient lady, more famous than any of the chiefs, more than Ramakukan or Tengani, more than the Company. She lived at Chimuara, close to where the Shire flows into the Zambezi, and no one, African, Portuguese, English, Indian, ever passed her compound without stopping to pay their respects. She had dozens of servants and a whole village of slaves. The canoe men had a song about her:

I have no mother,
I have no father,
I have no mother to suckle me,
Sinyala Mariya is my mother.

They all sang it, on the Shire and the Zambezi, especially when they were near her compound. Actually, she was Matekenya's aunt, so Mbewe could take refuge with her and be welcome.

But Matekenya was dead. He had been killed two years ago, just after Chipatula's raid.

'There's going to be war at Chimuara,' said Mbewe.

Masamanga looked astonished. 'Who would ever make war against the *Sinyala*?'

'Not against her. Against the Portuguese.'

Masamanga was still adamant. 'No one will attack *Sinyala* Mariya'.

'No. But who will protect her slaves?'

He was sitting in the middle of six wars. Chikusi's war with the English was only the most recent. That would involve him in war with Ramakukan. There was the existing Kololo war with Matekenya's people. Chipatula had already raided the Portuguese at Tete, and Matekenya's people had joined the Portuguese. The Portuguese would like nothing better than to attack the Kololo with the excuse that they were coming to rescue the English. But now Matekenya's people were preparing for war against the Portuguese, and Chipatula's death would give them their opportunity.

Next morning before dawn, he set out for the *azungu*, at the Company store in the highlands they called Mandala.

2 Maria Afonso

Maria Afonso Teixeira Rebelo de Carvalho was hungry and footsore, trudging in his mother's footsteps on a journey that had taken them two whole months. They had set out in March before the snows had fully cleared from their home in Cumeeira, carrying sufficient food for a week.

'God will provide,' said his mother.

It was what she always said. But she placed equal faith in the letter she was carrying. She couldn't read or write, but she was confident the letter, from a distant relative, would secure her son's future.

Cumeeira was a tiny village in the mountains north of Portugal's River Douro. Afonso remembered vineyards and olive orchards and a perpetual absence of men. None of his friends had fathers at home. They were in Brazil, like his own father, or in Africa or New England. The local wine was good wine and the olive oil excellent, but the farms had shrunk in size as they were passed from fathers to too many sons, until the land was insufficient to support the people.

Afonso and his mother had set out from Cumeeira on their long journey south one week after the priest brought the letter saying his father had died in Brazil. It was the priest who arranged the other letter, the one his mother was carrying. She left his elder sister Eulalia, named for the patron saint, to look after his little brother and baby sister, and departed in darkness before the village was stirring.

He recalled little of the journey, just the heat and cold and hunger. They must have avoided the towns for fear of being arrested. He remembered his terror at crossing the brand new railway bridge at Regua, treading carefully from sleeper to sleeper while the Douro foamed below with the spring rains.

He recalled rough tracks through narrow, rocky valleys. He recalled hot afternoons, and cold nights huddled together for warmth under hedgerows. He recalled over-curious goats trying to butt him, and vicious dogs to be pelted off with stones. He recalled oxen with patient brown eyes pulling carts, and one carrier with a donkey who gave them a ride for several miles before asking his mother to marry him. She had cursed him with a ferocity that startled.

He recalled being invited by a family planting their field to share their midday meal of bread and sausage and a cheese as hard as concrete. They drank wine from a leather bag with a spout, and poured some down his throat just to try it. He recalled sleeping in the porch of an old stone church, and being woken by the Easter procession, with the blessed Virgin decked with white lilies and his mother crossing herself with tears in her eyes. He recalled crossing another river, waist deep, and being told it was the Dão where the best vines grew. He washed his smock, and lay naked on a rock while it dried in the sun. He recalled somewhere near their destination seeing the sea for the first time from a rocky hillside. It was his mother's first sight too, and they stood together spellbound by the green infinity, till his mother dismissed it with the words 'That's where your father disappeared to, and where so many Portuguese have perished.'

He knew they must have passed by many towns his mother, through shame or policy, avoided. So he was not prepared for the enormous pale pink mass of the convent that turned out to be their destination.

It was more than enormous. It was colossal, like some fairy-tale giant's palace. There were two towers, like the tower on the parish church in Cumeeira but much higher. There were two bulky pavilions, one at each end of an immense façade with hundreds of windows. There were huge statues, their hair and clothes billowing in the wind. High above everything, a vast dome floated in the heavens.

The more he stared, the more he felt diminished by it.

'What is it?'

'It's the famous convent of Mafra,' said his mother.

'Am I going to be a monk?'

'If God wills,' said his mother. 'But your late father would never forgive me.'

She told him to wait by one of the stone lions at the foot of a wide semi-circular staircase while she went to make enquiries. She was gone for about half an hour, at the end of which he heard raised voices. A man wearing a long black cassock and black hat was waving his arms and shouting at his mother to 'Be Off'. When she rejoined him she was upset, and he was angry on her behalf.

'I have to sit down somewhere,' she said.

They made their way through a small rose garden to a bench in the town square, marked by avenues of plane trees.

'He is no man of God,' she muttered. 'Just because I have no shoes, I'm not supposed to walk on his marble floor.'

'You are not from here, daughter?'

It was an old lady speaking, a widow swathed in black, occupying the same bench.

'We have walked many miles.'

'If you lived here you would know that palace is only for the rich.'

'I want to see a priest,' said my mother. 'But these people are too proud.'

The old lady pointed to a dirt road leading steeply downhill from the end of the square where the plane trees stopped.

'Go and see Father Anselmo at Santo Andre's. He is a true father. Not like these Judases.'

They left the convent behind and followed a wide track between farms and labourers' cottages, to what felt like an altogether different town in the valley. It turned out to be old Mafra, with more cottages, a couple of *quintas* flourishing with grapes and oranges, built at the edge of an escarpment, beyond which the road fell steeply to a wide plain extending to the Atlantic and a razor sharp horizon.

At the centre of the village was Santo André's, the seven-hundred-year-old parish church. It was not like the church he was used to in Cumeeira, but more like an ancient stone fortress, gloomy with arrowslit windows, and badly in need of repair. They entered by a porch like the one they had sheltered in on Easter morning and Father Anselmo, in a white *batina*, with a shining skull and shaggy tufts of white hair above his ears, descended the altar stairs to greet them. He understood instantly that they were travellers and invited them to be seated on a bench.

'Do you wish to make confession, my child?'

'I need to, father. But first, there is the boy.'

Father Anselmo took the letter my mother had passed him and read it slowly, stroking his chin. He had startling light-blue eyes, and his face and manner were kindly.

'So you want to be a soldier?'

It was the first Afonso had heard of the idea. Better than being a monk. In fact, much better. Enormously better. Quivering with excitement, he glanced up at his mother, registered that she was as surprised as he was, then looked straight into those light-blue eyes and exclaimed, 'Yes, father!'

The priest folded the letter and put it in his *batina*'s pocket.

'Come and see me tomorrow morning. I will speak with the Director. Do you have a place to sleep?'

'Thank you, father. We will manage.'

But Father Anselmo insisted, 'Cumeeira is far. You are a good Catholic mother. Think of the boy.'

He led them to his presbytery and asked his housekeeper to take care of the young soldier and his tired mother.

How did one become a soldier in a convent?

No one explained anything, and he had had to work it out gradually for himself. The convent had ceased to be a convent with the abolition of religious orders. It remained a royal palace and a barracks and intermittently housed the Colégio Militar, a school for boys intending a military career.

He didn't know any of this when Father Anselmo told him to be ready at eight o'clock sharp.

'Military time,' he said. 'Not village time.'

Seeing the alarm he had caused, he broke into a smile.

'I will wake you after first mass.'

'We will be at mass, father,' said his mother.

The bell summoned them, and they were up before dawn, praying in the cold chapel. After breakfast, they climbed the hill to the convent. The housekeeper had washed his smock, and Father Anselmo had given him a bright green scarf.

They approached the façade and turned past the right-hand pavilion, then left along the convent's southern wall. He was shocked to realise the building was bigger than he'd thought the day before. It formed a vast square with hundreds of windows down the south side as well.

At an entrance, with sentries either side, the guard on duty greeted the priest.

'You are expected, father.'

Father Anselmo and his mother went inside, leaving him waiting with the guard. He stared at the dark blue uniforms and glossy boots of the sentries who stood motionless at attention. He wondered if they were statues like the ones he'd seen yesterday. Then he was summoned inside.

A tall man, again in uniform but with bright brass buttons, was standing with his back to a roaring fire. His face was as red as the fire, and he had a black moustache. He was holding in his left hand the letter his mother had brought.

'So this is the lad. What's your name, my boy?'

Father Anselmo had coached him in this.

'Maria Afonso Teixeira Rebelo de Carvalho, your excellency.'

'Ah, you come very directly to the point. It is a military virtue. Now tell me, who is this Teixeira Rebelo?'

He had no idea.

'He doesn't know, your excellency,' said his mother. 'Nor do I. It was his late father insisted on the name.'

'Quite correct. It is a famous and honourable name.'

The director stared for a moment, amused by the contrast between the name and the urchin before him, perhaps wondering if Teixeiro Rebelo had once looked like this.

'You are named for Marshall António Teixeira Rebelo, a hero, patriot, and founder of this college. This letter from your uncle declares you are a great-nephew of the Marshall and, like him, born of a peasant family from Cumeeira.'

Maria Afonso recalled this speech countless times over the next fifteen years, trying to imagine his youthful self responding more effectively than he did. It was a moment of grandeur, worthy of its surroundings in the convent.

Should he have been proud? Should he have been nonchalant? Should he have smiled slightly and modestly demurred?

He stared first at his mother, who looked as bewildered as he felt, then glanced at Father Anselmo, whose eyes shone with encouragement.

But he said nothing.

'Would you like to see your ancestor?' said the Director. 'He's right behind you.'

This frightened him even further. He turned, expecting to see a ghost, and saw nothing, just the door he'd come in by and a wall covered with photographs of military figures with lots of facial hair.

'That's him, to the right of the door. Marshal António Teixeira Rebelo, our glorious founder.'

It was a picture of a short, thin man with a large, long, stern face. He had a high forehead with wisps of grey hair, an aquiline nose and thin, pursed lips. His facial hair was confined to a tiny moustache and a short beard covering only his chin.

Not an ancestor to be comfortable with. He found himself still at a loss for words.

'One matter,' said the director, as though giving up. 'How old is this lad?'

The question was directed at Father Anselmo, who looked at his mother, who looked at Afonso. Then realizing her son had no idea, she blurted, 'He was born the same summer as Dom Afonso. That's why I named him so.'

'The Crown Prince? Dom Afonso Henriques? In that case, he's barely eight years old. I'm afraid he has to wait a bit. Entry to the Colégio Militar is from the age of ten.'

Something had gone wrong. Afonso's first thought was the old man on the wall was responsible. He hadn't proved good enough for that stern face. His second thought was he couldn't face that long journey home. So he hardly heard what Father Anselmo was saying.

'That's no problem. The lad can stay with me. It'll be a nice change for my parishioners to see an altar boy. In the meantime, he can learn to read so he'll be better prepared.'

The director nodded approval and shook hands, first with Father Anselmo, then with his mother, and finally with him.

'Come back when you're ten. We'll make you a soldier worthy of your name.'

3 Lorenzo

Our first harvest at the new mission station at Cape MacClear, wrote Lorenzo Johnston in his prison cell at Quelimane, was a portion of runner beans, pot-boiled, then tossed in rancid butter. 'A ground-opening crop,' said Mr Riddel, the gardener, which would 'give something back to the soil.'

The sand there looked in need of nourishment. Like the people. But at least Mr Riddel got something to grow.

Not like Mr Waller at Magomero. I remember him poring over his parsnip patch where the stream doubled back on itself. All it showed was some wild millet, with coarse black beads for ears. 'And I prayed so earnestly,' he said.

'Even for the Almighty,' said the Bishop, 'fine words butter no parsnips.'

Dr Laws declared the beans were the best he had ever tasted. That is how he always talked, like Moses encouraging the Israelites.

All this seems ancient history, wrote Johnston in his prison cell, though it came to pass only fifteen years back.

He was in jail awaiting trial for gun-running, for smuggling rifles and ammunition and even an artillery piece, to the Scotsmen fighting the Arab slavers deep in the interior. This was in breach of an official Portuguese blockade, and Dr Nogeiro Rato, the *advogado* hired by Tony St Claire to defend him, said the prosecution was claiming gun-smuggling was a capital offence. But Lorenzo should be in no fear of his life. He was a British subject, and the arms he had procured had protected British lives. In any case, as Dr Rato argued, the Portuguese had long since abolished the death penalty, and the more they insisted Mozambique belonged to Portugal, the more they had to obey their own laws.

Lorenzo´s cell was too small for such a tall man, heavy as a pugilist. He wasn't otherwise uncomfortable. His broad features extended upwards to a bald dome, with brushes of curly hair over each ear, and downwards to a thick black beard of which he was proud. He was proud, too, of his leather footwear which he liked to polish afresh first thing every morning in jail. He was perfectly capable of going barefoot, as in childhood or at the Bishop's mission—not for the Scotsmen, though, for whom he pointedly polished his boots each morning. Otherwise his dress was casual, with tight black trousers partly hidden by a loose-fitting smock.

He was able to make use of the books his wife Luiza had brought in, being careful to keep them hidden under his bed and guarded by his slop bucket, which the guards were squeemish about touching. The books were Livingstone's account of the Zambezi Expedition, Livingstone's *Last Journals*, edited by Mr Waller, Rev. Rowley's account of the Magomero Mission and Capt. Young's story of the Livingstone Search Expedition.

These were his stories. He'd been present over much of those thirty years. He'd been with Livingstone and the Bishop, with Capt. Young on his third expedition, with Dr Laws and the Scottish mission and with the African Lakes Company that was supposed to bring what they called 'legitimate trade.' Yet his name was scarcely mentioned. He was just Johnston, the Jamaican cook. Not cooking Jamaican food, of course. No ackee and saltfish, no cow foot and flour dumpling, no chicken foot soup. Just the tasteless dishes the *azungu* preferred, chicken boiled to blandness and, of course, those watery beans.

He needed to tell his own story. On paper. How had he come to help establish a Scottish colony, when white rule in Ethiopia was the last thing he believed in?

I start with the beans, he wrote, because the building of the new station was how the present pappy show began. I was thirty-eight years old and had taken a wife, who was with child. Not the used-up widower I am today, with a second wife who, whatever I try to teach her, considers herself my slave.

I never much liked the word missionary. It sounds too much like crusading. For me, slavery is the one and only issue. But I preferred those English missionaries to this new tribe of Scotchmen. They studied their own frailties. If something went wrong, like the parsnips, they made a joke about it. In the end, of course, they were hypocrites like all white men.

But before reaching that point, they knew how to laugh at themselves.

Dr Laws pronounced grace over the beans, 'thanking the Good Lord for providing our first African repast'. As though God cleared the land and did the hoeing and planting and twice-daily watering. As though he had a direct telegraph to the Almighty.

Dr Laws, though, was the first white massa ever to write down something I said.

The business happened like this.

We were sailing on Lake Nyasa in the new steamer, the *Ilala*. My friend Capt. Young was in charge. I call him my friend because he always treated me so, though I didn't always reciprocate.

When he commanded the Livingstone Search Expedition, after Musa lied about the doctor's death, he wanted me to join. I was living in Cape Town where Mr Waller left me, and he'd heard about me from Mr Waller. But I was in a rage about the news from Jamaica. About all those killings at Morant Bay. For a while, I didn't want to talk to any white man. All those people murdered, men, women and children, as the white militia ran amok. Just because poor Quashie trespassed on a long abandoned plantation. All those people hung by the neck, including Pastor Gordon, who was miles away from any uprising. He was a member of the assembly, and it was he taught me to read and write in his Baptist school. That didn't protect him from Governor Eyre, who showed less compassion than Pharaoh and broke every law in the book taking revenge. All because a landless ex-slave tried to grow provisions on some empty ground.

They made Eyre a hero when he should have been cashiered. All those famous men coming out in his support! Charles Dickens, who was supposed to be a champion of the poor, except when they are black. Charles Kingsley who called himself a Christian socialist. John Ruskin, with his hifalutin style. I know they abolished slavery, but you can't trust them not to revert to type when their interests are at stake.

So I was vexed plenty. But when Capt. Young sought me out a second time, and told me this time he was taking a steamer to the lake, I couldn't say no. I was married by then, and my wife expecting. But I couldn't turn down an appeal to return to central Africa and strike another blow against the slavers. No longer as just as cook, as I'd been for the Bishop. I was Capt. Young's jack-of-all-trades. Man Friday, he called me, like in *Robinson Crusoe*. I wasn't offended because I admired his competence and good humour.

The new steamer was the *Ilala*, after the village where Dr Livingstone passed away. We assembled it in the delta, bolting together its numbered parts, and sailed up the Zambezi and through Elephant Marsh as far as the first cataract. Then we took it apart and hired carriers to ferry the sections over the rocky defiles above the foaming river, until we reached smooth water and re-assembled it.

Not a bolt got lost! I have to admire that, and didn't object to joining in the heavy work when I saw Capt. Young taking the lead. He didn't mind getting his hands scratched and oily in a noble cause.

My cause, being suckled a Jamaican slave.

When at last we sailed into Lake Nyasa, we anchored for the night off Cape MacClear. That is where Mr Riddel afterwards planted his beans. At first, it looked a good site for the mission, with a sheltered bay ringed by mountains and a small river. However, Capt. Young didn't want to commit the party too soon, so next morning at first light we headed north to study more of the lake.

It was then the incident occurred that Dr Laws wrote down, quoting what he said I said.

We had been steaming for about a hour, when suddenly the lookout shouted, 'A slaver!'

It was a Arab dhow running under full sail. Capt. Young ordered the Ensign raised and buttoned his uniform. He turned to Dr Laws and said, 'I give you two minutes to decide whether we fight or not.'

'You are in command,' said the Doctor. 'Whatever you order me to do, I will do.'

I had yet to learn what bandulu words these were.

Capt. Young turned to me.

'Johnston, will you fight?'

31

'Yes, sir.'

I admit I was excited. This was like at Mbame's, when the Bishop was approaching Magomero and our party set free all those eighty-four slaves.

'Doctor, load your revolver and come with me into the boat. Johnston, take the wheel and stand across her bows.'

Long afterwards, this is how Dr Laws wrote about what followed.

'Me not got slaves in,' came in accents of terror across the water.

'I did not say you had,' shouted Young, 'but I want to have a look at you.'

Boarding the vessel, they found that the large open slave-hold was empty, and breathed a sigh of relief. The master, Mohamet, an Arab, and the crew consisting of four other Arabs and some natives, were in an abject state of astonishment and alarm.

'Yes, yes, me sabe English. Me no take slaves. Good evening. Thank you, sir, Massa.'

'You speak English?'

'Yes, yes. Me come from Zanzibar.'

'All right,' said Mr Young, 'you are free to go.'

When they returned, Johnston, who had been watching the scene, remarked, 'That Arab was never so near to being a white man in his life.'

It surprised me when I read this. Were these really my self same words? I don't remember. It sounded like something I might have said, much more than the 'Me not got slaves' and 'me sabe English. Good evening, sir, Massa' that Dr Laws attributed to Mohamet.

No Arab ever talked like that, though Mohamet had cause to scratch his head. An English steamship in Lake Nyasa was a big surprise. Just to cause him further botheration, Capt. Young circled him several times before heading for the western shore.

'Never so near being a white man in his life.'

Dr Laws and Capt. Young thought that hilarious. I meant, I suppose, Mohamet was frightened out of his skin. But joking about colour is never straightforward. Were they laughing because whiteness was impossible for people like

Mahomet? In that case, the joke included me. You will never see me white no matter how English I become.

Still, he reported what I said, or what he thought I said, and he credited me with good grammar. As you see, I feel mixed about Dr Laws. I still do, now he's achieved the colony he was ambitious for, with the help of the guns I provided.

The day after Capt. Young finally recommended Cape MacClear as the best site for the mission, Dr Laws asked me where I 'hailed from'. That's what he called it, 'hailed from'. He assumed I was one of the native Christians from the Cape and was surprised Capt. Young trusted me with responsibilities.

'I was born a Jamaican slave.'

He pulled a face.

'When I first offered myself for the mission fields, the committee tried to send me to Jamaica.'

He sniffed.

'I told them I had no desire to go there. Rather the reverse.'

He didn't explain, but I knew what he was thinking. After Morant Bay and the ruption about Governor Eyre, he'd read Carlyle on *The Nigger Question*. About Quashie surrounded by pumpkins and refusing to work. About the necessity for the whip.

Being Jamaican, I didn't understand the Scotch gospel of work.

He reminded me I was recruited as a cook and that was my responsibility, not gallivanting on the *Ilala*.

So I was back to doing what I did at Magomero.

All this was fifteen years back. That is how the present war began, with Mr Riddel's beans. Of course, you could say it started when the Portuguese first set foot in Africa, all those centuries back. Or when Dr Livingstone walked across Africa. Or when the good bishop died in Elephant Marsh. All that made part of the history. But no, it was when Dr Laws and those Scotsmen tried to put down roots at Cape MacClear, even if they were only runner bean roots, that what's happening today became destiny.

4 Mbewe

After Masamanga's warning that Chipatula's sons were determined to kill him, Mbewe set out at before dawn for the highlands. In the middle of six wars, the compound at Mandala seemed the best refuge.

First, he travelled by canoe upriver to the confluence with the Ruo river, where the bishop was buried. He had to be careful, because this meant entering Chipatula's territory, where he had his second capital at Chiromo. But he knew those streams and made it safely to Mangasanja's on the Ruo, where he could leave the canoe with a friend. From there, he could travel overland, entering the highlands from behind Mount Thyolo, well east of any danger. He arrived on the afternoon of the second day, getting his first glimpse of Mandala as he passed Soche's village.

He had seen Bonga's *arringa*—what the *azungu* call a stockade—at Massangano on the Zambezi above Tete. He had seen the *quartel* built by the Portuguese in Quelimane, which the locals called *Chuabo*, or fort. But he had never seen so strange a building as Mandala.

It was two huge rectangular houses, one on top of the other, with the tallest corner posts he had ever seen, and other posts—eight on the longer side, five on the other. The underneath house had a space where *azungu* were sitting and talking with the real walls of the house behind them. So there was a secret inside part and an outside part that was still part of the house.

The top part of the house was exactly the same, again with people walking about. How had they got up there? The only tree, a tall acacia, was too far away for them to climb from. How did they get the floor to stay up there? He was assuming it was the same beaten earth with cow dung as at the bottom. The building had a thatched roof, with freshly trimmed grass, and on top of everything a tiny brick house with four clay pots pointing to the sky.

He was puzzling over the meaning of this when someone shouted in English 'Seize him! Seize him!'

He stood still where he was.

'Seize him. He's a spy for Chikusi'.

A young white lady in a cotton dress and solar topee looked over the veranda rail at the man who was shouting.

'What's the matter, Philip?'

'He's Chikusi's spy. Hold him.'

Three men wearing hats like upturned pots ran from the block house Mbewe had passed through. They grabbed him by the arms, twisting them painfully behind his neck.

The person who was shouting was his brother, Chimtanda, same father, different mother. Mbewe stared at him in amazement. He was wearing a white shirt, khaki shorts and cotton socks with brightly shined shoes. His hair was cut very short, with a line like a furrow from above his left eyebrow to the back of his head.

'Who is it, Philip?' asked the white lady.

'He's Chikusi's slave. He's come to spy on us.'

The men with the pots tightened their grip. Three *azungu* approached from the lower floor of the house.

'Good afternoon, brother,' Mbewe said to Chimtanda. In English.

'You're not my brother, you're my slave,' he answered in Kololo.

'Chimtanda, we have both lost our father,' Mbewe replied, still in English. 'I didn't know you were called Philip.'

'Who are you? What are you doing here?'

It was Mr Morrison, another trader working with the Company whom he had also piloted through Dambinyi. He didn't recognise Mbewe out of the steamer.

'I've come to see Mr Moir.'

'There are two of them.'

'I mean Chindevu. Mr Frederick.'

'He's at Ramakukan's. He won't be back for a week.'

Mbewe was puzzled. Didn't they know anything? It was two days since Chipatula and Piri-Piri were killed. Yet Chimtanda was obviously in the know.

'Lock him up,' said Mr Morrison to the men with the head pots, 'until we can establish who he is.'

'Thank you, Philip', said the white lady. 'We can't be too careful.'

Chindevu returned that evening with the news. A messenger from Ramakukan's had intercepted him on the escarpment. Until then, all the people at Mandala knew was that Chipatula's sons had absconded from the school that morning. All except Philip. They hadn't known why, and they were alarmed. Chipatula's sons were the Mandala school's prized pupils.

Mbewe was pleased Ramakukan had sent a warning. He could easily have captured Mr Frederick. In the first of the six wars, Ramakukan was not going to fight against the English. Chindevu ordered Mbewe's release, and Mr Morrison had the courtesy to apologise. He didn't see the white lady again for many days. It turned out she was Piri-Piri's wife, Madam Fenwick.

Chindevu took him to see his brother, Mr John, the one they called Chemandala. Mbewe saw for the first time how the *azungu* climbed up to the top house. There were slats of wood, one above the other at an angle, called a staircase, and they led up to a room that Chemandala called his office.

Mbewe had acted as Mr John's pilot on at least three journeys upriver, but he had never talked to him the way Mr Frederick did. Chemandala was more like one of the missionaries, very private and very strict, his eyes hidden behind his gleaming spectacles. It was hard to know what he was plotting, or whether he was plotting anything. Perhaps it was all just happening.

Mbewe knew Chemandala had quarrelled with Ramakukan. He didn't seem to understand what an important man Ramakukan was. He refused to pay any tax for travelling though his territory on the river. When the porters stole some bales of calico, he demanded Ramakukan track down the thieves and repay the Company—as though Chemandala was now the owner of the country. He had even sent his ivory hunters, boys from the mission, poaching in Ramakukan's territory and, when they killed an elephant, refused to hand over one of the tusks as was Ramakukan's right.

'What really happened, Mbewe?', Chindevu asked him, as he stood there in the room called an office. Chindevu was also standing, Chemandala was sitting behind a wooden table he called his desk, and behind him the walls on three sides were covered with boxes holding books and papers.

'I only know Chipatula and Piri-Piri quarrelled over money and that they were both drunk.'

'Piri-Piri?'

'It's what we called Mr Fenwick.'

Chemandala gave a sudden snort.

'Because of his red hair?'

'His red hair, his red face and his bad temper.'

'Why on earth would Chipatula deal with a man like that?' said Chemandala. 'His last words to me, in a letter, were 'To hell with you'.'

Mbewe found it hard to explain the rules of trade to a man who'd come to teach Africans commerce. Piri-Piri offered Chipatula what he wanted, gunpowder and rum. The *kachasu*, the white rum, was bad. But it was obvious why Chipatula wanted powder. If he was going to kill elephants, to trade the tusks to Mandala, he needed powder for his guns. By this time, too, Mbewe had piloted enough steamers to know they were no good for river trade. Half the cargo space was taken up with firewood to keep the engines in steam. With his canoe, Piri-Piri could travel almost as fast, and could offer better prices by cutting his costs.

'They got drunk and quarrelled,' he told Chemandala, 'and Piri-Piri shot him. Piri-Piri ran to the island to hide among the reeds. But Chipatula's men tracked him and speared him to death. They cut off his head and put it on a pole.'

'You saw this?'

'No, Masamanga, my wife told me. She said Chikusi's men were looking for me because I was the first to pilot Piri-Piri to Mitengo.'

Chemandala was not a calm bearded presence like Chindevu. He looked irritated, as though Mbewe had just got him stuck on a sandbank. He took off his glasses, breathed on them and started polishing them with his handkerchief before replacing them on the end of his nose.

'If he blames you, why does he want to attack me? He says I commissioned his father's death. It makes no sense. I was Chipatula's friend.'

Mbewe explained patiently what again seemed obvious.

'Chikusi is Chipatula's heir. Born of Masambala, his senior wife. But he has to establish himself with his followers. If he can win over Ramakukan's headmen, so much the better.'

'So?'

'If he captures Mandala, he'll have enough to reward everyone.'

'Then,' said Chemandala, pushing his spectacles back, 'they must not capture Mandala.'

5 Maria Afonso

Afonso loved being an altar boy. Father Anselmo quickly became more like a real father than the father he barely remembered. He loved the clean, starched vestments, the aroma of incense, the strict liturgical rules about where to stand and in what posture. He loved extinguishing the altar candles after mass, the wax scalding his forefinger before hardening to a white film. He enjoyed sipping the sacristy wine when Father Anselmo wasn't looking.

He loved the seven-hundred-year-old chapel with its mixture of Romanesque and early Gothic, and he got used to the leaking roof and the broken window in the apse. He loved the sense of hierarchy, of fitness, taking as no more than his due the respect of old ladies who were as poor as his mother and who knew his story.

He never forgot the insult to his mother outside the convent, and believed the chapel devoted to St Andrew, the least ostentatious of the apostles, was nearer God than anything in the palace up the hill.

But he never saw his mother again. The winter after her return journey, she died of fever. By then he was able to read the letter sent him by the Cumeeira priest at his sister's dictation and was able to record his grief in his own hand.

A week after his tenth birthday, he entered the Colégio Militar at its new site in the village of Luz, just outside Lisbon.

Father Anselmo walked with him, first to Sintra, where they stayed with the priest of the tiny chapel in São Pedro, and then on next morning to Cascais to catch the boat. So his first glimpse of Lisbon was from the river, as was his last glimpse of Lisbon fourteen years later when he departed for Africa. But how different the two occasions—the first a thrill of inarticulate optimism, the second overwhelmed by homesickness expressed through the poetry he had come to know by heart.

He found the army was a bit like the church. There were similar rituals, a similar hierarchy, similar rules about movement and posture and the same love of colourful uniforms, along with a strict code of conduct. The big difference was he could make friends. There were other boys like him. Some were the orphaned sons of soldiers, others from backgrounds as poor as his, determined like him to make the most of this chance in life.

These were not his thoughts on arrival. He expressed them in an essay contributed in his fifth year to the college magazine, and they caused a stir. They were felt to be satiric, if not downright blasphemous. Friends expected a summons by the director. Expulsion was rumoured, or at least some kind of official reprimand. The matter rated a mention in *O Século*, Lisbon's newest right-wing daily, which invoked Teixeira Rebelo, his famous ancestor. In the event, the college chaplain put an end to the fuss, describing the article as a declaration of love for both institutions, church and army, which was what he had intended.

Meanwhile, in addition to his academic studies, he learned to ride, to fence and to play the cornet in the college band. He marched through Lisbon each founder's day, on March 3rd, wearing the distinctive *barretina* helmet with its green flash and shouting the college war cry *Zacatraz*. He learned that the stern old man Teixeira Rebelo was remembered with pride and affection by older generations of students. Pride for his conduct at the battle of Rossilháo in the Peninsular war against revolutionary France, when his direction of the artillery won the day, affection for his kindness to generations of homesick ten-year-olds. One day, in the college library, he came across his great uncle's translation of Muller's classic *Treatise of Artillery* and took a vow to follow more closely in his footsteps. In practice, though he loved riding, this meant opting for a career in the infantry rather than the cavalry. It was in this period that he simplified his name, from Maria Afonso Teixeira Rebelo de Carvalho to the more manageable, and infinitely more practical, Maria Afonso Rebelo.

His article had got him noticed and he was one of the students invited to dine with a famous old boy of the college, Major Serpa Pinto, the African explorer. Serpa Pinto, named for his maternal grandfather, another hero of the Pensinsula War and a lifelong Liberal, had achieved still greater fame by imitating Livingstone, crossing on foot from Benguela in Angola to Pretoria in South Africa. On his return to Portugal he was honoured by King Luís at a glittering assembly in Lisbon's Teatro da Trinidade, while the whole country went delirious about him, with avenues and squares named after him in the smallest hamlets. There were brands of *Serpa Pinto Cigarettes* and *Serpa Pinto Biscuits*. His book *How I Crossed Africa* was about to be published, in Portuguese of course, but also pointedly in English and German and, it was rumoured, he was shortly to be honoured with a Founder's Medal by the Royal Geographical Society in London.

The occasion at the Colégio Militar was in the great hall, with over one hundred guests, including the young Crown Prince Afonso, Afonso's namesake and age-mate. Major Serpa Pinto, a surprisingly boyish figure for someone so famous, wore his colonial dress uniform, with dark blue coat and light blue trousers, distinguished by his ceremonial sword and the Meritomilitar star pinned to his left breast. Neither he nor the Crown Prince made speeches. That was left to distinguished figures such as the historian Oliveira Martins and finance minister Barros Gomes, both passionately concerned with the colonies, together of course, with the Principal.

When the meal was over and the toasts drunk, Serpa Pinto came to join the lowest of the tables where the students were seated and talked of his own days at the Colégio Militar. He, too, came from a poor northern background, from a village near Cinfães, south of the Douro and slightly west of Regua. When Afonso told him of crossing the railway bridge at dawn at the start of his long journey south, the African hero embraced him, and asked what his plans were for the future.

Naturally, he replied 'Africa.'

6 Lorenzo

For a mission site, Cape MacClear was deceptive, wrote Lorenzo Johnston in jail at Quelimane.

'Like Ayrshire parkland,' said Dr Laws, meaning it sloped gently with trees dotted here and there. But the greenery was a tough kind of grass sprouting from root systems hard to disentangle from the sand, and the trees were thorny acacias, no use as building material. There was a shallow stream crossing the site, but the stream's head beyond the slope was a huge morass. It fact, the place was like a Jamaican beach, a sandbank between swamp and ocean—in this case, an inland lake as big as a sea. There were sea breezes at dawn and land breezes at dusk, but otherwise the air was hot and humid between the encircling mountains and the scorching sand.

Dr Laws was keen to write HOME on this place, and he began by marking out the settlement in the form of a Union Jack, paced out as one hundred yards across, parallel to the lake.

'If only we can get the idea of a straight line and a right angle into the natives' heads,' he pronounced, 'we shall have made a great stride towards civilization.'

He stamped out a St George's Cross of tracks, dividing the site into four and a St Andrew's Cross of narrow paths, halving each quarter. To avoid vexing the Portuguese, he didn't actually raise a flagpole.

Watching this, I had a sudden revelation. We weren't missionaries. We were pioneers of a colony. At Magomero, the Bishop didn't study to found a colony. He wanted to be archbishop to some local king, if only he could find one. Dr Laws's ambition was to become another Pharaoh.

At the head of the Union Jack in the sand, we built a rectangular bungalow, with rooms for stores one end, for dining and for prayer meetings in the middle and for sleeping quarters at the other. With the rains fast coming, it was too late in the year for brick making, so it was all done African fashion with reed walls and with grass for thatching. As cook, of course, I had my own sleeping quarters in a separate hut, which suited me fine.

At the start of November, Dr Laws felt restless. He decided to circumnavigate the whole lake to see if he could find a better site, one with a bit more milk and honey. So the whole party disappeared in the *Ilala*—Capt. Young, the engineers, the seamen and Sam the interpreter. I was left behind with Mr Liddel, Mr Simpson the engineer, George the carpenter and my two friends from Magomero days, Thomas Boquito and Fred Soromuti. That same week the rains arrived, and the three *azungu* promptly went down with fever. The swamp became an inland lagoon, breathing vapours, and with the vapours came clouds of mosquitos. I never saw so many, not even in Elephant Marsh, which was famous for them.

But for the first time, I was in charge. Thomas and Fred nursed the three *azungu* while they lay hot and helpless in their delirium, and I boiled soup, which was all they could hold down. For a whole month I ran the Free Presbyterian Mission to Central Africa on my own terms. I didn't go half idiot. I managed to stock up on dried *chambo* and *mlamba*, asking the fishermen to trade their supplies. I bought some live chickens, and built a hencoop. I made a trip to the villages five miles off and traded baskets of maize flour. This wasn't easy because it was the planting season and next year's harvest was eight months off. But the people were hungry for cloth and I was keen to show them they could obtain cloth without selling slaves. I told them the missionaries had come to put an end to the slave trade. Of course, this got me into trouble afterwards, but the point was made and Dr Laws could hardly go back and unsay what I had declared.

Oh, and finally, I planted the runner beans in the plot Mr Liddel and I had already hoed. By the time Dr Laws and the others returned, just before Christmas, the three *azungu* were back on their feet, looking very shaky, and the runner beans were showing their little white curls of flesh.

The voyage had reached the north end of the lake, two hundred miles further than they predicted. But they hadn't succeeded in finding any better site for the mission. Slave traders already occupied the few harbours that existed. Worse, they had steamed through terrible storms they were lucky to have survived. Capt. Young kept very quiet when Dr Laws reported this, because he had helped design the *Ilala*, which now turned out too small for the job.

They would have to remain at Cape MacClear, and they would need a bigger steamer.

That explained the botheration on Dr Laws face as he landed from the *Ilala* to confront the three gaunt spectres he had left, hale and hearty, just a month before. They prayed together, and he received a visitation that the swamp was the source of the fever. At 5.00 a.m. next morning, after the coffee with no sugar, we all, including me the cook, began digging a deep canal joining the swamp to the lake.

As I said, Cape MacClear reminded me of a Jamaican beach. I don't know if this is true of beaches in Scotland but at home, where a river meets the ocean, it makes a sandbank that all but dams the river itself. A swamp forms behind it and the river becomes a steady trickle, even in the dry season. If you dredge the river, which was Dr Laws's plan, you risk washing away the sandbank, no matter how many Union Jacks you stamp on it.

The next three weeks, I saw another side of Dr Laws. I'd seen hints of the same in Dr Livingstone, who was capable of sacrificing anything or anybody to achieve his goals, which he sometimes managed. Dr Laws flung himself into the canal project, working harder than the rest put together, toiling to dig sand.

It's not possible to dig sand. You shovel it to one side, then watch the landslides as the grains trickle back into the tiny depression you've made. A rainstorm at noon washes everything back into the gully, undoing hours of labour. After a week of this, Dr Laws had a new idea—to hammer stakes into the sand at six foot intervals either side of the gully and tie reed mats between them. The plan was to collect the sand in the baskets the village women use for storing flour and pile it up behind the flimsy palisades. Perhaps in the dry season, this could have worked, though only for a short time. But the mats weren't strong enough to hold back rain-swept sand. We woke from our sleeping quarters after a night of electric storms to find the mats and stakes all tangled in the shallow bed of the stream.

The rains were torrential, with high winds and bursts of forked lightning, like a Jamaican hurricane but without the respite you get in the hurricane's eye, or from knowing it has its own clock. The stream flooded, of course, washing away the last trace of Dr Laws's canal. Even the Union Jack became a maze of tiny rivulets, and where the main stream entered the lake a delta of its own built up, like a copy of the mission site.

With the rains came more fever. It don't bother me or Fred or Thomas, but all the *azungu* were affected, sometimes four at a time. Dr Laws dosed them with quinine, just like at Magomero. But it never did much good. I prayed Capt. Young wouldn't die, nor Mr Liddel who I'd helped in the garden. He was a Joshua, always open to ideas. When the pumpkins started sprouting with their umbrella leaves, I pointed out that the Africans ate the leaves too and showed him how to cook them with a little dried fish.

The fevers wore everyone out. They made the *azungu* ill-tempered, and they didn't just take it out on the servants as we tried to nurse them. They attacked each other. Again, this was different from Magomero. When fever made the Bishop and Mr Waller testy with each other, they argued about things like the word lists they were making. Mr Waller insisted *ukaka* was the correct word for sesame seeds. The Bishop said, no, what he'd written down was *umphedza*. In fact, they were both right. There's more than one word. But they argued like hot pepper until Mr Waller apologised for what he called his ill-humour, and the Bishop embraced him.

But these Scotsmen turned their very religion into quarrelling. 'You should strive', Dr Laws would say furiously, 'by the grace of God, to be more like Christ himself was and is.' There was no answering that, though I once heard Mr Liddel mutter, 'Mind your God and mind your Bible' as he walked off in a huff. Another of Dr Law's rebukes was 'Preach everyday that most eloquent of sermons, the Christian life'—this because Mr Simpson, shaking with fever, had forgotten to tell Thomas to clean the latrine. The fever seemed to bring out something stamped on their souls since childhood.

The worst of these quarrels erupted between Dr Laws and Capt. Young, and it helped me to my own decision. With the rains ending, Dr Laws hired a dozen men to dig an irrigation ditch to bring water to Mr Liddel's garden, promising he would pay them in calico. They were working rhythmically and chanting, their hoes striking the ground in time with the beat. I was close by, washing the breakfast plates, and Capt. Young, who was passing, caught me laughing at the song.

'What are they singing, Lorenzo?'

I translated:

> We bring ufa for sale,
> And yet he makes us work so hard!
> We bring fowls for sale,
> And yet he makes us work very hard!
> We bring maize for sale,
> And yet he makes slaves of usi.

Capt. Young roared with laughter, just as Dr Laws, who had heard everything, came round the corner of the main building. His face was redder than usual, and it was clear he was furious.

'In Christ there is no slave or free. His service is perfect freedom', he shouted.

He stalked off, then swiveled round after a few paces.

'Your work here is done,' he told Capt. Young. 'I will give you a letter saying you have completed what you were commissioned to perform.'

How this argument was resolved I never knew. Perhaps Dr Laws realised how short-handed he was, particularly in days of fever, and how there was no one else to captain the *Ilala*. Whatever, Capt. Young stayed until the cold season. But the quarrel brought home to me how my fate was bound up with Capt. Young's. Also, that my scripture was different from Dr Laws's. The four gospels make no provision for slavery.

One further thing confirmed my intention. We heard a slave caravan had been assembled, not twelve miles off at Ntondo's. Ntondo's was one of the villages I visited to buy fowls and maize flour when the *Ilala* was circumnavigating the lake. Rumours like this were constant, but this time the slaves included men who'd worked for us at Cape MacClear. Their families came to ask for help in rescuing them, describing the shackles and forked sticks in which they were held, ready for shipment across the lake. But Dr Laws refused, though he afterwards claimed their story 'made his blood boil'. What really made him angry was I had told them the *azungu* had come to put an end to the slave trade. I was instructed to curb my spiritual pride and mind my kitchen.

In July, a bundle of letters arrived, with the first news of the outside world in nine months. They told of reinforcements already at sea, a gardener, an engineer, a weaver, a blacksmith, and a group of *catequists* from South Africa.

So colonization was well under way.

Capt. Young announced he would leave as soon as the first contingent arrived. I decided to leave with him. Dr Laws would have to find another cook.

My own news was that my wife, Lottie, had passed away in April, giving birth to a stillborn son.

7 Mbewe

The *azungu* were fortifying Mandala, lining up packing cases between the pillars on both levels, with narrow slits between them for shooting through. Mandala was on a slight rise, and defenders firing from the upstairs house would have a huge advantage.

They all had powerful Winchester and Martini-Henry rifles. Coming upriver, they liked to shoot at things, hippos, crocodiles, even fish eagles. They called it sport and did it for pleasure, even if the result was something 'for the pot'. The first time Mbewe saw a Martini-Henry in action, he was staggered. Mr Faulkner, that elephant hunter who died of fever, could take a springbok in his sights when it looked no bigger than a cane-rat, and drop it with a single shot.

Chikusi's men had only flintlocks and bows and arrows.

As well as Mr John and Mr Frederick, there were Mr Morrison and Mr Fotheringham, who both worked for the company, Mr Buchanan who used to be with the mission but now had a farm near Mount Soche, where he was trying to find something that could grow profitably and Mr Rankin, an ivory hunter Mbewe had met at Sinhala Mariya's. He was surprised to see him at Mandala because, like Piri Piri, he usually preferred to trade on his own.

But there were two other men he didn't know. One was tall and portly and had a huge moustache. He talked very differently from Mr John or Mr Frederick, as though he had a pebble in his mouth, and there was another constantly in attendance on him. This second man was equally tall, but young and dark-haired and seemed anxious to please. At times, the two men laughed together as though they were brothers, though the laughter never included Chemandala or Mr Morrison. At other times, the young man, who always stood slightly behind his friend, seemed to be noting down whatever the first man said.

Another puzzle was that every evening, when they sat down to dinner with Chemandala and whoever was present, they changed their clothes, very smart in black cloth with ties like black butterflies, and sat at separate tables.

Mbewe was down in the yard wondering about these matters when an old man called Mphetomwanyama arrived. He knew him as one of Ramakukan's elders and greeted him in the proper manner, bowing and gently clapping his hands.

'Good morning, uncle. A message for Chemandala?'

'No. From Ramakukan to Mr Consul.'

'Who is this, Mbewe?' called Chindevu from the upper floor.

He told him, 'A messenger from Ramakukan.'

'For my brother?'

'For Mr Consul.'

'Ah! He must see Mr St Claire first'.

He beckoned us inside. Mphetomwanyama was staring in astonishment at the house wondering, as Mbewe had done, how it stayed up and how the *azungu* had got up there.

'Can they fly?' I heard him muttering.

He studied the staircase with deep suspicion.

'It is for climbing up,' said Mbewe, as though he had been doing it all his life. Mphetomwanyama began on his hands and knees, then rose to his feet on the sixth step, managing to climb the rest without leaning on Mbewe and taking the last two stairs in a single stride, grinning as he looked back down the staircase. They entered the room used by Mr John. The young dark man was sitting at the desk with Chemandala standing beside him, looking very cross.

'Is this Mr Consul?' Mphetomwanyama asked Mbewe in Manganja.

Chindevu understood him but replied in English, 'It is Mr St Claire, his messenger.'

Mbewe translated, and Mphetomwanyama said at once, 'Ramakukan's message is for Mr Consul.'

'Only Ramakukan can talk to Mr Consul,' said Chindevu. 'Ramakukan's messenger must talk to Mr Consul's messenger.'

Mbewe translated this and Mphetomwanyama thought for a moment. Then he spoke to me rapidly.

'He says Mr Consul is the Queen's messenger. So Ramakukan's messenger must talk to Mr Consul.'

'Such protocol,' said Mr St Claire. 'This is worse than the Portuguese. Wait here. I'll see what I can do.'

He left the room, and we heard laughter from somewhere inside the house. He returned after a few minutes, following the tall man with the moustache, who was apparently Mr Consul. He was still laughing as he entered but changed it quickly to a smile and a handshake for Mphetomwanyama.

'Please inform Chief Ramakukan that as Her Majesty's Roving Consul—no, that will be impossible to translate, say as the Queen's messenger I am very happy to receive his messenger.'

Mbewe turned this into Manganja, and Mphetomwanyama made a long reply, waving his arms for emphasis.

'Ramakukan says there will be no war,' Mbewe told Mr Consul. 'But the period of mourning must be respected. There must be no river travel for forty days.'

'Is Ramakukan in control?'

'There is no control during mourning. It is a time without rules.'

Mphetomwanyama interrupted with another long speech, looking from Mr Consul to Mbewe, and back again.

'Chikusi is still making war. He wants to be chief instead of Ramakukan. Katunga and Mlauri are supporting Chikusi. The other headmen are still loyal.'

'We heard Mr Frederick has been killed.'

Frederick was the Company agent at Katunga's.

'Mr Frederick is well, but the store has been burned.'

Chemandala wanted to interrupt but Mr Consul held up his left hand. Mbewe was impressed he could silence Mr John with a gesture.

'Please tell Chief Ramakukan that the Queen knows about his kindness to Dr Livingstone. We have no wish for any war.'

He paused while Mbewe translated.

'Please tell the chief we will respect the period of mourning. The steamers will remain where they are until we hear from him.'

He turned to Chemandala.

'Where are they at present?'

'The *Ilala* is at Livingstonia. The *Lady Nyasa* is waiting at Chiromo.'

'They will remain there for the time being.'

Mr John looked black as thunder.

'Tell the chief we fully respect his rights as chief. When it is possible to travel, I shall come to him and settle the dispute about the tusks of ivory.'

So Ramakukan was dealing directly with the Queen in England. The two messengers, Mr Consul and Mphetomwanyama, shook hands.

8 Maria Afonso

Afonso had no immediate prospect of going to Africa. First he had to complete his studies. After his sixth year, he left the Colégio Militar for the Escola do Exército, founded by the redoubtable Marquis Sá da Bandeira. He made this move because of the Escola's curriculum and facilities. But it had the effect of associating him with the Reformist Party, which Sá da Bandeira had served five times as prime minister. The Reformists had recently lost power to the Regenerators. At the time, Afonso gave no thought to the consequences, but for the next few years he found himself on the wrong side of a division that was more than political, reaching bitterly into all levels of society.

From the half-starved boy who had stood before the Principal of the Colégio Militar in Mafra, Afonso had grown into a short but big-boned lad, with large capable hands and the slightly bowed legs of someone descended from generations used to walking across ploughed fields. His face was oval, the features grouped close together as though drawn on an egg, with room to spare either side. He had abundant curly hair and, for the time being, was clean-shaven. It was not a face he enjoyed seeing in the mirror, wishing he had the razor sharpness of his famous ancestor. No matter what he did, his uniform never fitted properly, though it was immaculately kept.

Sá da Bandeira had died while Afonso was at the Colégio Militar but the Escola's curriculum was infused with his legacy. Like Serpa Pinto's maternal grandfather, he had first become famous in the Peninsular War against the French, reinforced by his key role in the War of the Two Brothers, between Pedro's constitutionalists and Miguel's absolutists. He lost his right arm in the defence of Porto. His liberal principles were next expressed as Overseas Minister and five times as Prime Minister. His record included the founding of polytechnics and schools of fine arts in Porto and Lisbon, along with the Escola de Exército and countless agricultural and industrial associations. Most notably, his name had passed into history for his abolition of colonial slavery. To Afonso, he was a supremely romantic figure. Left for dead at the battle of Viella in southern France, he was rescued and nursed by two French ladies, with whom he subsequently maintained a lifetime's correspondence. Afonso dreamed of something similar happening to him, except, of course, that it would be a single French maiden, beautiful and modest, whom he subsequently would marry.

The days had gone when Sá da Bandeira had dreamed of turning Portuguese possessions in Africa into a second Brazil. The Portuguese did not enjoy the technological supremacy over African fighters that would compensate for long lines of communication. In Zambezia, three campaigns against Bonga's *arringa* at Massangano had ended in 1869 in utter disaster, and for the next two decades the whitened skulls of Portuguese soldiers were displayed on Bonga's stockade as a terrible reminder to travellers by the river. A shift in policy was inevitable, but it left Afonso, as he began his new course at the Escola, with little prospect of ever becoming a soldier in Africa.

'Comércio livre,' insisted his friend Alfredo de Sá Cardoso, thumping the wooden table in the student *refeitoria*. 'Now slavery's gone, free trade will make the creoles prosperous. They're loyal Portuguese, after all. Their wealth will be our wealth, securing the colonies for Portugal.'

Alfredo, who tended to dominate discussions with his high forehead and purposeful face, had been a fellow student at the Colégio Militar but one year ahead of him. He had taken up with Afonso after the episode of the essay comparing church and army, and now at the Escola, though still separated by a year, they had become firm friends.

'You sound like a *rosebife*,' said Manuel de Oliveira. He spoke with an exaggerated Coimbra accent, regarding anyone from Lisbon as little better than an Arab.

'What did Napoleon call them? A nation of shopkeepers.'

'With their methods, they're going to rule the world,' countered Alfredo, his deep-set eyes out-staring Manuel. 'Why shouldn't we copy what works. It's not as if we can afford anything else.'

That point scored, there was silence round the table. It was Tuesday, the day the cooks served cod with cream, a favourite with the students, and the tables were crowded

Diminutive Zé Miguel, who already sported a pale moustache, was mumbling. His full name was Alfred José Miguel, Alfred, that is, in the English fashion, but since meeting Alfredo had modestly resorted to the shorter form of his name to avoid confusion. He had the habit of rehearsing his phrases before he uttered them. At last, he piped up shyly, 'What goods are they going to trade in?'

Alfredo waved his hand grandly.

'Oh, palm oil, sesame, groundnuts, cotton, wild rubber, the usual stuff. The crisis of capitalism is a crisis of raw materials. The Africans will grow them, or collect them, our people will trade them, and Portugal will buy them.'

'What if it's the English who buy them?'

'No matter. Our people, Portuguese people, will still profit. And the colonies will prosper.'

Afonso took no part in this discussion. Though he and Alfredo were friends, he was a year younger than the other speakers, and at the Escola hierarchies were strictly observed, at least in public. He listened with fascination. In his heart, he felt Alfredo was wrong, but he couldn't pin down his objections.

Mumbling again before coming out with it, little Zé Miguel had a go.

'What of our glorious history? Francisco de Almeida? Afonso de Albuquerque? The *barões assinalados*? The conquerors of Mombasa and Calicut and Macão?'

Zé Miguel, who was part Indian, was from Portuguese East Africa, from a large estate, or *prazo,* south of Quelimane. The Portuguese empire was a matter of trust to him.

'What of them?' said Alfredo excitedly, knowing he was being outrageous. 'It was only about trade. What did Vasco da Gama go in search of?'

He looked round the table, challenging each in turn with his thick eyebrows.

'Pepper. That's all it was about. Pepper, cinnamon, cloves, cumin, and the rest. What do you do with spices? You eat

54

them. And when you've eaten them, you have to cut down two whole forests to built a couple of caravels to sail to India and pay out African gold, to buy some more. It was always a fool's game.'

'So Camões was a fool?'

Alfredo smiled condescingly.

'Camões was a great poet. Perhaps the greatest the world has seen. But he was no man of business. Look at the way he managed his own life. Even his love affairs were a disaster.'

But he had gone too far and was losing his audience. As they finished their cod with cream and returned their plates to the kitchen hatch, some preferred to take their sweets and coffee to other tables.

After coffee, Alfredo, Zé Miguel and Afonso walked downhill into the heart of Lisbon. The Escola was based in the magnificent Palácio de Bemposta, built by Catherine of Bragança, Charles II's widow, on her return to Portugal in 1693. It was located on a small range of hills to the north-east of the city, a little beyond the church and convent of Graça, which were in turn a little beyond the castle and the church of St Vincent. To get to town, the friends had to cross the Martyrs' Field, where Gomes Freire and his fellow patriots had been hung by the English in 1817, descending into the old Arab quarter of Mouraria. Beyond that, they were met by rubble.

Alfredo had been born in Lisbon and knew the city inside out. It was one of the things Afonso most enjoyed about their friendship, since his own visits had been infrequent and usually to specific destinations, in excursions from the Colégio Militar—to the castle, to the arsenal, to the Terreiro do Paço, to the Jerónimos Monastery. Alfredo showed him the back streets, with their steep staircases, the delights of travelling by horse-drawn tram and the tiny cafes in the grid of streets built by the Marquis of Pombal after the earthquake. But in sharp contrast to his colonial iconoclasm, Alfredo was conservative about the city. He didn't like change, and change lay before them.

The whole area in front of the *Baixa Pombalina* had been ripped up. Where there had been a long park and garden, with public walkways to east and west, reaching as far as the Praça de Alegria, there were now earthworks. The fountains Alfredo remembered so well, the waterfall, the gardens with their flowering trees and allegorical statues in the eighteenth century manner, were all gone, at least for the time being. The city council was building a ninety-yard-wide boulevard, in blatant imitation of the Champs d'Elysée, extending one thousand yards north-east from the *baixa*, between the heights of Graça and Penha to the right and the Bairro Alto to the left, as far as the green hills and smallholdings of the Vale de Pereiro. Two years they'd been at it, and they'd progressed hardly two hundred yards with their diggings.

Secretly, Afonso was impressed, but he didn't want to irritate his friend. 'It's a big project. Who's paying for it?'

'Oh, borrowing, borrowing and more borrowing. That's how everything's done these days. Bankruptcy doesn't matter.'

They crossed to the Rua de Santa Justa and climbed up the Chiado past the Bertrand Bookshop to the Loreto, sitting outside a small bar opposite the melancholy statue of Camões, with its sleepy, pacing sentry. Coach drivers waited patiently for fares. On one corner, a group of shabbily dressed loafers stood smoking. At the entrance to the Havanesa, another group of loafers smoked, but these wore frock coats and talked politics.

Camões's statue stood on its high pedestal, ringed by Portugal's lesser poets. They were drinking the wine of the house, a rough red from Setubal. Zé Miguel, fingering his tumbler, was mumbling to himself.

'Can you have meant what you said about *The Lusíads*?'

Alfredo was unrelenting.

'it's a grocer's poem,' he declared, 'a parody of an epic we Portuguese have been fooled into taking seriously. Vasco da Gama is a hopeless hero. He never even gets out of his boat, except briefly in India for some incompetent diplomacy, and then he spends half a canto trying to get back into it.'

Once again, Afonso felt an impulse to protest, but instead he recited, half under his breath so that the words were barely audible:

But while in your blind, insane frenzy
You thirst for your brothers' blood in Christ,
There will be no lack of Christian daring
In this little house of Portugal.
In Africa, they have coastal bases;
In Asia, no one disputes their power:
The New World already feels their ploughshare,
And if fresh worlds are found, they will be there.

No one interrupted. He had created a respectful silence. For three hundred years, the Portuguese had been a nation of emigrants. The fact was enshrined in the national epic. Alfredo raised his tumbler to the statue with a respect that was only partially mocking.

'You win, brother', he said, and it wasn't clear whether he was addressing Camões or Afonso. 'You always win.'

He ordered another carafe and for a while the silence continued, though Zé Miguel began to mumble.

'That's just it', he burst out. 'There's no part of the world where you won't find Portuguese'.

'What? Governing? Or just integrating?'

'What difference does it make?'

Three fishwives with flat baskets on their heads swayed past, swinging their hips. One of the horse-cab drivers began arguing loudly with a customer about a fare. Their angry dispute was clearly audible at thirty yards distance. Draped in pigeon guano, Camões maintained his pose, staring across the heads of his fellow poets, his one eye endlessly ambiguous.

'It makes all the difference,' said Alfredo wearily. 'Camões painted our past in such colours we're all seduced. We think we were glorious then and can be glorious again. But it's poetry, nothing more. The English call it punching above your weight.'

The argument across the street was getting nasty, and two policemen with their dark-blue uniforms, peaked caps and sabres had arrived. The cab driver was instantly docile. But the customer, apparently unaware that bribing the police was going to cost him more than the fare in dispute, continued shouting. Eventually, they led him round a corner into an alley on Rua Flores. All the by-standers, including the frock-coated gentlemen outside the Havanesa, knew what was being negotiated and that the cab driver would get nothing.

Alfredo drained his wine and refilled the three tumblers.

'Our strength is precisely that we're not governing. We don't have the power to conquer and rule. But we're there. Everywhere you go, in Brazil or Africa or India, even China, there's a small Portuguese shopkeeper, married into the community, speaking the language and speaking Portuguese. They know what's produced locally, they know the markets and the routes. That's why, however Manuel de Oliveira sneers about shopkeepers and *rosebifes*, that's why this free-trade policy makes sense.'

Then he added, as an afterthought, 'It also happens to be government policy. You know I'm not normally an admirer of governments. But this time they are talking sense.'

Afonso wanted to ask, 'What role is there for a soldier in this?', but he kept his peace.

9 Mbewe

Chemandala had sent letters to the captains of the *Ilala* and the *Lady Nyasa,* warning them not to enter the Shire River. Mr Frederick arrived from Katunga's with nothing but his own clothes, but proving Mphetomwanyama had not lied. Mr Consul exchanged messages with Ramakukan, settling the dispute about the ivory and agreeing that, in future, the Company would pay a tax for passing through his land in return for an end to thieving by his followers. Everything seemed to have calmed down.

Mbewe knew all this because it was common knowledge. No one panicked, but they just couldn't stop talking to anyone who would listen. About what had happened, what was going to happen, what might already be happening. There was supposed to be a letter from headman Changara at Matope, demanding Mrs Fenwick be handed over to him.

The third afternoon, Mrs Fenwick started screaming. Mbewe hadn't seen her since the day he arrived and told Chindevu about what happened to Piri Piri. People said she had locked herself away and would only consent to see Philip when he brought her some food.

Now she rushed out to the top veranda in her nightclothes, shouting over and over again to the yard below.

'Philip's gone! They've taken him to be a slave!'

She had a letter in her hand.

Mr Morrison calmed her and led her back inside. She could be heard moaning and repeating, 'They've taken him to be a slave.'

Mr Morrison came downstairs, holding the letter. He wanted to ask Mbewe if he recognised Philip's handwriting. Mbewe replied no, he didn't know how to read. Mr Morrison said the letter was in English and it read, 'Madam, Goodbye. They have captured me.'

Mbewe's first thought was he was lying. He'd just gone to join his brothers, the ones who left when Chipatula was killed. Then he wondered, why had he stayed behind in the first place? Why leave then, and why leave behind a letter? Was he hoping the *azungu* would rush after to rescue him and be drawn into a trap?

He was puzzling over this when the noise of a crowd came blown on the wind from the escarpment road. As it grew louder, he could see four bearers carrying someone in a hammock. They were running, chanting in rhythm, and behind them was a line of excited children. Gradually, the words they were singing became audible:

> Ichi ndi chiani?
> Ife se na chione
> Nzungo o vala bark cloth.

Women gathered, joining in the song, ululating and clapping as they formed two lines for the bearers to pass through.

> What is this?
> We have never seen this,
> A white man wearing bark cloth.

The bearers stopped in the yard. The occupant of the hammock seemed to be trying to urge them to carry him into the house, but they laid their burden down, and he had to walk. At first, the man seemed quite naked, no shirt, no shorts, no shoes. Then Mbewe saw he had indeed a triangle of bark cloth covering his manhood. In the same moment, he recognised him. It was Mr Gouk of the *Lady Nyasa*.

He staggered inside, followed by hoots of laughter, and the crowd waited in the courtyard for explanations. They didn't have to wait long.

'Sunk! What do you mean sunk?' Chemandala's voice echoed. There was a barely audible murmur, then, 'Why didn't you obey my letter?'

Another murmur. There was absolute silence in the courtyard as everyone strained to listen.

'I told you, stay where you were. On no account were you to enter the Shire till further instructions. And when you did, to make sure you maintained a full load of firewood and kept the main gun primed in the bow.'

After a longer period of muttering by Gouk, Chemandala shouted again. 'I never wrote that!'

Two of the women started up the song again, but they were told to keep quiet. Chindevu appeared on the veranda and beckoned Mbewe to come upstairs. He climbed to the office where Chemandala was sitting behind his desk, with Mr Morrison standing beside him. Mr Gouk was still in his bark cloth.

Chemandala ignored his entry. He was pointing at a book with metal rings, open on the desk before him, holding another paper in his hand.

'Here's the carbon copy of what I wrote. This missive's not even in my hand.'

'I'm sorry, sir', said the captain. 'I thought I was obeying your orders.'

'This is a disaster.'

'I'm very sorry, sir,' said Mr Gouk. 'I don't believe I have ever seen your handwriting.'

Mr Consul came into the office, accompanied by Mr St Claire who looked as if he'd just woken up from a nap.

'I understand there's been a development,' said Mr Consul. 'Hello, do I recognise Mr Gouk?'

Chemandala was too furious to be polite.

'The *Lady Nyassa* has been sunk. We have a spy in our midst.'

He started directly at Mbewe and held out the paper.

'Is this your doing? Did you write this?'

Mbewe couldn't read the letter but he recognised the neat marks covering the middle of the paper.

'Sir, I am not educated, sir. But I think Mr Morrison might know.'

He returned the letter back to Chemandala who passed it on to Mr Morrison.

He read aloud, 'The river is open. No problem. Proceed immediately to Katunga's. Praise be to the Lord.'

'The signature,' he added, 'is illegible.'

'Did you really believe I wrote this?' shouted Chemandala.

Mr Gouk looked like a beaten dog. Chikusi had made him wear bark cloth, like the lowest of the low, and now the company was also treating him like a dog.

Chindevu intervened.

'The question is, what is Chikusi demanding?"

It turned out there was another letter, brought by the Mr Gouk and written in Manganja. Mbewe couldn't read this either, but Chindevu knew enough Manganja to pick out the sounds so Mbewe could interpret.

'He demands you send him all your guns and calico, and hand over Piri Piri's woman. Otherwise, they will break up the steamer.'

'Piri Piri's woman?'

'Mrs Fenwick'

'Is he crazy?'

'I suppose he wants to stick her head on a pole. Next to her husband,' said Mr Morrison.

'No,' said Mbewe. 'It is just our custom. If you kill a man it is only fair to take his woman as your wife. Otherwise, who will protect her?'

'Chikusi wanted to kill me,' said the captain. 'Only Mlauri stopped him.'

'Who's Mlauri?' asked Mr Consul.

'One of Ramakukan's headmen,' said Chindevu.

'All the same,' said Mr Consul, 'it doesn't look as though Ramakukan is completely in control.'

'Well that's,' began Chemandala furiously, then swallowed the rest of his remark.

'So who was responsible for this forgery?' he asked instead, brandishing the first letter.

'Philip,' said Mr Morrison.

In all his voyages, Mbewe had never seen the *azungu* so completely out of their depth.

10 Tony St Claire

Tony St Claire had been much taken by his new title, First Under-Secretary to Her Majesty's Roving Consul for Central Africa.

'Where the devil, for a start,' he chuckled to his guests in the smoking room at Pratt's, 'is Central Africa?'

The Foreign Office knew where Portuguese East Africa was located and the Queen already had a consul there. They knew where Portuguese West Africa lay, though it wasn't yet honoured with official representation. Presumably, central Africa was the bit in between, though it seemed the Portuguese didn't accept for that for one minute.

'Where do they think it is then?' asked one of Tony's guests with a yawn.

'They don't reckon it's anywhere. For them, Portuguese East and Portuguese West join up.'.

'But there must be somewhere in the middle. It stands to reason'

'Not for them. They reckon it's Portuguese all the way across.'

Tony signalled to the waiter.

'Two more bottles of claret, George. Can't you see we're dry?'

All the waiters at Pratt's were, by tradition, known as George. It saved having to remember faces.

'That bishop,' he continued, 'the one we used to hear about at St John's. You remember all those prayers about our modern martyr? He was consecrated Bishop to the Tribes dwelling in the neighbourhood of Lake Nyasa and the River Shire. Maybe that's where Central Africa's supposed to be.'

'My uncle was a bishop,' said another of the guests. 'Bishop to the tribes dwelling in the neighbourhood of Truro.'

'That's also pretty remote,' said Tony. 'But did he have to declare war against some of them. I mean, real war, with guns and assegais?'

'I don't think so. He just preached some very pointed sermons.'

'Did they kill him?' asked the first guest.

'Who? My uncle?'

'St Claire's African bishop.'

'No,' said Tony. 'He died of fever and was buried by that River Shire. I know where that is. It's on maps nowadays.'

'Is that possible?'

'What?'

'Becoming a martyr when you died of fever.'

'I've no idea,' said Tony. 'George, what do you reckon?'

George was pouring claret into five clean glasses. Clean glasses for a fresh bottle was *de rigeur* at Pratt's, even though there had been no time for the wine to stand.

'I believe, sir, that violence against the person is not a theological necessity.'

This was recorded as one of George's best *mots*.

The other words of Tony's title were 'First Undersecretary', as though there existed a second and third and fourth. Or even a secretary for him to be under.

'No way,' said Tony. 'It's going to be just me and him.'

'Him' was Consul Doveton, the man who, six months later, he had got into the habit of calling 'Mr Consul', following the example of Ramakukan's messenger Mphetomwanyama. He'd enjoyed the diplomacy over Ramakukan, which he thought Mr Consul had handled very well, avoiding a war with the Kololo and also avoiding any interference by the Portuguese. He'd also found Mphetomwanyama as impressive as any member of his own diplomatic corps.

Consul Doveton was a Roving Consul, which meant he was part diplomat, part spy and part amateur explorer, sending papers to the Royal Geographical Society about the sources of obscure rivers or the characteristics of harbours he reckoned to have discovered. He also enjoyed hunting big game and was assembling a 'bag' of the major fauna, to be sent to the Science Museum.

St Claire found himself more interested in plants, especially plants that might turn out to be exploited commercially. He was a clergyman's son, raised in a Yorkshire parish and a minor public school, a little inclined to view the world as an eternal cricket match that could always be interrupted by an tea interval. At school, he had turned out to be adept at turning Tennyson into Latin verse but had shown no other intellectual interests. He had bright blue eyes, broad shoulders, and the slight stoop from being taller than his contemporaries. But he made friends easily and kept them, being endlessly good-humoured.

Plants were an unexpected enthusiasm, acquired on a visit to the Governor's botanical garden at Cape Town, where Tony had waited three weeks for his onward passage. The first day he was simply stunned, even disturbed, by jacarandas and strelitzias, aloes with their perfect symmetry, and succulents like the spreading fingers of the Hottentot fig. For the first time in his life, he felt his habitual understatement failing him. Standing under the avenue of flamboyants—no other possible name for them with their cool green fronds and exploding stars of scarlet flowers—irony had no place. He felt the need to gush but lacked the vocabulary and was reduced to 'good Lord' and 'phew'.

On subsequent visits, he began to learn from their labels that some of these plants, like the coral trees or the elephantine baobabs, were indigenous while others, like the wild dates, the Norfolk island pines or the ancient Saffron pear tree, had been imported for the sake of the collection.

He had landed in what he thought would be a third rate version of Plymouth, albeit overlooked by the huge mass of Table Mountain, and had begun to discover a vocation. In the greenhouses, there was an active search for new plants able to survive in the sub-tropical hot summers and mild wet winters —especially types of cotton, rubber, coffee or sisal that could be grown commercially. This was not merely a matter of importing seeds and seeing what could grow. It involved breeding new types, as Mr Darwin had described pigeon fanciers and race-horse breeders doing. He learned that, just as in France, the local vineyards had been destroyed by the phylloxera aphid, so the local gardeners were experimenting with American root-stocks as cultivars. By the time Tony boarded the frigate to sail to the delta of the Zambezi River, he was no longer joking about his job description or his destination. He had a cause.

His own 'bag', as he accompanied 'Mr Consul' on his hunting safaris, was of seeds, berries and dried tubers, with a notebook sketching the living trees and shrubs and delineating carefully where they had been encountered. He didn't much enjoy killing animals, but hunting was a good excuse for venturing into the forest to collect his own specimens.

After their meeting with Ramakukan, Mr Consul and Tony were combining business with pleasure on their return safari to Quelimane when, in Maindo, a *prazo* to the south west of the town, they had a nasty encounter with a buffalo. With his first shot Doveton wounded it in the cheek. When he put his hand out for the second rifle, his bearer tripped and the gun dropped between them. The buffalo charged and the small party scattered. As the wounded animal turned, Tony grabbed the gun and tossed it to Doveton who fired again, this time mortally. But Tony was caught in the buffalo's second charge, and its horn glanced against his right thigh, just below the hip.

In no danger but in considerable pain, he was carried by improvised hammock to the nearby house of a widow called Dona Esmeralda.

The Consul knew her slightly. Until his death eighteen months earlier, her husband Augusto had been one of his best sources for the clandestine slave trade, still maintained from hidden creeks in the vast Zambezi delta. He wasn't sure whether she blamed him for her husband's troubles. But she welcomed the small party generously, ordering refreshments and making Tony comfortable on a long, cool veranda, surrounded by plants and shut in by mosquito netting.

The Consul prepared to leave for Quelimane.

'I'll get the naval doctor here tomorrow,' he promised.

He was referring to a British anti-slavery corvette, patrolling the Quelimane bar.

'We have a doctor here, too,' she said. 'Very good with wounds,' she said. 'Not so good with love potions.'

Consul Doveton pulled a face.

'No mumbo jumbo, please.'

'What is this mumbo jumbo?'

'Never mind. Just look after him. Help will be here tomorrow.'

Knowing which house he had been summoned to, Jiwa the doctor—or what Consul Doveton would have called the witchdoctor—left most of his customary paraphernalia behind. That meant discarding his bag of divining bones, his spirit bottle, his flakes of tortoiseshell (good in curing rickets), his patch of porcupine skin (to repel thieves), his tiny bundles of wild rice (to keep families united), all normally hidden under his cloak made from skins of monitor lizards. His ivory-handled flywhisk he brought with him (after all, it had practical uses), and the necklace of leopard's teeth he was too proud to remove.

Despite Dona Esmerald's comment that he was no good with love potions, he was universally nicknamed Faz Tudo (literally, 'does everything'), and in crises he was much in demand.

Calling for a lantern in the dying light, he examined Tony's wound carefully, cutting a hole in Tony's trousers and picking out some fragments of khaki.

'It has not been washed,' he remarked, and asked for a basin of warm water.

Tony was in much pain, but Jiwa could not have been gentler as he bathed the exposed skin, clearing the dried blood.

'There is bone,' said Jiwa, holding up a thin splinter. Then remarkably, he asked for a urine sample, which he held up to the kerosene lantern, studying it for some moments.

'There is no inside bleeding. That is good. But we will check again tomorrow.'

It ended with him mixing a paste of pounded seeds and herbs which he smeared over a banana leaf and bound securely over the open wound. Almost immediately, Tony felt the pain easing.

'O que é?' he asked his host, in his halting Portuguese.

'That is Jiwa's secret,' said Dona Esmeralda. 'Now you must eat and take a little wine and then rest.'

11 Lorenzo

When Capt. Young departed from Cape MacClear, continued Lorenzo in his notebook, I left with him. I took the line that he recruited me and that I should leave when he left. Dr Laws couldn't argue. He was glad to see me go but reluctant, because I was making the decision. He'd have preferred to sack me but didn't have any reason. My cooking was not at fault. It was my character. I was Quashie, even down to the pumpkin which I taught them to eat in the African manner.

So we left together for Cape Town, down the River Shire through Elephant Marsh, down the Zambezi to Mazaro, down the Quaqua to Quelimane, and from there by steamer to Cape Town. This gave plenty of time to talk, and Capt. Young outlined a plan.

I had nothing to hold me in Cape Town, beyond visiting a grave. He came with me and I honoured him for that. Afterwards, he suggested I should sail with him to Scotland where I 'would be an eloquent campaigner in the fight against the slave trade'.

'You mean make speeches? I've never done that.'

'Just tell your story, and describe what you've seen in Africa.'

So I agreed. We sailed to London, caught the train to Carlisle and the connecting train to Buchanan Street, Glasgow, where Capt. Young booked me a room in the Sailors Home on the Broomielaw.

Glasgow was an awful place. Over the next few days, I'd plenty of free time to look around, beside the Clyde along the Broomielaw, turning in towards the city, walking the length of Argyle St., turning left into Queen St. as far as George Square and the Tron Church, then back across the river into the Gorbals. I saw many fine buildings, as fine as those twenty years before in London, some of them new, like the Stock Exchange and the Fish Market. next to Buchanan Street Station, which remained for me a landmark. There was wealth there, I could see that, from shipbuilding and engineering along with the cotton industry and the glassworks.

But the place stank. The air seemed heavy with some kind of gas, combined with other smells of sewage and rotting vegetables. It made breathing a effort, while I never studied such pallid, stunted people, as though they never saw sunlight or tasted fresh lentils. This was November, and there were days when the breeze from the sea was fresher after a shower. But even the poorest people in Africa, even in the days of the *magumanya* famine, never looked so dirty or ill-made as the inhabitants of the Gorbals. They were friendly enough. The children lined up behind me, giggling and shouting 'Blackie', but I didn't mind that. Children are children everywhere. What I did mind, because it was dangerous, was Argyle St. after ten o'clock at night. Every other building was a public house, like rum houses in Jamaica, except this was beer and whisky. When the drunks turned out on the street at closing time, there was no knowing what could happen. After one night when I saw six drunk women fighting, over what I have no idea, but they were pulling each other's hair and scratching with their fingernails, I decided enough was enough and spent my evenings in the Sailors' Home. There I could sit with the day's newspapers, puzzling over how people who lived like this could want to go to Africa, to tell the people there how they should be living. I don't mean they were hypocrites. Just that it seemed, well, an aggravation.

After five days, Capt. Young called on me with a strange request. He took me to a house in Mason St., near the Cathedral and the Necropolis, to meet a huge man with a big face, full head of hair and a long beard. His name was John Mossman, and he a was sculptor, a maker of graven images, working on a statue of David Livingstone. This was interesting, and I studied he wanted to talk about Livingstone, since I knew him from Magomero days. But no, Mr Mossman wanted something more. He wanted to use me as a model. He planned to include several African figures round the plinth of the main statue and asked if I was willing to pose for them. He even offered to pay. It would take, he told me, an hour or two most days, for several weeks.

I liked Mr Mossman. He was cheerful and ebullient and not in the least condescending. Capt. Young told me the payment was 'handsome', and I admit I was flattered. It always irritated me to be invisible in the histories in which I played a part, and here was a famous sculptor wanting to include my face in a statue to stand in the very middle of Glasgow. So I agreed, and for the next three months I visited Mason St. whenever I was free.

He began by making endless chalk drawings of my head and shoulders from every side. I was asked to look up at the ceiling and hold the pose for an hour without moving. Then down at the floor, then to left and to right, smiling, frowning and grimacing till my face felt as stiff as a real statue. All the while, he kept up a cheerful banter, which of course I couldn't join in, about what a filthy place Glasgow was, how it needed some better designed buildings with monuments and sculptures to make the place tolerable, about how the commerce was shrinking due to the state of trade with Europe and America, about the Scottish Presbyterian church with their idiotic divisions over tiny points of doctrine and ritual—yes, ritual, he said, even though they were supposed to be against Popish rites. Sometimes, I felt like laughing but, of course, I had to keep a straight face.

With Capt. Young to instruct me, I began my career as public speaker. Three nights a week, but never on Sundays, we went to different churches—some of Reformed Presbyterian, some Wee-Frees, some Established Presbyterian, and I don't know what else, all as Mr Mossman had said, quarrelling about small texts of the Bible. To me they looked exactly alike, gloomy caverns of stone-built or brick-built churches in which, from the carved table below the pulpit where I gave my talk, the congregations were barely visible. I was never the main speaker. Usually, the local minister opened with prayer and a talk about the Scottish missions his own particular church was supporting, then one of the sponsors of those missions talked of the fight against slavery, in the middle of which, I made a fifteen-minute speech about what it was like to be a slave.

At first, I didn't do very well. I didn't manage to say what the organisers expected. They had set positions which they wanted me to confirm, and they were vexed when I didn't. I don't mean they weren't open to argument. When one man in the newly built St Jude's claimed abolition was a disaster for Jamaica, I rounded on him fiercely, speaking as a ex-slave, and lots of people spoke up for me, coming up afterwards to shake my hand.

But there were other, smaller matters I couldn't question without undermining the cause—which was my cause—the abolition of the Arab slave trade. Capt. Young had to coach me on these, because I was disposed to argue.

They believed Africans had to be taught about commerce, and that Livingstone had been the first to introduce the exchange of trade goods. In my first talk, I described African specialists—the blacksmiths, the weavers, the salt-makers, who traded their hoes and rough cloth, even bark cloth, and punnets of salt. But Capt. Young said, no Lorenzo, don't speak of that. They believed the slave trade and what they called 'legitimate commerce' couldn't exist side by side, and that once half a dozen 'honest' businessmen arrived, the slave trade would wither of its own accord. I told them the trade in ivory ('legitimate') and slaves ('illegitimate') had always worked side by side.

'Ah,' said a man with a grey beard. 'But that is the exception that proves the rule. The slaves convey the ivory to the coast, and the white ivory and the black ivory are sold in the same transaction.'

'So who carries the calico and beads and guns and alcohol back into the interior?' I asked.

He digested this point, and I explained. 'There are professional porters who make one, perhaps two trips a year. They carry the ivory, and then they carry the trade goods back to where they started from. As for the slaves, many are women and children who can't carry anything.'

'I was surprised to hear you saying that,' said Capt. Young, after one such dispute. 'It doesn't help the cause.'

So I realised that in the cause, my cause, I had to be a politician. This was even more the case when I met some of the men who gave their backing to Dr Laws and wanted to be told Cape MacClear was succeeding.

'This is Mr James White of Overtoun,' said Capt. Young, after one session. 'He's a big industrialist in the chemical sector.'

So I found myself telling Mr White of Overtoun about the new buildings at Cape MacClear and the first operation ever performed in Africa using chloroform.

'I want you to meet Mr James Young of Kelly, F.R.S. He owns the patent for paraffin, and it was he who put up the money for the *Lady Nyasa*.'

'I've already seen the hull,' I told him. 'A steamer on the lake is going to be worth its weight in gold in the fight against slavery.'

'You must shake hands with Sir John Gowan of Beeslack. He's a leading paper manufacturer and a friend of Mr. Gladstone's.'

'I explained to Sir John how the *Union Jack* was laid out in the sand, and how the swamp behind Cape MacClear had been drained to eliminate mosquitos.'

'You're getting better at this,' Capt. Young told me.

Then he let me into a big secret. The industrialists I'd met, big-shot money-men, were planning a new venture. A trading company, the African Lakes Company, was being established 'to operate in conjunction with the mission at Cape MacClear but staffed independently and intended to make profits.' It would have its own steamer and would operate in all the waters of Lake Nyasa, the Shire and the lower Zambezi, trading in ivory, rubber, cotton and oil seeds, in return for whatever the Africans wanted—cloth, obviously, but beads and mirrors and anything else that could be traded. Not alcohol, though, nor guns. Those were strictly forbidden.

So it came about, two years later, I was installed as manager of the A.L.C. store at Matope, just above the rapids on the River Shire. This appointment was not straightforward. The directors consulted Dr Laws and the reply they received was not flattering. I was regarded as insubordinate and a deserter. But they already knew I had a mind of my own, and my defence that Capt. Young had recruited me and obliged me to leave when he left, to continue the fight against slavery in Scotland, was hard for them to dispute. By then, I'd met influential people, whom Capt. Young persuaded to speak up for me. Mr Mossman wrote a splendid letter, saying I was far more naturally intelligent than any clergyman he'd ever met—this, despite the fact that, holding my various poses, I had barely said a word in his presence.

Also, I had already spoken to too many congregations. It was known I'd posed for Mr Mossman's statue, already being cast in bronze for erection in George Square, in a role highlighting the doctor's fight against slavery. If the story got out that the Company had refused to employ me, especially if that 'natural intelligence' or my anti-slavery zeal became issues, they would look bad. Sending me off to Africa to take charge of a remote store seemed a good solution. At Matope, I would sink or swim on my own account.

Before I set sail, in the second batch of company recruits, I was present when Mr Mossman's statue was unveiled to the public. Mr James White of Overtoun pulled the string that drew the cloth back. The statue showed the doctor much larger than in life, holding the Bible in his left hand, while his right reached out behind him to collect his famous cap from a small tree trunk. By his left foot lay a sextant, an astrolabe and some shackles scattered on the ground, symbolizing his other concerns.

On the plinth were other carvings, one showing him as a explorer, another as a missionary reading the Bible to two African men and two women with babies, all listening eagerly. A third showed an African woman, shielding her baby as an Arab threatened her with a whip. I didn't recognise my own face in any of them, though I wondered if one of my scowls had contributed to the Arab's countenance.

12 Maria Afonso

Afonso's question about the role of soldiers in Africa continued to worry him.

'So you want to be a soldier?', Father Anselmo had asked when, unknown to himself, he was eight years old, his profession apparently already chosen. Why did he respond with such enthusiasm? He supposed it seemed better than joining the convent, where his mother had just been insulted. The name his late father had bestowed on him, without explanation, turned out to be his destiny. He had no regrets about that. But ever since his meeting with Serpa Pinto, he had assumed soldiering meant Africa, and Portugal seemed to have lost interest in her colonies. The English, the French, even the Germans and Belgians were more active. Was his role to be simply putting down political unrest at home?

The country seemed in a state of undeclared civil war. The old Reformists (now the Progressive Party) and the Regenerators were no longer on speaking terms, and Republicanism was an increasing force. But labeling the parties in this fashion didn't bring any clarity to the turmoil. All sides invoked the African Empire, but antagonism took precedence over doctrine with no regard to consistency or even loyalty. Afonso didn't know where he stood, or what his future might hold.

The Overseas Minister, for instance, was a maverick called Manuel Joaquim Pinheiro Chagas. He'd studied at the Colégio Militar, back in its Mafra days and had gone on to the Escola do Exército. Afonso had met him once, in the library at the Bemposta Palace. He'd been catching up on his reading with a view to completing an essay on infantry tactics, when the Principal stepped out from behind a shelf with Pinheiro Chagas in tow. What they were doing there Afonso never discovered, but the Principle seized the opportunity to introduce him as the great nephew of Marshall António Texeira Rebelo, founder of the Colégio Militar and translator of Muller's *Treatise of Artillery*, a copy of which he produced from the shelves. This was a bit overwhelming, and Afonso was conscious afterwards of missing an opportunity to impress. He was reminded, in fact, of his shyness when confronted with the photograph of his famous relative in the Principal's office in Mafra.

'Mountebank,' exclaimed Alfredo, when Afonso told his friends of this encounter. 'Saltimbanco. Charlatan.'

When little Zé Miguel looked puzzled, he added, 'Politician!'

They were following what had become a Friday evening habit, drinking red wine at their customary café opposite the Camões statue, opposite Chiado. As usual, they had wrangled briefly over the bill until, as usual, Alfredo insisted on paying. His grounds were that Lisbon was his territory. If ever he were in Mozambique, he would let Zé Miguel stand the honours. As for Cumeeira—he let the sentence dangle.

'You will be received like a man from another planet,' promised Afonso.

'Speaking of other planets, how was Pinheiro Chagas dressed?'

'Impeccably,' replied Afonso. 'Stiff shirt, pleated waistcoat, double-lapelled suede jacket, tie like a large yellow butterfly.'

'His hair?'

'Not a grey one in sight.'

'When a man dyes his hair,' declared Alfredo, 'it's a sign his mistress is much younger than him.'

Zé Miguel began the lip movements that indicated he was about to make a statement.

'He's our Overseas Minister,' he said.

'So?'

'He's the minister I have to deal with.'

Zé Miguel's home in Mozambique was a mystery to Afonso. He sensed something was wrong, mainly because of his friend's complete silence on the matter. He knew only that his mother was widowed and that he had a younger sister.

Alfredo refused to be impressed.

'Why do we need an Overseas Minister? Why particularly do we need him?'

'Someone has to be responsible for the colonies?'

'Free trade's the anthem these days. Why do we need a Minister to conduct the choir? Especially one who's tone deaf.'

Afonso wasn't surprised Zé Miguel had no immediate response to this. In any case, Alfredo was continuing relentlessly.

'Is there a single position he hasn't adopted and abandoned? A single party or a single constituency he's remained loyal to? He's been conservative and progressive, he's been pro-reform and anti-reform, he's been monarchist and constitutionalist, he's been for colonial intervention and against colonial intervention. Even now he's serving as Minister in a government he was elected to oppose.'

This was true. Pinheiro Chagas was supposed to be with the Progressive Party, not the Regenerators.

'He's a turncoat and a timeserver, a tub-thumping gasbag. Fortunately, he's about to get his come-uppance.'

Alfredo's scorn for his homeland could be coruscating but was normally expressed through elaborate and witty fantasy. His friends had rarely heard him so bitter. He seemed to sense this, refilling their glasses and giving Afonso and Zé Miguel one of his joyous smiles.

'They've got the wrong bones,' he said.

The sentence conveyed nothing to either of them.

'Vasco da Gama's bones. They're the wrong ones.'

Slowly, it dawned on Afonso what Alfredo was talking about. Three years before, in a tumult of national fervour largely orchestrated by Pinheiro Chagas, Vasco da Gama's skeleton had been exhumed from where it had lain since 1590, in the Alentejo town of Vidigueira, for reburial in the Jeronimite Monastery at Belém. After much patriotic ceremonial, the cortège had left Vidigueira on a slow train, stopping for further speeches at Cuba, Alvito and Barreiro. There the coffin was transferred to an official armada, conveying it to Lisbon's Terreira do Paço where, amid yet more speeches, it was united with another coffin containing what was hoped were the remains of Luís de Camões, exhumed from the Church of Santa Ana, destroyed in the earthquake of 1755. Everyone knew the Camões identification was uncertain, but about Gama they were confident. The two coffins then were conveyed to Belém, and after processions involving national and municipal dignitaries, along with members of the Royal Academy of Science and the Geographical Society, and accompanied by massed military bands, they were received at the monastery by Dom Luís and the Queen, for reburial in two expensively-wrought tombs.

'I was there at Belém,' said Afonso. 'All the finalists at the Colégio were on parade.'

'Unfortunately, they took the wrong bones. Gama was buried on the Gospel side of the nave. The bits of skeleton they dug up were from the other side.'

'So what's going to happen?'

'They're going to have to repeat the whole burlesque. The gasbag will have to dust down his speeches. But never mind. They're endlessly re-usable. He just needs to shift a few positives and negatives.'

Zé Miguel was mumbling something.

'As our compatriots are fond of saying, this could only happen in Portugal.'

Alfredo smiled again and gave his arm a quick squeeze.

'Always the *mot juste* from little José.'

None of this gave any shape to Afonso's thoughts about his future. But his question about soldiers in Africa was partly answered when, several months later, the Escola mounted a dinner for one of its former students, back from a career in Public Works in Mozambique. This happened once, or perhaps, twice a year, and Afonso always enjoyed the occasions for giving him a practical sense of what his own future might hold.

This particular evening, the guest of honour was Caldas Xavier, a pale diminutive figure with haunted eyes as though recovering from fever and, as it turned out, easily excited. He was introduced as one of the Escola's most brilliant students, graduating as lieutenant in 1875. But he had made engineering his specialty, and his career in Mozambique had been entirely in civil construction—road-building in Inhambane in the south, and working on the new railway linking Lourenço Marques with the Transvaal. Undeniably useful work but hardly heroic. Afonso was not sure he was impressed.

It was after dinner that matters got lively. Caldas Xavier's speech was devoted to attacking the Regenerators, the free traders currently in power. Whereas Sá da Bandeira's Progressive party had abolished slavery and promoted colonial development, especially in Mozambique, the Regenerators were focusing all their attention on the metropole. New roads, new railways, new bridges, new boulevards were all very well. But how were they being financed? It was all being done through massive foreign loans, raised by secretly mortgaging the African colonies.

This charge produced uproar as students shouted their approval. When a loan voice demanded evidence, Caldas Xavier was adamant he had evidence. In fact, he had no need of evidence. The facts spoke for themselves.

'Where's the money coming from?' he roared. 'That massive Avenida just below us, with its obelisks and monuments and palm trees and lavish gardens almost a mile long. Who's paying for it all?'

Britain and Germany had been promised that when Portugal defaulted on their loans, they would be compensated with parts of Angola and Mozambique.

'What our heroic ancestors fought for is being bartered so the decadent bourgeoisie, those Jews and Jewesses, can have fine houses and parade along the avenue in the latest fashions from Paris.'

Afonso was wild with enthusiasm, embracing Manuel de Oliveira as the whole hall rose to its feet applauding. Then he noticed Alfredo had remained seated, staring woodenly ahead, and he lowered his hands uneasily.

'I return to Africa,' Caldas Xavier concluded, shouting above the clamour, 'to a small town called Mopeia, on the banks of the River Zambezi, to contribute to the colony's commercial development by promoting the growth of opium.'

A smile of contempt passed across Alfredo's handsome features.

'Opium,' he muttered derisively. 'It's not religion. It's empire that's the opium of the Portuguese.'

But he kept his voice low in the general excitement and only Afonso heard him.

13 Tony St Claire

Tony was woken next morning by the sound of stealthy movements. His eyes made out a slender girl in a long, shapeless dress, aged about seventeen, her hair twisted in strips of paper fastened with pins. She was taking a watering can from plant to plant. Careful not to betray he was awake, he saw for the first time that the mass of colour he had noticed the previous evening were separate leaves and flowers, rising from a variety of clay pots, old tins, kettles, tubs, a couple of sawn-off wine-barrels, lined up all sides of the veranda, leaving space only for the entrance, two doors and a sewing machine. Some he already recognised, the blue plumbago, the euphorbia with thick spiny stems and tiny red flowers, various fleshy begonias and a scarlet hibiscus, whose fresh blossoms the girl was stroking as though welcoming them with the new day.

But there were others he must have seen but not attended to—leaves of every kind, heart-shaped but like painted shields, red or purple or white at the centre, fading to green at the edges along the lines of their veins, or serrated or with holes like a Swiss cheese, climbing the veranda supports. There were ferns curving in perfect symmetry, delicate as lace in their tracery. There were orchids bound to pieces of dead wood and hanging from the cross-beams. As the girl drew closer, she looked extremely pretty, bowed over the plants, with an earnest olive face and green, cat-like eyes.

Aware suddenly that he was awake, she squealed and scurried off but returned after a few minutes with a plate of boiled sweet potato, a boiled maize cob, and a mug of strong bitter chocolate.

'Bom dia', he said cheerfully. 'My name's Tony. What's yours?'

'I am christened Maria Antónia.'

'Oh, you speak English. That is very good.'

'Só um poco.'

'And we have the same name!'

'I know,' she said, and withdrew again from the veranda.

He had just finished this breakfast when Jiwa Faz Tudo returned. He brought with him a broom for Tony to use as a crutch, sticking the broom head under his armpit and helping him to the steps, where two African men carried him down to the yard and sluiced him with several buckets of cold water. Back on the veranda, Jiwa made him take a few paces.

'Dói?', he asked. 'It is with pain?'

'Just a little.'

'That is good. It is the exercise.'

Only then he removed the dressing, washing and inspecting the wound again and taking another sample of urine.

'It is good,' he said, binding up the wound, with the same mysterious ointment. 'Four weeks you will walk.'

'Four weeks!' exclaimed Tony.

'You are welcome as guest,' said Dona Esmeralda, who had orchestrated the ablutions.

Jiwa left, promising to return the next morning. Mentally, Tony resolved to take a second opinion when the naval doctor came. But he didn't wish to appear ungracious.

'You are being extremely kind. But how can I repay you?'

'You can teach English. Me, Maria Antónia, and Father Espírito Santo.'

When Tony looked nonplussed, she added, 'Maria Antónia, bring the books. Not all of them, just the first ones.'

Maria Antónia, whose hair was still pinned in papers, returned with a small pile of magazines. Tony was amazed to be handed *All the Year Round, a Weekly Journal Conducted by Charles Dickens*. Specifically, he was holding numbers 84 to 86, dated the 1st, 8th and 15th of December, 1860. The pages were yellowing, and some were being eaten by white ants. But among other contributions, each of the journals contained two chapters, the opening chapters of Dickens' novel *Great Expectations*.

'My husband used to read these. It is how we learn some English. Me and Maria António.'

'And the Father"

'He, yes. But he is concerned at the catequismo'

'The orthodoxy? You mean whether Dickens is a heretic?'

'*Sim*. But I enjoyed'.

Tony had never read any Dickens, though he had heard of him as a popular author. He read now *My father's family name being Pirrip, and my Christian name Philip, my infant tongue could make of both names nothing longer or more explicit than Pip. So I called myself Pip, and came to be called Pip.*

'Your husband read this? To all of you?'

'We didn't understand everything, but he explained.'

'I want to know,' said Maria Antónia, shyly.

'What?'

'I want to know what happens to Pip. After he go to London.'

'I'm afraid I don't know,' said Tony. 'I have never read this story.'

'But you could', she said eagerly. 'It is all here.'

'We have the full set,' said Dona Esmeralda. 'To the very last chapter.'

Tony read a little further. *I give Pirrip as my father's family name, on the authority of his tombstone and my sister—Mrs Joe Gargery, who married the blacksmith.*

'We have also Oliver, how you say, corkscrew?'

'Oliver Twist'.

'And David Coppermine?'

'Copperfield'

'Field, yes.'

Tony laid the down the magazine and sighed.

'You've been very kind, but I'm sorry, I don't believe it will be possible.'

He was about to add 'official duties', but the words died in his mouth. His post as First Under-Secretary to Her Majesty's Roving Consul for Central Africa Secretary had brought him with a wound to this mosquito-proof veranda in Portuguese East Africa surrounded by hibiscus and succulent plants, being cared for with great kindness and some skill by people, including a very pretty girl, who wanted him to read Dickens with them.

'Let us see,' said Dona Esmeralda, 'what the English doctor says.'

'Just so,' said Tony eagerly.

The English naval doctor failed to appear. Instead, mid-morning, while Tony read on in *Great Expectations*, finding it, to his surprise, increasingly engrossing, he was interrupted by Father Espirito Santo, bounding on to the veranda, his *batina* billowing behind him.

'So where's the wounded heretic?' he demanded.

Tony laid down the journal and extended his hand in welcome.

'Wounded, yes. As for heretic, I'm sure it's nothing the Holy Spirit can't deal with.'

Father Espirito Santo chuckled as he pulled up a chair alongside Tony's pallet.

'If I'm dealing with a saint, I suppose I have to be humble.'

'A saint?'

'I understand you're Sr Santo Claire'

Tony was nonplussed. He was used to saying 'Sinclaire', and never realised he was claiming sanctity.

'Espirito Santo is actually quite a common Portuguese name,' the priest continued. 'It probably means my ancestors were Jewish, before the expulsion. Those who stayed took Christian names, and it's said Espirito Santo was the part of the Holy Trinity least offensive to them because it's disembodied. Though that hardly applies to me.'

He folded his robe over his stomach and winked.

'When I was in London, some people laughed at the name. Others looked very pious. I think I preferred the laughter.'

'How long were you in London?'

'Oh, I was very young, so it seemed no time at all. The ambassador had a wife who missed Portugal and thought London was Babylon. They sent me to be her confessor. To try to cheer her up a bit. But it didn't work. I wasn't holy enough for her, so the Archbishop had me replaced.'

Maria Antónia came from within the house, bringing a jug of freshly-squeezed orange juice. Tony noticed she had taken the papers from her hair, which hung in neck-long curls. She was wearing a long pale-blue dress with a high waist-line, in vaguely Regency fashion.

'Oh Father,' she blushed, 'we didn't hear you come. I'll bring you a glass'.

'Don't worry, *menina*. I'll come in and greet your mother.'

He stood up, straightening his robe.

'You've got a great vantage point for watching today's events. Do you know Aesop's fable about the lion, the bear and the fox? You'll see Aesop's characters here today, *Senhor* Corvo, *Senhor* Pombo, *Senhor* Rato and *Senhor* Raposo. Watch out especially for Raposo, the fox.'

Through the fine wire mesh, Tony could see the approaches to the house. His bed was in a corner of the verandah to the right of the entrance. Behind him, to the side of the house, was a yard of hard-trodden sand where domestic servants were washing clothes, surrounded by an orchard of bright green citrus trees interspersed with coconut palms. To his left, leading from the entrance, was a long driveway, raised above fields of millet and bordered impressively with royal palms and hibiscus.

Left alone, Tony resumed reading *Great Expectations*.

Mr Wopsle, the clerk at church, was to dine with us; and Mr Hubble, the wheelwright, and Mrs Hubble; and Uncle Pumblechook (Joe's uncle, but Mrs Joe appropriated him), who was a well-to-do cornchandler in the nearest town, and drove his own chaise-cart. The dinner hour was half-past one. The time came and the company came. Mr Wopsle, united to a Roman nose and a large shining bald forehead, had a deep voice which he was uncommonly proud of; he himself confessed that if the church was 'thrown open', meaning to competition, he would not despair of making his mark in it …

There was a commotion at the end of the drive, and the first of Dona Esmeralda's guests arrived in a palanquin, called locally a *machila*, carried by four Africans panting a song in unison. They stopped beneath the short flight of steps, and Dona Esmeralda came to stand at the top in greeting, joined by Father Espirito Santo.

For a few moments, nothing happened. Was the newcomer sleeping? Tony wondered. Dona Esmeralda looked puzzled and then unmistakably irritated. Finally, a swarthy, corpulent man in uniform lowered himself from the *machila*, satisfied he had kept his hostess waiting. His hair and moustache gleamed suspiciously black, and his gold earrings gleamed.

'Ah, my beautiful hostess,' he intoned, as though his rudeness was the norm. As he stepped on to the veranda, he noticed Tony and stopped in irritation.

'*Quem é?*' he peered closely. '*É um Inglês?*'

'I am First Under-Secretary to Her Majesty's Roving Consul for Central Africa,' said Tony, asking the Father if he would be good enough to translate, while the newcomer tapped his cane impatiently.

'Ah, the spy! It is of no importance'

He waddled into the house, followed by Dona Esmeralda.

'The *capitão-mor*,' said Father Espirito Santo, 'our distinguished police commander and magistrate, also known as *Senhor* Corvo. Though this is one fable where the Crow and the Fox are allies.'

He went inside, and Tony resumed his reading.

Mrs Joe,' said Uncle Pumblechook; a large hard-breathing middle-aged slow man, with a mouth like a fish, dull staring eyes, and sandy hair standing upright on his head, so that he looked as if he had just been all but choked, and had that moment come to; 'I have brought you as the compliments of the season—I have brought you, Mum, a bottle of sherry wine—and I have brought you, Mum, a bottle of port wine.'

Tony laid down the journal, reflecting inconclusively on Aesop and Dickens and wondering whether his feeling that all was not well was induced by the priests' words or by the tale he was reading.

Two *machilas* arrived more or less together and were greeted this time in friendly fashion. *Senhor* Pombo, with a trim white beard and startling blue eyes in a tarnished coppery face, was evidently a favourite, both with his hostess and with Maria Antónia, who hugged him as he kissed her cheeks and then took his arm as they went inside. *Senhor* Rato, a shrivelled Indian of uncertain age, was already known to Tony. He was a public notary in Quelimane whom Doveton used occasionally to authenticate signatures on bills of exchange. He had already heard of Tony's accident and greeted him with a grin.

'I speak seven languages perfectly, Sr António,' he declared with proud emphasis, adding, 'We overtook the doctor on the road. He'll be here in two shakes of a rat's tail.'

Perfection indeed!

Tony glanced at Father Espirito Santo, but the priest had stepped inside. For the second time that morning, he had been outdone in irony by people he would never have suspected.

Sure enough, the next *machila* to arrive was carrying the English doctor. Not an Aesop character, thought Tony, as he watched him straightening his uniform and combing his hair, before collecting his medical bag from one of the bearers. Nor especially a Dickensian one, with his red face and red knees, suggesting all the skinny parts in-between must be red as well. He looked the very epitome of irritation as he mounted the steps and was greeted by Dona Esmeralda.

'This,' he declared, 'is beyond the call of duty.'

Ignoring her outstretched hand, he walked over to Tony's pallet and stared down at him.

'Your excellency,' said Dona Esmeralda, 'you must be very tired from your journey. May I bring you some refreshments?'

'No, thank you,' he said brusquely. 'I carry my own. I don't trust anything you'd have to offer.'

Tony bridled, but Dona Esmeralda spread her hands pacifically. 'Let me know if there is anything you require.'

'Do you have to be so damn rude?' he said, as she withdrew.

'Do you have to drag me out on this wild-goose chase? I'm a naval doctor. I don't treat adventurers.'

'I'm Consul Doveton's secretary.'

'So, what are you doing hunting buffalo?'

Conceding the point, Tony stopped him as he was ripping off the banana leaf dressing. 'Careful with that,' he said, 'I want it.'

'What? This rubbish? Have it your own way.'

He set the bundle to one side and proceeded, Tony observed with some pleasure, to do more or less what Jiwa Faz Tudo had done—bathing the wound, inspecting it for bone splinters, binding it up—though this time with ointment and a bandage—and taking a urine sample, on which he didn't deign to comment.

'I've ordered you a palanquin. If you'll gather your things together, we'll be off'.

Tony watched him reassembling his medical bag but made no move.

'Are you coming?'

He took a deep breath.

'I'm staying here.'

'Blast you, I might have known it would be a wasted journey.'

'It wasn't wasted,' said Tony. 'You helped me make up my mind.'

The doctor's desire for a professionally discourteous exit was frustrated by the simultaneous arrival of Dona Esmeralda's last guest. Tony knew, of course, this could only be Sr Raposo. His first surprise was the sight of Raposo's *machila*. Unlike the normal hammock slung between poles, this was an elaborate carved affair, like a sedan chair, with parrots perched on each of the corner posts. His second surprise was that he knew that heavy figure, that anaemic face with the stubble and close-set eyes, along with the sense of menace that preceded him and hung in his wake. They had crossed only briefly in the lobby of the hotel in Quelimane, and Doveton had whispered, 'That's the one they're after'.

Doveton was referring to the anti-slaving patrol, whose doctor was briefly blocked from leaving by Raposo's arrival.

Dona Esmeralda and Maria Antónia both greeted their guest, and Maria Antónia led him inside, her face an unreadable mask.

'I don't admire the company you're keeping,' was the doctor's final taunt as, ignoring Dona Esmeralda, he clattered down the steps.

'You're not going with him?' exclaimed Dona Esmeralda.

'If that's acceptable to you.'

'You're very welcome. Maria Antónia will bring you something from our table.'

'One thing. Is it possible to ask Jiwa to come? My thigh is hurting again.'

'Com certeza.'

14 Mbewe

At Mandala, nothing happened for three weeks. Then a message came from Ramakukan. Once again, Mphetomwanyama delivered it personally.

'The river is open'.

Mbewe was summoned to Chemandala's office where they were making plans. Mr Morrison, Mr Rankin and Mr Gouk would go to meet Ramakukan. He was to go with them as pilot, in the hope it was possible to travel downriver. Mandala, by this time, was getting short of supplies.

They journeyed to Ramakukan's as arranged, taking down a load of ivory for transport to the coast. The store had been burned, but Mr Frederick was left there to guard the ivory in a small hut, and they continued down river in canoes with Ramakukan and his men.

Mitengo, Chipatula's capital on the left bank, was deserted except for a few women. His house was draped in yards of calico, some of it belonging to the Company and the rest confiscated from Piri Piri.

Piri Piri's head, or what the crows had left of it, was still there, grinning from the pole as though pleased at all the trouble he had caused. There were still wisps of pepper-coloured hair on the scalp. While Mr Morrison was taking it down, Mbewe went to visit Chipatula's grave. After all, despite Chikusi and despite Philip, Chipatula was his father. He bought a gourd of millet beer from one of the old women and made his sacrifice, saying prayers for him.

The *Lady Nyassa* looked much bigger than normal, lying in shallow water under the headland. The decks were awash, but the two paddle wheels and the bridge were clear of the water. Mr Morrison soon found the hole Chikusi's men had punched in the flat bottom and fitted a temporary repair.

After that, re-floating her was a matter of baling out the engine room and the cargo holds. Ramakukan himself took the lead, raising a gourd of water from the engine room to pour over the side.

Mr Gouk found a crocodile in the hold. It wasn't a big one, just four foot or so, but it didn't like being disturbed. Mr Rankin wanted to shoot it, but the captain said 'No, you'll damage the plates.' Ramakukan's men held it at bay with spears until the steamer had surfaced enough for it to slide overboard. Then Mr Rankin shot it.

Back at Katunga's, Mr Morrison had the steamer beached for a thorough examination.

'It'll take some days,' he told Mr Gouk. 'I'll have to strip the engine and scrape the whole hull.'

Chindevu was in command as they sailed from Katunga's a week later. Mr Gouk had loaded up with firewood, three tons of it and, as usual, that left room for only half the ivory that had been left with Mr Frederick.

Though the cold season had begun, the river was still full, gleaming silver under the overcast sky. Every few miles, they passed through a chilly shower, the raindrops pitting the surface like tiny pebbles. They passed Mitengo, which was still deserted except for the old women, and steamed on through Dambinyi marsh by channels that hadn't changed much in the meantime. It was just as they were leaving the marsh, approaching Chiromo, Chipatula's new capital, at the Ruo junction, that Chikusi's men attacked.

North of Chiromo, the river was only one-hundred feet wide, curving to the left under a high bank lined with borassus palms and fever trees. Chikusi must have reckoned it was a good place for an ambush, and he had his men stationed on both sides.

But the current in the narrows was fast, hugging the high bank. It was hard for the warriors on that side to see more of the steamer than the top of the funnel and the masts. Those across the river had a better view but their weapons were too feeble to do much harm. Stones fired from muskets flew wide, and some arrows fell harmlessly on the deck.

Mbewe was concentrating hard on the river. Opposite Chiromo itself, the river widened, the current racing mid-stream. The yelling and firing followed them as the two islands Mbewe was looking for came into view, and he made Mr Gouk steer between them. One paddle was stopped, swinging the steamer hard right. This meant leaving the main current to take the narrow passage between the islands. Mbewe was gambling it was deep and free of snags. For the next five hundred yards or so, Chikusi's men couldn't see them.

As the island to the left receded, he indicated hard left, dodging the backwater between a third island and the right bank, then hard right again as they regained the main river. Mr Gouk didn't argue. Mbewe's heart was in his mouth as they bumped on a sandbank, but the steamer didn't run aground.

They were well ahead of the ambush by this stage, and almost at once they passed the confluence with the Ruo river, into water flowing faster and deeper. The danger was over.

'Did you see them?' said Mr Morrison excitedly. 'Five hundred with guns and another thousand with bows and arrows.'

He was pacing up and down the deck, excitedly.

'Did you see the Mandala boys? Still in their shirts and khaki shorts?'

Mbewe had seen nothing but the sleek, boiling surface of the river as he watched out for snags.

'Mbewe, you're a pilot in a million,' said Chindevu.

'She's not built to be hurled about like this,' said Mr Gouk. 'I worry about the old girl.'

'I thought she responded very well,' said Chindevu.

Mr Morrison shook his head.

'The Company needs a better steamer. This heap of scrap iron will never do.'

Mbewe was still studying the river, though with a new worry.

Had he been seen? Almost certainly, he thought. He had done what no slave should ever do. He had taken sides.

The rest of the journey down river was as usual. They covered the normal fifty miles a day, stopping only at the wooding stations. Mbewe didn't step ashore anywhere, so heard no talk of the war Masamanga had spoken of. What he could see was that the gardens had been harvested. The maize had been stored and the houses had splashes of maroon and yellow on their roofs where sprays of millet had been spread out to dry. Only the cassava had been left in the ground.

If war was planned, everything was ready.

Then at Mthumbi's, he saw men preparing the war drums, heating the goat skins with resin in front of fires. The riverbank paths leading south were marked with green branches.

They reached Maruro, the Company wooding station, after four days, and Mr Gouk stayed with the steamer while Chindevu continued down the Kwakwa to Quelimane. From Mazaro to Quelimane was only seventy miles, but by boat on the muddy Kwakwa the journey took six days. Chindevu asked Mbewe to accompany him but didn't explain why.

Every mile of the way, Chindevu complained. About the paddlers, all brought down from the highlands by the Company and not worth their pay. About the Portuguese, unable, after four hundred years, to provide proper access to God's highway. About exorbitant custom duties levied by the Portuguese and about chiefs like Ramakukan demanding tribute to pass through their territory. About the heat, the mosquitos, hippo flies and the fever caused by the bad air of the swamps they were passing through.

'It's called malaria', he explained. 'The word signifies bad air.'

He went on complaining about a steamer so feeble that its main cargo was the firewood needed to keep the engine working. About the river which wasn't a highway at all, just a series of pools between sandbanks. All this when the Company was trying to bring civilisation and commerce to an Africa wracked by the slave trade.

Mbewe listened, thinking the *muzungu* is learning.

Then approaching Quelimane, the *muzungu* sprung his surprise.

'Mr John wants you to come and work for the Company.'

Mbewe didn't understand. He thought he was already working for the Company.

'No, no. He means full time. Permanently. For a regular wage'

He could see his companion was baffled.

'You know how the Reverend Scott at the mission is training catechists? He wants Africans to be part of the work.

Mr John wants you to do the same for the Company. He's very impressed by your 'commercial acumen'. Those were the words he used. He means that you understand trade.'

There was a long pause while he lit his pipe. It was shaped like a spoonbill's beak, and Mbewe sometimes wondered if was going to set fire to his beard.

'You understand trade. You speak the languages—Manganja, Lolo, English, some Portuguese. I agree with my brother. You'd be ideal. '

'You mean be the Company's slave?'

'Ach no, man. How could you say such a thing? You'd be well paid. Or paid, anyway. Regularly, cash-in-hand every Saturday. Or after every trip, if you prefer.'

'But if the Company doesn't survive?'

Mbewe was thinking of all those complaints in the canoe coming from Mazaro.

'Ah well, in that case, we'd have to let you go, of course.'

So it was a bit like being a slave but without the advantages. A slave always had a master. Unless his master sells him, so maybe it was much the same.

'There's no reason why the Company should fail. There's lot of goods to be traded. Not just the ivory. Mr Buchanan's started to grow coffee. Coffee's much more valuable by weight. We can expand the trade in oil seeds. I'm trying to lease an estate near Quelimane to grow coconuts. You can sell every part of a coconut, from the milk to the fibre. Then there's that Portuguese company growing opium near Mopeia. There'll be big trade from this region once it gets established. And those who are here first will reap the advantages.'

His pipe had gone out while he made this long speech, and there was another pause as he re-lit it.

'We have a great teacher in Scotland,' he said. Adam Smith, *The Wealth of Nations*. That's his book. It's about how trade makes everyone rich.'

'The Reverend Laws says it's the Bible made the *azungus* rich and powerful.'

'Ach, well, that too.'

'We're getting a new steamer,' he added quickly. 'It's called the *James Stevenson*. Bigger than the *Lady*. Rear-wheeled, so less trouble on the Shire. Able to carry more and much faster.'

Suddenly, Mbewe understood. They needed a pilot they could trust, and permanently. Working for the Company meant not working for any of the other traders. He would lose his freedom to pick and choose.

'I'll have to talk with Masamanga,' he replied. But he didn't need to. He already knew his own mind.

15 Maria Afonso

That year, the Feast of San António fell on a Friday, so the college was closed from Thursday afternoon for the Lisbon marches. Alfredo, who never seemed to be short of money, invited Afonso and Zé Miguel to spend the weekend in Sintra. The old Larmanjat single-track rail link had gone bankrupt, but they took the early omnibus through Porcalhota and Queluz and reached Ranholas, on the leafy outskirts of Sintra, by mid morning. Alfredo had been there many times, Afonso once only at the age of ten, on his journey from Mafra to Lisbon with Father Anselmo, and Zé Miguel never.

As they stepped down in the square outside the royal palace, Alfredo burst into delighted laughter.

'Oh, *meu Deus*, I'd forgotten,' he said, 'I'd completely forgotten.'

He grabbed Afonso's arm.

'What would you take as the appropriate symbol for the Portuguese royal family? A pair of scales promising justice? A coat of arms with its five shields, vowing to protect the nation? The open hand of charity? No, look at it.'

He pointed dramatically.

'Two huge kitchen chimneys, signifying the royal stomach!'

It was true. The palace's most striking feature was two enormous brick cones rising much higher than the tallest pines.

Alfredo was still chuckling as they walked a short distance uphill to the Hotel Lawrence and had sandwiches on the veranda overlooking the wide, green valley. The trees were so densely packed that only their tops could be seen, with occasionally a square of red pantiles and a glimpse of white walls indicating a secluded house.

'Didn't Byron stay here?,' asked Afonso.

'He did,' said Alfredo.

'I heard he was very insulting about Portugal,' said Zé Miguel.

Alfredo laughed again. He was in the highest spirits, getting away from the Escola.

'He was an English lord, so he took it for granted he had the right to any woman he took a fancy to. When one of the Portuguese husbands objected, he wrote us off, quite correctly, as a nation of thieves and murderers. But he loved Sintra, so there's no harm in our staying where he stayed.'

That afternoon, they hired donkeys outside the hotel to carry them up the steep, rocky path to the Moorish castle on the mountain top, just across from the neighbouring peak crowned by Pena Palace, Sintra's other royal retreat. Pacing the castellated walls and climbing the turrets, they could see for miles in every direction. The whole Tagus estuary lay below them, as far inland as the Torre de Belém, with Cabo Espichel and the Arrabida mountains on the far side. To the north, the wild Atlantic coast could be traced as far as the peninsula of Peniche, along with a strange building like a large white wedding cake, a few miles inland.

'I didn't know you could see Mafra Convent from here,' exclaimed Afonso.

For the first time, he told his friends about arriving on foot from Cumeeira with his mother, and how she had been insulted by one of the basilica priests for walking barefoot on the marble floor. The story led naturally on to their encounter with Father Anselmo and how the priest had adopted him, before he joined the Colégio Militar. It turned out Alfredo and Zé Miguel knew Mafra too. They had spent the first part of their course there, before the Colégio moved to Luz outside Lisbon, where Afonso joined them a year later.

Descending the mountain, Alfredo led them, apparently aimlessly, through the maze of narrow streets and staircases of the town centre and of the linked villages of Santa Maria and São Pedro, already absorbed by the town but on separate peaks. Everywhere they went, Afonso was dazzled by the great masses of purple bougainvillea, or dark blue plumbago, or ancient writhing wisteria vines, some of them still flowering as late as June. The grounds of the Escola do Exército were beautifully laid out, as befitted its origins as the Bemposta palace, with many of the same flowering plants Afonso recognised in Sintra. But in Sintra they seemed natural, self-seeded and centuries old and in control of their own destinies.

Even the bright-red geraniums, overflowing their pots or their hanging baskets, seemed independent of human help, so brilliantly did they go about being what they were.

At every turning, there was a vista—impossible just to call it a view, so much like a painting did it seem, whether looking downwards over red-tiled roofs with their chimneys and wrought-iron cupolas to the massed forest of the valley, or upwards through trees crowding the mountainside but this time seen from below, with ferns and orchids drooping from their gnarled branches, until the eye was drawn to the battlements of the Moorish castle on the summit. Every fifty yards or so, they crossed a narrow gorge of white water, plunging precipitously through more ferns. An avenue of jacarandas led past the Trindade Convent to the São Pedro church, where Afonso had stayed. He found he couldn't remember the priest's name, but he was reminded again, with a rush of love, of Father Anselmo, whom he hadn't seen for six years.

Back at the Lawrence, where dinner was served from six in the evening, the friends found themselves sharing the dining room with two pairs of German tourists, to whom they took an instant and patriotic dislike.

Nothing about the menu, on which they were well advanced, seemed to please the Germans. Not the *caldo verde* (a shredded cabbage soup with a slice of *chouriço*), not the cod with cream, not the *cozido á portuguesa* (a stew of mixed meat and sausage, again with cabbage), nor finally the *pudim flan* (a rich egg pudding with cinnamon). The white wines were sour and the red Dão was without body. None of this was said in Portuguese, for they had come touring without learning a word of the language. It was conveyed through scowls, half-touched plates and Teutonic explosions, with the odd phrase in guttural English, evidently the *lingua franca* of their travels.

Alfredo responded to all this by openly relishing, in English, each of the courses in their turn, pronouncing the soup 'excellent', the *bacalhau* 'superb', the *cozido* 'impeccable', and the pudim flan 'a masterpiece'. These comments, coming as they did several minutes apart, seemed at first private to the trio of friends. But at that initial 'excellent', Afonso couldn't resist stealing a glance at the German table. He caught the eye of one of the wives who in turn nudged her husband's elbow. By the time the *cozido* was declared 'impeccable', all four Germans were aware they were being provoked. Their scanty dinner was over, but the despairing proprietor had managed to unearth a bottle of Schnapps for the men and Amontillado for the women, and they were lingering over their drinks. When the *pudim flan* was judged 'a masterpiece', the Schnapps bottle was banged hard on the table by way of warning.

But Alfredo was incorrigible.

'These are the people,' he told Afonso and Zé Miguel in English, 'who want to steal our colonies.'

'Careful,' said Zé Miguel in Portuguese.

But he was too late. One of the Germans, revealed now as a heavily-built man with a loose jacket and tweed waistcoat, approached their table.

'We Jarmans,' he said in heavily-accented English, 'will have our place in the sun.'

He nodded, as though in confirmation.

'If some Portuguese-speaking half-breeds don't like it, pfiu.'

'Ludvig!' warned a blonde woman, evidently his wife.

He made as though to spit at their feet, but restrained himself, adding only 'Boy soldiers!' before returning to his companions, who left the dining room together.

Alfredo was jubilant.

'We drew them out as to their intentions, and they quit the field.'

'I don't like being called a boy soldier.'

'Sheer envy, Afonso, my friend. That man would give his right arm to be once again as young as you.'

'All the same,' said Zé Miguel, 'I wouldn't like to meet them again.'

There he had a point. The night was still young and it was too early to retire. Sintra was not like Lisbon, a place of innumerable bars and fado houses. It would be pleasant to sit on the veranda, but not if the moonlight had already been colonised by the Germans. Afonso went to conduct a reconnaissance. The veranda was free, he reported. But where was the enemy? Had they gone to bed?

'No,' said Afonso, 'they're leaving.'

'What?'

'They've paid their bill and ordered a carriage to take them to the Nunes.'

The Nunes was the other hotel for international travellers. Alfredo beckoned to Damaso, the elderly waiter.

'What's happening?'

'Ah, *senhor*,' said Damaso, chubby and worried-looking. 'The kitchen appreciates your compliments, but the management does not like losing custom.'

'There are times,' Alfredo declared sententiously, 'when patriotic feeling must take precedence over self-interest. Please bring us a bottle of champagne and three glasses. We will celebrate on the veranda.'

Night had now fallen, though a toe-nail moon drifted above the battlements of the Moorish castle like a symbol of other faiths, other dynasties. Bats were making weird, darting spirals from under the hotel's eaves and, down in the garden and the nearest part of the forested valley, a million fireflies were flashing their Morse codes. Damaso brought the champagne and they raised their glasses.

Zé Miguel was mumbling something to himself. He was rehearsing another of his phrases, and his friends waited patiently. Eventually, he came out with it.

'So you believe empty patriotic gestures matter more than free trade?'

Afonso frowned, not immediately getting the point of the question, but Alfredo whooped in delight. He far preferred the twists and turns of an good argument than settling to any consistent position. To say something memorable was far more fun than to say something that was true.

'Never underestimate little José,' he said. 'You're right, I'm beginning to sound like your hero Caldas Xavier. I must apologise to the Lawrence management.'

Then suddenly he turned serious.

'You're also right that free trade is dead. The bi-lateral treaties with Britain will never be ratified, not even by our own

Cortes, which has so much to gain from them. Germany and France want their share of Africa, and they're going to take it. So patriotic gestures are in order.'

He was referring to the treaties, signed in February 1884, between Portugal and Britain. Effectively, in a triumph for the Regenerators, Britain had accepted Portuguese sovereignty in the African interior. Had the treaties been accepted, there might have been no African scramble. Germany and Belgium, in particular, would have had no leverage in central Africa. But Germany and France denounced the bi-lateral treaties, leading to demands for another international conference at which they staked their claims.

'The strange thing is,' continued Alfredo, 'that if we do go to war, I believe it will not be with Germany or France. It will be with England.'

Afonso was shocked.

'England? Our oldest ally?'

'Their missionaries, I mean the Scottish ones, are the only people actually occupying a portion of our territory. The question is, will they fight? And will we?'

Next morning at breakfast, Alfredo had a fresh proposal, presented as always with a mixture of seriousness and light irony. They should catch the omnibus and visit Mafra. He was curious to see once again the town where he had misspent a year of his childhood, and it was high time Afonso paid a dutiful son's visit to Father Anselmo. Finally, it would avoid Zé Miguel bumping into the Germans, with who knows what consequences. He had already established they could return directly from Mafra to Lisbon that evening.

Afonso felt the kindness in this and was grateful. The omnibus ran from Sintra palace to the Mafra palace-convent, and took just under an hour via the stone masons' town of Pero Pinheiro. The journey would have been faster but for the steep descent into Cheleiros, then the even steeper climb to Igreja Nova and the Carapinheira turn-off.

'Do you realise,' said Alfredo as they were crossing the humped Roman bridge in Cheleiros, 'that all the marble to build the convent had to travel this way from Pero Pinheiro to Mafra? Imagine conveying those massive columns and cornices and entablatures and lintels and quoins and transoms, all the way down this hill without the carts running away from them, then over this bridge and up the other side, yard by yard, without the carts running backwards. Doing that day after day for thirteen years. One wonders how many people were killed.'

They reached Mafra by mid-morning and Afonso immediately announced he would be attending the 11.00 o'clock mass at Santo André's.

'You don't need to come, but I want to take Father Anselmo by surprise.'

'Of course we'll come,' said Zé Miguel.

They walked down the narrow track directly from the convent to old Mafra and, while his friends entered the Romanesque church, Afonso went round to the door of the sacristy, where he found Father Anselmo putting on his vestments.

'Who's that?' he said. 'Ah, God be praised. I don't believe it. My dear, dear boy, how you've grown. And how smart you look.'

There were tears in Afonso's eyes as he embraced the old priest.

'Can I be your server?'

'Do you still know all the responses?'

'Of course I do, father. We have a chapel at the Escola. It is dedicated to *Nossa Senhora de Conceição*, and I attend mass there.'

He almost said 'regularly', but honesty intervened. Father Anselmo noticed, and his pale-blue eyes sparkled at the omission.

'Let's find you a surplice. Your old one will be far too small for such a grown man.'

Bearing a lighted candle, Afonso led Father Anselmo into the tiny, ancient church. As the flame illuminated his face, the old ladies making up the Saturday Mass congregation were quick to recognise him, with a buzz of appreciation. Afonso went through the various postures of the mass, holding the liturgical books open at the correct pages while Father Anselmo prayed with his arms extended, holding the

99

scriptures for the readings from the Old and New Testaments, presenting the wafers and the chalice to be blessed, ringing the bell for the consecration of the Host and leading the congregational responses. He had always enjoyed doing this and especially enjoyed doing it before his friends. It was as though he had brought them home. Noticing their uniforms as they came forward to receive the wafers, Father Anselmo gave Afonso a quick glance and took more than usual care with his blessing.

As he stood with Father Anselmo at the door after the Mass, his various 'aunties' fussing over him, Alfredo whispered 'I'd no idea you were so famous.'

16 Tony St Claire

Tony had discovered a little more about that Aesop-like lunch party. He learned partly from stray remarks in English by Dona Esmeralda or Father Espirito Santo and partly too because he was beginning to pick up some elementary Portuguese. This was especially the case with the two men who carried him down to the yard each morning for his shower. They were called *macayayas*, which he soon realised was the local equivalent of the colonial English 'houseboys', meaning a man who did a servant's work. He established their real names were Doto and Paulo and, simply by thanking them for their services, lessened their wariness of 'o inglês'. In short, they relaxed in his presence, chatting between themselves, and though their conversation was only half in Portuguese and half in something else, he learned they were worried about their future.

The lunch had ended without incident. There had been no raised voices and, apart from Sr.Raposos who muttered again about English spies, each of the other guests had complimented him at their departure as he lay on his pallet. But Dona Esmeralda looked preoccupied and Maria Antónia was especially subdued.

He had already concluded the occasion had something to do with Dona Esmeralda's new status as a widow. That presumably explained Sr Rato, the notario's presence. A will requires a lawyer. But what about the Fox and the Crow? Plainly, there were not there as family friends, and were it not for Father Espirito Santo, he wouldn't have considered them allies.

Was the will, perhaps, being disputed?

All he could add to this, from stray remarks of the priest and the Dona, was that *Senhor* Raposo leased the neighbouring *prazo* and that relations between him and her late husband had been bad. There was a still festering boundary dispute, arising from her husband's attempt to dam a stream. The experiment had gone wrong, creating a swamp, desirable as a dry-season garden, but unfixed as to its boundaries.

The morning after the lunch, he asked Maria Antónia about her veranda garden. Knowing she had been watched the first morning, she made a point of greeting him 'Bom dia, *senhor*' as she began her routine of watering.

'Maria Antónia, my name is Tony, not s*enhor*.'

'Tónio.'

'Okay Tónio. Are all these plants yours.'

She looked surprised.

'Of course not. Some are much older than me. This one,' she said, pointing to an ancient gnarled cactus, 'belonged to my grandmother. It must be so old and still flowers every year.'

Tony recognised a spiny striped marrow he had seen in the governor's garden in Cape Town. There were other cactus-like pin cushions with tiny purple flowers, or prickly tea cosies, or pink sea urchins, or spiny gherkins, or with moon-shaped panda faces and tiny panda ears, or chains of fleshy diamonds with cascades of red flowers at the tips. One of the sawn-off wine barrels held a prickly pear, its thick pulpy leaves inscribed with family names, Zé Miguel and Manuel and Belinha. From another of the barrels a purple bougainvillea climbed to the ceiling.

'People bring me,' said Maria Antónia. 'They know I like, and I remember them. That is Zé Miguel, my brother', pointing to a pink and white orchid dangling from a cut branch. 'He find it in the bush and bring me.'

'Your brother? Where is he?'

'Alfred José Miguel is in Lisbon. My mother send him when my father dies.'

She turned away, unwilling to discuss this, pouring water on what Tony knew to be a waxy anthurium lily.

'But I'm sure some of these must be yours? That Persian Shield, for instance.'

She followed his finger to a bushy shrub with iridescent purple leaves, planted in an old copper cauldron.

'What you call it?'

'Persian Shield. That's its name.'

'I did see it in Quelimane in *Senhor* Pombo's garden and he give me. I plant all these ferns and leaves.'

'Including that kettle?'

This time she smiled. 'I did save that. It has a hole and my mother was throwing it out.'

It held a small ginger plant.

'What are they all called, do you know?'

She had emptied the watering can and looked directly at him for the first time.

'Does everything have to have a name?'

'Yes,' said Tony firmly. 'Everything should have a name. When Adam woke in the Garden of Eden, the first thing he did was give a name to all the plants.'

He held her gaze briefly as her green eyes widened.

'But this was before Eve was created. So perhaps he never told her.'

'Chi-sah!' The momentary spell was broken. 'I will bring your breakfast.'

'No, he didn't,' she said, ten minutes later. 'He named all the animals and all the birds, and then God made Eve from one his ribs. It says nothing about naming the plants.'

Tony burst into delighted laughter as she handed him a crimson slice of water melon, along with chunks of boiled sweet potato and a cup of chocolate.

'You're cheating. You asked Father Espirito Santo'.

'No I didn't. I read it in the Holy Book.'

'But the padre is here for the reading?'

'He is coming.'

Tony had caught up with the back issues of *Great Expectations*. He was ready with volume 96 of *All the Year Round* for Saturday February 23rd, yellowing and a little frayed at the edges but perfectly readable, beginning the second part of the novel with Pip's arrival in London. Really, he thought, chapters one to nineteen were very well done, like a fairy tale for our times, but funny and gripping. Dickens may not have been a university man, but he could write.

After Jiwa had dropped by, to supervise his exercise and ablutions and change his dressing, he was ready to begin. Dona Esmeralda and Father Espirito Santo sat on one side of his pallet, and Maria Antónia on the other.

The journey from our town to the metropolis was a journey of about five hours ... We Britons had at that time particularly settled that it was treasonable to doubt our having and our being the best of everything: otherwise, while I was scared of the immensity of London, I think I might had had some doubts whether it was not rather ugly, crooked, narrow and dirty.

Tony had glanced ahead, so knew he would be reading these words. He did so with panache, imagining to his friends at Pratts this was his first secretary's diplomatic message to the tribes dwelling in the neighbourhood of Lake Nyasa.

But his audience didn't react. He discovered they were more interested in character than opinion, and the first character to impress them was Mr Jaggers, Pip's guardian. How could a notário be so powerful?

'He's more than a notary, ' said Tony. 'He pleads causes.'

'You mean like a juiz?'

'No, not a judge. But someone who influences judges and juries by the power of his arguments.'

'What is juries?', asked Maria Antónia.

'Let's read on', said Father Espirito Santo.

Tony continued with Pip's meeting with Herbert, the pale young gentleman who had challenged him to a fight back in the garden of Satis House. Over dinner, Herbert told Pip for the first time the story of Miss Havisham and her worthless brother, and of the bridegroom who deserted her on her wedding day.

'At twenty past nine,' said Dona Esmeralda, 'while she was still dressing. I knew it was like that.'

'English women must be very strong,' said Maria Antónia.

'Strong?' said Father Espirito Santo. 'She was certainly headstrong.'

'I mean not to give in. To defy men like that. To get her revenge.'

The priest laughed ruefully and patted her left shoulder, shaking his head. She glanced at him, then looked at her mother, appealing for support.

'Don't you have strong women here in Africa?' asked Tony.

'Well, there was Dona Ines', said Dona Esmeralda.

Dona Ines was the notorious proprietor of the neighbouring *prazo* during the eighteenth century. Immensely wealthy, with a standing army of five-thousand slaves, she had murdered husbands at will, like a Catherine the Great of the Zambezi valley.

The priest laughed again, as this was explained to Tony.

'I hope, child, she's not your model.'

'I don't understand,' said Maria Antónia. 'This man, the one who courted Miss Havisham and stole money from her, why did her abandon her? If she was so rich, why didn't he just marry her and get everything?'

Tony checked the journal, following the text with his forefinger, not because he needed to but to show he was taking the question seriously.

'Here we are, ' he said. 'Pip asks the same question, *I wonder if he didn't marry her and get all the property.* And Herbert answers, *He may have been married already.'*

'So why would that stop him? How many wives has *Senhor* Raposo got? It doesn't stop him wanting more.'

She waved her hands indignantly.

Tony said, 'Herbert continues. *Her cruel mortification may have been a part of her half-brother's scheme.'*

His audience looked blank, so he added, 'Her brother hated her, so it was his idea she should be deserted on her wedding day.'

Even as he said this, his voice faltered for lack of conviction. Why, after all, should the suitor have obeyed the brother when there were such rich pickings to be had?

'I believe,' said Father Espirito Santo, 'the first explanation makes better sense. In England, the law matters. That is why Mr Jaggers is so important. We have laws here, but they are Lisbon laws. They lose their force in the African heat.'

'Is that why the English navy is here? To make us obey our own laws?'

Dona Esmeralda addressed the question generally. But she was staring at Tony.

'*A perfect fleet,'* said Tony, quoting Herbert.

17 Mbewe

For Mbewe, there was only one word for war, the Manganja *nkhondo*. It meant a lot of shouting and gunfire but usually not many people were killed. Maybe five or seven, while the rest ran away, knowing they had lost. The Portuguese word *guerra* was much more terrible. Bigger guns, hundreds of dead people.

Matekenya's war was *guerra*. News of it started with Portuguese women running barefoot through the streets of Quelimane, sobbing to anyone who would listen about how they'd escaped through the reeds, how they'd left the old people behind, or dropped their babies and couldn't find them in the darkness and confusion. About how the Africans on all sides had risen in revolt. About how the forts at Sena, Mazaro, Mpassu and Chironje had been attacked and every Portuguese soldier murdered.

There was a steamer in the harbour—British, since they were the only ones that called at Quelimane those days. Governor Palma Velho was the first to take refuge there, his police repelling other Portuguese who clamoured to get on board. Was this really the end of Portuguese rule? How could Matekenya's few hundred men have achieved this? Was it even what they wanted?

Chindevu pooh-poohed the idea, making a comment of which Mbewe took careful note.

'You should never,' he said, 'try to tax people unless you've the power to do so. As soon as they find they don't have to pay, they'll go back to their villages.'

He was more worried about the *Lady Nyasa*, waiting at Maruro.

'I hope Gouk's got the sense not to hand it over this time,' he muttered, as he pored over a list of the foreign traders in Quelimane. There were German, Dutch, Prussian, French, Swiss and Italian houses in town, as well as the many Indian houses.

'You know these people, Mbewe.'

It was true he'd acted as pilot for most of them.

'Tell them I've sent you. Call them to a meeting this evening. We need to protect our businesses.'

So Mbewe spent the afternoon visiting the stores. He saw Mr Scholmann of the Dutch company, and Herr Deuss, from Hamburg. They both agreed to come. Monsieur Rossier, manager of Régis, was as nice to him as usual. He remembered the first time he was guiding his canoes and they stopped at his late mother's village. The monsieur said he was 'charmed' to meet 'your dear wife', and gave Masamanga a piece of silk to prove it.

Herr Gubler of Fabre et Fils also swore he would be part of it and would tell Rudolph and Jean and Ippolito about Chindevu's meeting. Ippolito, who was Signor Lamagna the Italian, didn't seem very likely to join, being short and fat and always complaining about the heat.

Next morning they embarked on the Kwa Kwa with Chindevu in command. His army was fifteen Europeans, a dozen Indian traders and eighty African soldiers armed by the Governor.

Not a single Portuguese, Mbewe reflected. Their mission was to secure the different trading posts, beginning with the Dutch post at Mutu and the station at Mururo, where the *Lady Nyasa* was anchored. Nothing beyond that. It wasn't their fault they ended up saving the colony for the Portuguese.

These things happen. What you intend isn't what follows.

Despite the rumours, Mazaro hadn't been attacked. But they could hear gunshots from the direction of Mpea and set off immediately, all except Signor Ippolito, who said he was unwell and returned to Maruro.

It turned out the Opium Company was being besieged. Mopeia, as the *azungo* call it, was on a hill, but the company office was down by the Zambezi where the poppy fields were. The manager was called Caldas Xavier, a Portuguese major, and he, his brother, Mr Henderson his engineer, and twelve Indian workers along with their wives, had been surrounded in the office for several hours. The rescuers were just in time, for the defenders were running out of ammunition. The manager's brother saw them from the roof and waved, and

Chindevu and the Company men shouted 'Hip Hip Hurrah' in return.

Matekenya's people were hopelessly outgunned, and they retreated back north, leaving fifty of their men dead. Mbewe was heartsick so see men that he knew lying among the reeds. The column lost just two of the African soldiers.

Chindevu, with Mbewe as pilot, followed the retreating army up the Shire in the *Lady Nyasa*. They stopped at Chironje and went ashore. The people said they had no quarrel with the company, only with the Portuguese, and they returned several canoes that had been taken. So the first part of the war was over. They were very afraid and with good reason.

What happened next was much, much worse. The Portuguese brought one of their warlords from the south side of the Zambezi, a man called Gouveia with a huge army of slaves. Four thousand of them ravaged Matekenya's land, burning and raping and killing as far as the Ruo confluence. In the days that followed, Mbewe attended many funeral wakes. Each lasted a whole seven days, so he could only travel between them, visiting the families he knew best, pouring millet beer at so many graves. This happened not once but twice, first for the main war at Mopeia, then for the second war when the Portuguese came back, burning and killing. The village where Mbewe lived with Masamanga, his late mother's village, was among those destroyed. The people appealed to the Kololo for help and Chikusi wanted to respond, but Ramakukan refused.

So once again it was Ramakukan who brought peace. Because of his attitude, Mr Consul was able to persuade the Portuguese to tell Gouveia to stop. That way everything calmed down.

But it was the Portuguese who had started the war, by trying to make Matekenya's people pay them taxes. Mbewe was clear in his mind about that. It was like Chemandala trying to deny Ramakukan his rights, as a chief, to tax people crossing his land or to have his share of the ivory. That had almost started a war between the Kololo and the Company. It had only ended when Mr Consul was prepared to be reasonable.

For the time being, there was a truce. Nothing was really settled. War could break out any time between the Kololo and Matekenya's people, and the Portuguese would call it a war against them. Then what would the British do? In any case, Mbewe didn't think all these *azungu* would be satisfied with just being traders or missionaries. Like the Portuguese, like Chemandala, they would want seize the land and impose taxes. When that happened, there would be a big war.

Determined to remain his own man, Mbewe resolved he was not going to work exclusively for the Company, as Chindevu wanted. As soon as it could be arranged, he would join the *azungu's* school at Mandala. He had been impressed by Philip's letter. The future was going to be very different, and Philip's skill, which had deceived the *azungu*, was something a slave should acquire. Even if he continued as a pilot, he wanted to know how to read and write.

18 Tony St Claire

One morning, as Tony was enjoying his shower, he asked Doto and Paulo to pause to allow him to look around the yard. Surprised by his interest, they became interested themselves as they helped him, half-carried, half-hobbling on his broom crutch, as he made his small tour.

There were two wells, one serving the household, and a larger one for industrial purposes. Both were accessed by large metal pumps, and Tony was amused to see *Made in Sheffield 1874* embossed on the stumps.

Against the side of the house, but out of sight of the veranda, was a domed construction, newly whitewashed, with a small metal hatch. Peering inside, he saw it was lined with fire bricks.

'Fugão,' said Paulo.

'Ah, yes, of course. A wood oven.'

In an adjacent shed were stacked logs of eucalyptus, along with others he identified from the scent as laurel, presumably for flavouring. In a mixture of Portuguese and English and with many gestures, his guides explained how the stove was stacked with firewood and lit at first light until it was cleared of ash and stacked instead with a suckling pig, or a haunch of gazelle or kudu, or a goose, along with pies, cakes and bread loaves.

'It stay hot-hot, long time,' said Doto.

'Yes, yes, I see.'

Behind the house, at some distance, was a large fenced enclosure containing more kinds of domestic fowl than he knew existed—hens and geese and turkeys, but also several types of ducks and what Paulo called *nkanga*, a kind of purple and blue chicken with white dots on its side feathers. From the dovecot he had already sampled fried baby pigeons. Within the enclosure was a covered run for keeping quails. At the far end, well away from the house against a retaining wall, were a couple of pigsties.

'You have cows, too? Vacas?'

'They die. The tsetse kill them.'

The retaining wall continued on three sides of the house and presumably the fourth. It was a good two hundred yards back, so the whole area enclosed was about two acres. Part was given over to a vegetable garden, with sweet corn, beans, sweet potatoes, casava and half a dozen different types of red and green peppers. Part-formed a small orchard, with orange and clementina trees, a few bottle-green mangoes, several pawpaws, a guava and a dwarf coconut palm no taller than the pawpaws. A narrow stream divided the garden from the orchard, bubbling from underneath the wall to the north and passing out of the enclosed area under an arch near the pigsties.

Against the wall to the east were several brick outhouses. Outside one was a huge pile of coconuts which five women were de-husking, sitting on the bare earth and ripping the fibre with their hands. The clean coconuts were stacked inside and the fibre stored in sacks. The second building contained agricultural equipment, a gleaming plough and a harrow looking new but unused. Paulo commented, 'It is for *cavalos*, horses, but they die.'

'Tsetse again?'

'*Sim, senhor.*'

The third outhouse was stacked high with ivory tusks. He counted fifty-three pairs and a few single tusks, a small fortune.

'Are there elephants here?' asked Tony in surprise.

'No, not *hôje em dia*. Was longtime. But the Chikunda bring.'

The Chikunda were professional elephant hunters in the interior. The brought caravans of ivory and slaves to the coast. The slaves, these days, were sold secretly for export.

'Who buys the coconuts?' asked Tony.

'It used to be Mr Sulemane from Quelimane,' said Paulo. 'But since the *patrão* was killed, no one comes.'

'The ivory too?'

'Is the same.'

Back at the house, he found Doveton had dropped by, to enquire what had happened to his First Under-Secretary. He kissed Dona Esmeralda on both cheeks, then repeated the operation, a little more slowly Tony noticed, with Maria Antónia.

'Thank you for looking after this wretch,' he said cheerfully.

'No trouble, He's been entertaining us.'

'Entertaining you? How?'

'Reading to us. Shall I bring you a drink?

'Just orange juice, if you have it.'

Doveton pulled up a chair and opened his briefcase. Tony shoved the latest number of *David Copperfield* under his pallet, hoping Doveton hadn't noticed.

'Sleigh said it would take six weeks, so I didn't call earlier.'

'Sleigh?'

'The ship's surgeon you sent packing. He took great umbrage.'

'He was abominably rude,' said Tony.

'He's certainly no diplomat. But how are you? Are you being looked after?'

Tony had mentally noted that six weeks and was careful not to rush his recovery.

'Capitally,' he said, 'but it'll take a little longer before I'm up and about.'

'Actually,' said Doveton, 'your accident gives me excellent cover. I've been lying low for a day or two.'

'Why? What's the matter?'

'Haven't you heard? The whole country's in uproar. Matekenya's people have attacked Chimuara, in another of these revolts over taxes. Really, the Portuguese are great idiots. They shouldn't try these things when they haven't the power to back them up.'

'We've heard nothing down here,' said Tony.

'I'm sure Dona Esmeralda's people know very well what's going on. But they don't want to get involved, any more than I do.'

Tony reflected, not for the first time, how out of touch a white man could be in Africa, especially when surrounded by smiling faces.

'Anyway,' continued Doveton, 'there's been a great panic in Quelimane. The Governor's hiding on a British steamship. He had the cheek to send me a letter saying the English are behind everything. By the English, he means Ramakukan. As if the Kololo would have anything to do with Matekenya's lot. The Company people put together a small army of traders to protect their various factories. I gather there was a big stand-off at Mopeia yesterday. Obviously, I want none of it.'

Doveton had brought a sheaf of correspondence and some notes on a journey to the Lugela River to be written up. The correspondence had fallen behind and, with a frigate calling at Quelimane in five day's time, needed urgent attention. The main item was a report, also to be compiled from notes, on the state of the slave trade on the lower Zambezi, for dispatch to the Vice-Admiralty Court in Natal. There were other pieces concerning the increase in trade with the highlands since the arrival of the new steamer, and on the attempts of the Portuguese authorities to prevent the missionaries importing guns—guns they needed for their own security against Arab slave traders to the far north of Lake Nyasa. Fortunately, added Doveton, in what was to be a confidential appendix, a sugar planter in the delta region was helping them import arms secretly.

'Who is this?' asked Tony.

'Oddly enough, he's a Jamaican. I spent last night at his place. Extraordinarily interesting man. He's been here longer than any of us—came with the original bishop, came with the search expedition, came again with the Scottish lot, and decided to settle and plant sugar which, of course, he's known all about since his childhood.'

'This will take me a couple of days,' said Tony.

'Yes, of course. I'll send a couple of the sepoys to pick the stuff up. Just wrap it so it looks of no consequence.'

Doveton lit a cigar and, wafting the smoke aside, stared without recognition at the various plants in the various pots, tins, kettles and barrels lining the veranda. His thoughts, Tony could see, were on Whitehall and his messages' destination.

'I understand you had Raposo here?'

'Not me. There was a lunch party.'

'Sleigh made it sound he was your personal guest'.

'There was Raposo, Rato the notary, whom you know, Corvo the capitão-mor, and Pombo, a family friend.

Like Aesop's fables, he was about to add, but Doveton interrupted.

'Did you join them?'

'No, I was out here. I just saw them coming and going.'

'You didn't pick up anything? From that priest, for instance?'

'I just assumed it was something to do with Augusto's will?'

'His will? Why?'

'Well, there was the notary, the military governor, a close neighbour and a family friend. I guessed they were concerned about the future of the estate.'

Doveton got up suddenly and walked to the far end of the verandah. He stood there for a few moments, puffing on his cigar and staring idly at the pots and the plants. Once again, his mind was elsewhere, but not this time in London. Then he strode back quickly and shuffled through the papers he brought for Tony, selecting the report on the slave trade.

'I wish I could make it stronger,' he said. 'I'm certain Raposo's in it.'

He meditated, running his finger over what he had written, then put the papers aside, speaking confidentially.

'It's not like that here,' he said. 'These estates, *prazos* they're called, are not owned by the men. They're awarded by the Portuguese Crown to women, to be inherited by their daughters and granddaughters. Three generations was the original condition, with a requirement to marry men from Portugal. The conditions have long since lapsed, but this estate is Dona Esmeralda's. Augusto's will is neither here nor there.'

'How did Augusto die?' he asked.

Doveton sighed in exasperation.

'Officially, it was a hunting accident. They brought him back dead.'

'In reality?'

'Augusto was no hunter. He hated killing animals, even for the pot. He used to joke it was the Indian in him, overriding the British.'

Maria Antónia appeared in the doorway, enquiring whether Doveton would stay for lunch.

'Please thank your mother, *meninha*, and say, yes, I'd be delighted.

He stubbed his cigar out in a pot of cactus, and rose to go indoors.

'Do what you can with the report about Raposo. You know what I mean. Hints. Innuendos. Make it appear to say more than it really does.'

Tony was lost in thought as Doveton left him. For the first time, he felt a sneaking sympathy for those absurd Scotsmen he remembered by their African nicknames—Chemandala and Chindevu—with their leaky steamer and Presbyterian self-regard. How could a region with such agricultural potential still be exporting slaves? These Aesop characters—Mr Fox, Mr Crow, Mr Rat—how could a European power allow them to dictate policy, manipulate the laws, commit murder?

19 Maria Afonso

Looking back over his career at the Escola de Exército, for all the pleasure he had taken in his courses, that moment in Mafra when his friends and surrogate family had come together without planning was the most memorable. They lunched, of course, with Father Anselmo, who took great interest in their hopes for the future and was quick to recognise in Alfredo a student of unusual promise. They visited the Convent and especially the rooms, still belonging to the military, where Afonso had been interviewed and where Alfredo and Zé Miguel had begun their course at the Colégio Militar. On the Saturday evening, they returned to Lisbon.

That summer, it was confirmed that Vasco da Gama's skeleton was back in Vidigueira. A tomb on the Epistle side of the altar was opened and contained a single skeleton, which might have been Gama's or was perhaps that of his grandson, who had also been Viceroy of India. There was some evidence that their mutual gravestones had been exchanged during restorations of the church in 1841. Embarrassingly, the casket already transferred to Belém turned out to contain two crania and at least eight femurs. Newspapers speculated these were the mixed remains of Dom Miguel da Gama, Dona Leonor de Távora, and Dona Guiomar de Vilhena.

Alfredo's scorn was vindicated, and there were no speeches from Pinheiro Chagas who, for once, kept his mouth shut.

'Are they going to try again?' asked Afonso.

'Even this government is not impervious to shame.'

That same summer, too, came news that the Opium Company, which Major Caldas Xavier was administering in the small town of Mopeia on the left bank of the Zambezi River, had been destroyed in an African rebellion. Caldas Xavier himself had survived the attack, along with a Scottish engineer and a dozen Indian workers, but only after holding out against three thousand Africans in a battle lasting twelve hours. At first, the Regenerator papers described him as the 'villain' of the affair, the man whose methods of recruiting labour had sparked off the revolt. Slavery had been abolished under Sá da

Bandeira's reforms. Caldas Xavier had attempted to reintroduce it, under the guise of forced labour for the state.

However, when the scale of the revolt became clear, with Portuguese sovereignty at stake, the Regenerator newspapers were forced to eat their words. Caldas Xavier was hailed as 'the hero of Mopeia'. It was like the battle of Little Bighorn, except that this General Custer had won. Not only had he put down an African revolt, he had confronted head-on the agents of feudalism in Portugal's African colonies, setting an example for future economic development. His opium plantation, and his labour policies, were models for imperial regeneration.

Even Alfredo conceded this, a little grudgingly.

'He's right about plantations. I just wish it was with paid labour and that it wasn't opium.'

This about-turn coincided with events on the international stage, in particular, the Berlin Conference of 1884. That conference established the principle of 'Effective Occupation'. Powers could hold colonies only if they had treaties with local leaders, flew their flags there, had established an administration backed by an army and a police force, and were running a viable economy. Failure on any on these points could justify foreign intervention.

Alfredo had foreseen that free trade was redundant. The crisis of capitalism had taken a fresh turn as Germany eyed southern Angola and northern Mozambique, King Leopold seized the Congo, and Cecil Rhodes made plans for a British territory from the Cape to Cairo, all in pursuit of materials such as the vast seams of gold that had been discovered at Johannesburg. Along with Afonso, he became a student member of the Lisbon Geographical Society, where they mingled with the liberals of the day, like the historian Oliveira Martins and soon-to-be finance minister, Barros Gomes, both passionately concerned with the colonies. In 1887, the Society published its *mapa cor-de-rosa*, showing its version of southern Africa, with a solid belt of Portuguese territory joining Angola in the west to Mozambique in the east.

After graduating with the rank of subaltern, Afonso served for two years in Porto, which was heavily garrisoned against rising Republican sentiment. This enabled him to visit

Cumeeira for the first time since he was eight, meeting his sister's husband who was about to depart for Brazil, and trying belatedly to get his younger brother into the school in Régua. He contributed articles to *O Século* on Lisbon's defenses, based on the reports written by his ancestor, Teixeiro Rebelo, who had refurbished the line of forts from Carcavelos right round to Cabo da Rocha. He became a passionate defender of Major Serpa Pinto, who was under attack for having deserted his former colleagues, Hermenegildo Capello and Roberto Ivens, just twenty days into their African exploration, choosing to follow a well-established trade route from Bié in Angola to Pretoria in South Africa. Jewish, Indian, Mestiço and Afrikaneer traders had all made the journey which Serpa Pinto claimed to have pioneered. Capello and Ivens had just returned from a second exploration, mapping rivers in the area covered by the *mapa rosa*. Meanwhile, Serpa Pinto was serving as consul in Zanzibar and unable to defend himself.

Otherwise, Afonso kicked his heels, growing increasingly bitter. He began to share Caldas Xavier's contempt for the Lisbon petit-bourgeoisie, the clerks and small shopkeepers whose concerns never rose above daily finances. As he watched them parading on Sundays with their over-dressed wives in the half-constructed boulevard, he felt despair at how far Portugal had sunk from her former greatness.

He had trained to be a soldier, and that career had been focused on serving the empire in Africa. But for almost two decades, nothing had happened. While other European powers circled, like those Africans attacking the company in Mopeia, Portugal had done nothing except make fine speeches and issue diplomatic protests.

Unexpectedly, the Progressives were returned to power with plans for colonial intervention. Within a year, Alfredo was dispatched to Angola, to join the Luanda campaign. Zé Miguel prepared to return to help administer the family *prazo* in Mozambique. When a new expedition was launched with the twin aims of pacifying Zambezia and developing the economy on the English model through a Chartered Company, floated on the stock exchange, Afonso enlisted with enthusiasm.

20 Lorenzo

It was dusk at Quelimane, and in his cell in the old fort the sunset yellow was humming with mosquitos. But Lorenzo Johnston was content. His wife Luiza had brought to the prison a pot of dried fish cooked with coconut, one of her best dishes, along with a bottle of rough red wine. She had instructions to bring this only when Isidoro was on guard duty, which happened three times a week. The other guards confiscated any food and drink for themselves, but Lorenzo and Isidoro had been neighbours in Mlambe. When Luiza appeared, Isidoro waved the items through.

It was a big thing for me, he wrote, compiling his own record while surrounded by books describing the same events but barely mentioning him, a big event when I met Mbewe and became his friend. For a long time, I hadn't had anyone to share my thoughts with. Of course, he was younger than me, maybe twenty years. I tell people I was born a Jamaican slave. That's not strictly true. I was born in 1837, the year before complete emancipation. Legally, slavery was abolished in 1834, followed by a apprentice system, so I could never grow to be a slave. But who cares? I was born the year before the slaves were actually freed.

It came to pass when I was travelling upriver to my new job at Matope. I already knew who Mbewe was, and it wasn't the first time I had travelled with him as pilot. He was the first African I ever saw white men defer to. When he expressed an opinion about the river, about taking this or that channel, or stopping at this or that village for the night, they took his advice. They knew they were dealing with a master, and I never encountered that before with any black man, in Africa or Jamaica.

The first time this happened—I can't remember when exactly, but I remember the exact bend in the river, just after we left the Zambezi river to join the Shire. A wall of papyrus blocked the way, one hundred and fifty yards across, worse than anything I ever saw back in Magomero days. It seemed impossible to know where to break through, but Mbewe told

Mr Gouk to get up steam and point the prow to the left side, and Crash! Bang! Boom! while we ducked to avoid getting our faces slashed, the steamer was clean through into clear water, running fast and deep under the obstruction.

I was impressed, but it wasn't then we became friends. It was when I was travelling to my new job at Matope.

We had stopped ten miles beyond Tengani's to buy good river *chambo* with coconuts we'd brought up from the Zambezi delta. One of the fishermen in his dugout canoe was playing an *mbira*, with two rows of metal keys fastened to a wooden board. It was small enough for him to hold in two hands while he used his thumbs to flick the keys. I remembered how Sinjeri used to have one at Magomero and how he taught me to play it. That was, oh my Lord, so many years past! Anyway, I asked the fishermen if I could take a look, and he passed the *mbira* to me. I leant against the rail, trying to pick out one of the tunes I remembered.

Mbewe interrupted me.

'Not like that.'

He took the instrument from me and began playing like a real master, with notes bubbling over a repeated bass he made with his left thumb. He was good, and even better I remembered the song he was playing from my first time on this river. *Sina Mama, Sina Baba, Sina Mama wakulewa naye, Mama ndiwe Mariya.* I began singing the words under my breath, and it Mbewe's turn to be surprised.

'You know it?'

'I recall.'

So we got talking. The steamer got under way and we gave the *mbira* to the fisherman with many *zikomos*. I joined Mbewe in the prow, and immediately, he said something very strange. I asked him about his family and he replied, no, he had none, he was *kaporo*, a slave.

I'd heard the word *kaporo* many times but never heard it translated like this. What he said make no sense to me.

'How can you be a slave? On this boat, you are the man in charge.'

As if to confirm this, he broke off to give the correct course to steer between three islands. Then, as we passed under the high bank at Chiromo, he answered me.

'A slave is one who has no family. Like in the song, I have no father, I have no mother.'

'You mean they are both dead?'

'They have joined the ancestors. But that is not what I mean.'

He waved back towards Chiromo.

'My father had his capital there. He was called Chipatula.'

I remembered how Chipatula got killed by Piri Piri, the angry *muzungu* with the red hair.

'My mother is dead too. She was not one of Chipatula's real wives. She was his slave wife. So I was his slave too.'

'You have a wife yourself?'

'Yes, she is called Masamanga.'

I felt confused.

'A father. A mother. A wife. You have children?'

'Three boys, and a daughter.'

He called out instructions again to avoid a sunken log, and the steamer veered sharply to the right.

'How can you say you have no family?'

'I have no lineage. I will never be an ancestor. My sons will not be my heirs. I will never have any country.'

By now, we were approaching Elephant Marsh, where we were all completely in his hands. The place terrified me. By then, I'd sailed through it, what? Seven times? With the Bishop, with Capt. Young, with Dr Laws and other times. A place of fast currents and stinking vapours. A place where deadly snakes coiled right there in the reeds brushing the side rails. A place where, if you relieved yourself between the rails, you risked a crocodile seizing your member. I never saw anywhere like it. For hours on end it made me shudder, and I was always glad to emerge at Katunga's.

Yet Mbewe treated it like it home.

'I used to catch fish here,' he said. 'With my brother Mbiti.'

'So you have a brother too?'

'Chipatula had lots of boys by different mothers. Mbiti was my brother by a different wife. My father sent us to set his fish traps. But we used to catch for ourselves. Even dry them and sell them. My friend Kashkinya showed us how to do it. Afterwards, he got taken by a crocodile and I was very sad. But that's really how I started as a businessman.'

'You never had to herd goats?'

At Magomero, and in the villages around Cape MacClear, that was what most of the boys did.

'Only my father's sons by his real wife were allowed to do that. Goats are valuable. He wouldn't entrust them to a slave like me.'

At the time of this talk, I'd spent, dear Lord, more than half my life in Africa. But Mbewe was describing something I never considered. It intrigued me we were both born into slavery and we were both now free. His slavery was different to mine. I was freed by the British. He seemed to have somehow freed himself. After Chipatula was murdered by that madman Piri Piri, he became Ramakukan's slave. But already he was a wealthy man and when Ramakukan died there was no one he had to fear.

At times, I felt being a Jamaican gave no assistance in understanding this country.

But there are some things you never forget. I have never forgotten that evening at Matope when Mbewe and myself and two Muslim traders sat drinking whisky and discussing what was going to befall us all in Africa.

No river exists in Jamaica like this Shire. A waterway a thousand miles long, counting the lake where it starts. At Matope it is wide and placid, with green islands of reeds and papyrus, where hippos snuffle and crocodiles sleep with their mouths open and the *chambo* are succulent. A hundred yards past the station, it narrows to the first cataract, in fact a double cataract with a tiny island where I liked to sit, chasing off the monitor lizards and staring into the turbulent pool below. You could see fish leaping, trying to climb the waterfall, and some would succeed and some fall back. After a long journey upriver, at Matope you could feel you had arrived somewhere. The Zambezi delta with its channels, the winding serpent of the Shire confluence, the mysteries of Dambinyi marsh, the slog past the cataracts, all these gave way to a Shire that posed no further problems. You still needed Mbewe, but even he could relax. You were just three days from the lake.

I was back beside the Shire at a difficult time—difficult, that is, for the Scotsmen I was involved with.

Dr Laws had finally abandoned Cape MacClear for a new site at Bandawe, high in the hills north-west of the lake. By then, too many people had died at Cape MacClear. Only Mr Benzie, the new captain of the *Ilala*, was personally known to me. He was taken ill at Matope, and Dr Laws removed him to Cape MacClear where he died of blackwater fever. The rest were the man who replaced Mr Ridell as agriculturalist, the new doctor, a sailor and one of the Lovedale catechists—five graves in all. Yet it was not the deaths that provoked the change of site, not according to Dr Laws. It was the death of the cow and three calves he imported from South Africa. The tsetse fly prevented him keeping livestock at Cape MacClear, or using horses for ploughing. Up at Bandawe, where the Africans have big herds of cattle, the mission could make a fresh start, free from tsetse, at a cool altitude—and many, many miles from the slave caravans. He was pleased that problem no longer concerned him while he built his colony.

When Mbewe stopped by Matope, guiding the two Indians who had asked him to take them as far as the lake, we talked about these matters.

I told him how the *azungu* were clamouring for a colony, getting chiefs to sign bits of paper and let their land be stolen, even starting a war with the Portuguese. In my opinion, it was all wrong. White rule would never solve Africa's problems.

Mbewe laughed at my concerns.

'Let me pilot you to Massangano,' he said. 'You know it? It's after Sena, on the way to Tete. Bonga's stockade. The Portuguese tried three times to capture it. Bonga has their skulls lining the stockade posts. You can see them from the river, grinning at you.'

'The English are stronger than the Portuguese,' I objected.

'You think so? Have you heard what happened six months ago at Isandhlwana?'

The whole of Africa had heard of it, even to the tiniest village. Chelmsford's army tried to invade Zululand, and it ended with one and a half thousand English dead. With just spears and knobkerries, the Zulu massacred them.

'I like the English,' said Mbewe. 'Not all of them, not Chemandala, not Dr Laws, they're not friendly. But they can't trouble us. Half the time we have to look after them. They don't know how to catch fish, they don't know how to skin animals, not properly anyway, they don't know how to bring the rains, and they don't know how to cook *nsima*. Every three weeks they go down with fever and have to have one of us nurse them. They can't do us any harm'

Mbewe and I were sharing *nsima* and fried *chambo* from the river. The Indians were eating some chop of their own on the veranda outside the store. After they finished and washed their hands, they came to join us. They introduced themselves as Sacur Latif and Selemanee Abdullah and, when they found I spoke English, they asked if I was a believer. When I said no, I was Christian, which sounded a funny answer but was one they understood, they asked if I had any whisky. As matter of fact, I did. I wasn't allowed to trade in alcohol, but every time an English hunter or trader passed by Matope he expected a glass or two. So I kept a small supply and produced a square bottle with a slanting black and gold label that read Johnnie Walker.

They had changed garments since I saw them arrive with Mbewe, and now they were wearing white tunics that draped loose to the ankles, tied at the waist with a chord. They had already washed the ones they wore for travelling and draped them over the red-flowering euphorbia bushes in the yard, along with their turbans. Sacur Latif was short and slim, with eager eyes, and a face quick to smile above a thick and very black beard. His friend Selemanee seemed older, moon-faced and heavy, with an identical beard. Their cleanness was a bit intimidating, so I fetched a cotton tablecloth from the store to spread on the tea chest where Mbewe and I rested our plates. I also brought four china teacups to drink the Johnnie Walker.

'We overheard your talk,' said Selemanee Abdullah.

He spoke in a sing-song Manganja that was perfectly clear, mixing it with some expression in English.

'The Zulus have not seen the last of the English. In fact, they are already back. Zululand will soon be another part of the British Empire.'

'Why do they have to do it?' asked Mbewe. 'They're not like the Kololo or the Ndebele or the Ngoni. They already have a land of their own.'

'They're back in Zululand because they have suffered a terrible defeat. The most powerful nation on the earth can't accept that. Their pride won't let them just sit back.'

'But why go there in the first place? With armies, I mean? Traders, I understand. Missionaries, I partly understand. But why do they want to rule everywhere?'

'Mbewe, my friend, it is the question of our times. I have given the matter much thought. It is because they are a trading nation, and they are no good at trade.'

Sacur Latif give a sudden grin and nodded to us vigorously. It was evident he'd heard this before. I could imagine the many hours they spent together travelling by canoe, the evenings in the bush without companions and without whisky. I made a point of refilling their teacups, and so drew attention to myself.

'How long have you been a trader?' Selemanee asked me.

'Just five weeks.'

'Five weeks. And what did you do before?'

'I was a cook.'

'And before that?'

'Oh, a jack-of-all-trades.'

'A handyman,' said Sacur Latif, unexpectedly.

'What did your father do? And your grandfather?'

'They were slaves in Jamaica.'

That threw him off balance. He stopped and examined me carefully. 'I assumed you were English.'

'I've lived in London. And in Glasgow. In between in Cape Town.'

'But you speak Manganja.'

'I've lived here too. With the missionaries. It was them I cooked for.'

He nodded slowly, sipping his whisky and smoothing his tunic over his slightly protruding stomach.

'Now you're a trader,' said Sacur Latif, and I sensed he was getting the conversation back on track.

'My father was a trader,' Selemane continued. 'My grandfather and great-grandfather were traders. On my mother's side and on my father's side. It's my fate, it's in my blood.'

He paused, and asked me.

'When you close the store, when you are free to do things for yourself, what do you think about?'

What do I think about? I think about what to eat that evening. Should I go fishing? Shoot a duck or a pigeons? I think about locking up safely.

'I mean,' persisted Selemane, 'when your mind wanders. When you lie awake at three o'clock in the morning. What matters to you?'

I hesitated, but I told him, 'I think about abolishing slavery.'

'Precisely. That's the kind of thing the English think about. How to change the world. When I awake in the morning, while I'm brushing my teeth with a twig, I think about trade. When I'm sitting in the canoe, I think about trade. When I retire each evening, I'm still thinking about trade.'

'You don't think about your family?'

'Of course. If the gold is flowing in Africa, my first thought is I must do something for my children.'

Against my will, I was impressed.

'Gold flowing in Africa? King Solomon's mines?' Mbewe laughed. 'Those days are long finished.'

'There is always wealth, ' said Selemane. 'When your father and grandfather were slaves, what did they know about?'

It was a question I had never asked myself.

'I suppose they knew about growing sugar.'

'They knew about sugar. But because they were slaves, that is a business you want nothing to do with. That is why your Jamaica is poor. It is rich with sugar, but you do not want to grow it. Even though it's in your blood.'

I was shocked. This was another Thomas Carlyle, the Nigger Question, but without the insulting language. I wanted to tell him how the estates were still owned by the whites, how there was no land for people like me. But part of it was true. We refused to work for the slave-owners, even for wages, so the island's richest resource was wasted.

The sun was falling and the river with its reeds and the store where we sitting were bathed in yellow light. I got up and threw some pieces of cow dung on the small fire I always lit some late afternoon in the yard a little beyond the door. This helped with the mosquitos.

'It will be dew fall soon,' I said. 'You'd better pick up your clothes.'

But Selemane wasn't finished.

'Do you think you are a good trader?'

'No, I said firmly. 'I don't have the skills. But in any case, I'm not allowed to be a proper trader. People bring me ivory. I pay them well in calico, more than you do. But they don't want just calico. They want ammunition, and I'm not allowed to sell that. They say to me, what nonsense is this? How can we kill elephants without ammunition for our guns? I have to say to them, it isn't Company policy.'

'Precisely, The English put things before trade. That's something we never do.'

'You trade in alcohol?'

'Ah, no, that is forbidden by the Prophet.'

I wanted to laugh, but he would have been offended. He didn't see any contradiction. He even held out his teacup for a refill of Johnnie Walker.

'Anyway, that is why the English will take over. Because they can't compete with us as traders. So, they will take everything by force and then impose tariffs and taxes and transit duties to give themselves the advantage.'

'Same as in India,' concluded Sacur Latif with a grin. 'They came as traders, and now they own the land. So we Indians have to travel elsewhere to trade.'

That evening left a deep impression on me. The argument was obviously rehearsed many times, but their overall message made a deal of sense.

21 Tony St Claire

Three months after his recovery but still needing a stick to walk with, Tony was travelling with Consul Doveton back from a meeting with Portuguese officials in Sena, the provincial capital. The subject of the meeting was the continuing illicit slave trade. But one of the officials present was *Senhor* Corvo, the *capitão-mor*, who raised so many objections that the meeting ended without progress.

They crossed the Zambezi by canoe between Caia and Mopeia and continued along the river bank, single-file in their separate *machilas*, until a stream forced them to dismount. As they waded through water no more than a foot deep, Doveton remarked, 'I think this is Dona Esmeralda's boundary.'

'What, the *prazo* boundary? This far?'

'I reckon the house is about sixteen miles from here.'

Doveton was climbing back into his *machila*, but Tony hesitated.

'Do you need me? Do you mind if I look around?'

'Go ahead. I need you tomorrow but not especially early.'

They continued along the same path together for a couple of miles, then Doveton took a left turn to join the Quelimane road and pointed Tony straight ahead.

'The farm's that way,' he said. 'About another six miles. Then ten or so to the house.'

Tony had never before approached from this direction and had never heard of the farm. He and his four bearers continued alone, stopping first at a small cocoa plantation with perhaps two dozen trees. Was this the source of those morning cups of chocolate he had so much enjoyed? He had seen an isolated specimen in the governor's garden in Cape Town. What struck him now was the beauty of the trees with their fresh wine-coloured leaves darkening to green on the same trees, while the cocoa pods, shaped like tiny rugby balls, were every colour from green to yellow to crimson to purple as they ripened individually.

Four men were weeding between trees and, to his surprise, they greeted him as a *bwana* they already knew. Not for the first time, he wondered at the way news travelled here. The pods, the men told him, were picked throughout the year as they ripened. They picked one and slashed it open with a machete to reveal thirty beans packed inside. Next, he was shown a shed where the drying and fermenting of the pods was carried out. It had a moveable roof, opened as soon as the sun was high, but closed at night on during the rains. There were a several dozen jute sacks packed with dried beans, ready for shipment. Like the ivory and the copra back in the yard of the house, no one had collected them since Augusto's death.

The dirt track turned to sand as it led through several miles of coconut palms. In the dappled shade cast by the pale-green fronds high above his head, the light was distinctly gold, with black stripes like a zebras, as he stared into the distance past countless bare trunks. They seemed to jog up and down with the movements of the *machila*, and at the farthest point of the vista, they merged like parallel lines into a diaphanous wall. Every few hundred yards, they crossed a wide drainage ditch with pale blue water lilies, and in one of them they surprised a girl bathing breast-deep.

Tony was struck by how tall the trees were, a good eighty feet or so, in contrast to the short version beside Dona Esmerald's house. Lying back, staring upwards, he saw no two trees identical, all curving slightly in their individual struggle for light. Yet each looked perfectly poised and in each case the crown of palms was symmetrical.

After half an hour of this, during which Tony estimated they had covered four miles, the bearers keeping up a steady jog aided by a rhythmic, barely audible chant, they stopped in a small clearing beside a warehouse and half a dozen huts.

'You must be tired,' said Tony to the head bearer and then laughed as the man was too breathless to reply.

Descending from the *machila*, he walked with his stick towards a bench beneath a giant mahogany tree, the first tree not to be a coconut since they entered the plantation. There, too, the workers knew who he was, and one of them brought him a young, green coconut, hacking the end off with a machete and handing it to him to drink. It was semi-sweet and delightfully cool, not at all like the thick coconut milk he had known as a child at Christmas. Other coconuts were brought for the bearers, together with a bucket of water for them to splash themselves.

Above the warehouse door was a sign reading *Secção 3*.

'Four sections,' said one of the men. 'This one and three others.'

Inside the warehouse were large stacks of coconuts, waiting to be transported to the house for de-husking. Once again, it was obvious business was slack.

'How do they pick them', asked Tony, 'or do they just fall?'

'No, no, these men climb up. Otherwise, they spoil. Even these already pick, they spoil already. They keep too long.'

It was mid-afternoon, and the sun was still high as they resumed their journey, continuing under coconuts palms until, quite without warning, the sky overhead was clear of fronds and Tony realised they were following a river.

It wasn't a large river, an overgrown stream really, though the high banks spoke of a much deeper flow during the rains. It was lined by papyrus, with heads like maps of the delta, and by the grey plumes of reeds. Every hundred yards or so, the carriers made a diversion round the trunk of a bloated baobab tree, its stunted branches looking like roots thrust in the air. When Tony could glimpse the stream, it appeared green in the gaps between peninsulas of lilies and water hyacinths, a funny kind of water plant looked like tiny cabbages. It wasn't hard to imagine pythons and crocodiles.

The carriers had maintained their soft chanting, but suddenly they increased their volume to announce an arrival, and Tony found himself, quite unexpectedly, at what he immediately recognised as the farm. As he alighted before a substantial brick house with a thatched roof, he caught sight of several dozen workers, and his first surprise was that they were all armed. Most carried muskets, muzzle-loading weapons they must have traded from the Arabs, but he noticed a few rifles, some with more than one barrel. His second surprise was that Doto emerged from the house, greeting him warmly and taking his arm as he climbed out of the *machila*.

'It's okay, I have a stick these days.'

Nevertheless, he accepted Doto's support as he made a tour of inspection.

The farm itself had fields, divided by irrigation ditches connected to the river, and each was devoted to a different type of plant. Cocoa, as well as sisal, which he had seen at the Cape, he already knew. Sugar cane, like purple-veined bamboo, he guessed at. A field of waist-high bushes, sprouting a dry white foam, could only be cotton. Another field, with shrubs similar to the cocoa trees but with bright berries, had him puzzled until he picked and rubbed a berry and recognised kidney-shaped coffee beans.

Tony was in his element. This was plainly an experimental farm. His opinion of *Senhor* Augusto soared.

'What is this?' he asked, pausing before another field of waist-high, lush-leaved shrubs.

'*Chá, senhor.*'

Of course, tea bushes. Tony's admiration was complete.

Knowing little about any of these crops, he looked again more closely. The tea bushes were rather like a larger version of privet, but it was evident that they were very thirsty plants and the older leaves were brown at the edges. Perhaps they needed shade. The coffee shrubs appeared healthy, but the beans were not numerous. He had no idea what an economical crop would be. Sisal, he had been told at the Cape, was extremely slow growing, and these plants were still dwarfs. But the cotton looked promising. He had a vague notion the fibre length was crucial in competing with American plantations but had no idea how Augusto's cotton measured up. The most obvious success seemed to be the sugar cane, revelling in the conditions with stalks as thick as bamboo. One of the men hacked him a piece to taste and its sweetness was confirmed.

In the brick house, he found records of these experiments —varieties, dates of planting, types of fertilizer, notes on growth—but no one maintaining them.

'Isn't there someone in charge?'

'Diogo too scared. He run away when the *patrão* is killed.'

'Why are the men carrying guns?'

'I will show.'

131

Doto helped him back outside, and they walked a hundred yards to the river bank, to a point where there was a gap in the reeds.

'That side,' Doto pointed, 'Raposo's land.'

'So close?'

'Big trouble,' said Doto.

'Big, indeed.'

Climbing back into his *machila*, Tony hadn't planned to call at the house, but his path led past it and he couldn't resist seeing Maria Antónia again. It was three months since he had called, and the warmth of his welcome made him feel he had been remiss. Father Espirito Santo was with them, apparently negotiating some matter, and Maria António seemed a little subdued. But he was easily persuaded to dine with them, with the prospect of another session of *Great Expectations* afterwards on the front veranda.

They were now up to volume one-hundred-and-three of *All the Year Round*, dated April 13, 1861. For some reason, the others were slow to join him. While he waited Tony turned the long-yellowing pages, glancing over an article about the Arctic and Antarctica, and dwelling on a anonymous poem in couplets about Mohammed that ended with a curious footnote, denying any authenticity for the tale it related, which it attributed to an 'uncharitable Christian source'. Eventually, Dona Esmeralda and the others settled, and the reading began, with Maria Antónia still looking out of sorts.

Pip had long since settled in London with Herbert, embarked on the process of becoming a gentleman, with all that that entailed by way of snobbery towards Joe and dissatisfaction with himself. Father Espirito Santo had sighed over several of these episodes, especially over Pip's assumption that he was destined to marry Estella, for which he saw no evidence. Even Herbert's insistence that Mr Jaggers would not give Pip the attention he did were he nor sure Pip was destined for great things, carried no weight with the priest. Mr Jaggers was, after all, only a lawyer, acting on instructions.

'But whose?' he remarked to Tony, after one of their readings.

Maria Antónia, on the other hand, passionately sympathised with Pip. She felt herself orphaned and feared for her own future, knowing the confused hopes and disappointments of adolescence. When Herbert calls Pip *a good fellow, with impetuosity and hesitation, boldness and diffidence, action and dreaming, curiously mixed in him,* she wanted 'diffidence' explained—the word had no echo in Portuguese—but clapped her hands at the description.

Then, at the beginning of chapter thirty-two, just over half way through the story, Pip receives a letter which, he says, *threw me into a great flutter; for, though I had never seen the handwriting in which it was addressed, I divined whose hand it was. It had no set beginning, as Dear Mr Pip, or Dear Pip, or Dear Sir, or or Dear Anything, but ran thus:*

I am to come to London the day after tomorrow by the midday coach. I believe it was settled you would meet me? At all events Miss Havisham has that impression, and I write in obedience to it. She sends you her regard. Yours, Estella.'

Maria Antónia drew in her breath at this, frowning, and Tony paused in his reading, seeing she was going to demand another explanation.

She wrung her hands in exasperation and then broke out, 'What is this 'I am to come', and 'I believe it was settled.' Why can't she just say, 'I am coming to London and it would be nice if you could meet me'?'

'It is the passive voice,' said Father Espirito Santo. 'In English, it is used for politeness.'

'Ye-es,' said Tony. 'But this isn't a legal letter, or a diplomatic note. It isn't even an invitation. There's no need to be formal.'

'Dear Sir, Yours Faithfully,' said Father Espirito Santo. 'Or Dear Mr Jones, Yours Sincerely.'

Tony had to laugh.

'You're quite right, Father,' he said. 'Those are indeed the rules. But there's no need for that here. This is a friendly note, signed Yours, Estella.'

Three faces looked at him, expectantly. He hadn't thought a great deal about what he was reading, and he had a sudden feeling that Maria Antónia was following and understanding the story more fully.

'The situation is that Pip feels his future is mapped out for him. He has been chosen to receive a fortune and to marry Estella. He doesn't mind being given no choice in the matter.'

'Because he is in love with Estella', said Maria Antónia.

'Precisely. But Estella also has no choice. These passive form 'I am to come' and 'I believe it was settled' indicate she is acting in accordance with what has already been decided. Everything happening to her is pre-ordained.'

'By Miss Havisham?'

'Presumably. She says she writes 'in obedience' to Miss Havisham's impression.'

'And if she disobeys?'

'I don't know. Perhaps she feels Miss Havisham will disinherit her.'

But Maria Antónia wasn't satisfied.

'She is beautiful and she has been brought up to be rich. But she cannot choose.'

'We shall have to see what happens,' said Tony, preparing to read on.

Pip was so anxious about the meeting that he couldn't decide what to wear, his appetite vanished, and on the appointed day he arrived at the coach station in Cheapside before the coach had even started out from the Blue Boar in his home town. Bumping into Wemmick and with time on his hands, he accepted an invitation to visit Newgate Prison where one of Wemmick's clients was being held on a charge of robbery. Four pages followed, describing the inhabitants of 'Wemmick's greenhouse', which Tony was reading with some relish, putting his best acting voices into the dialogue, when suddenly Maria Antónia suddenly stood up, exclaiming 'It's horrible', and rushed off, sobbing. They heard her slamming her bedroom door and the bed squeaking as she threw herself down.

Dona Esmeralda made haste to follow, leaving Tony and Father Espirito Santo staring at each other in dismay.

'What's the matter?'

'Ah, it's a sad tale,' said the priest, but refused to elaborate.

22 Lorenzo

I was managing to muddle through at Matope. Some elephant ivory was brought in, along with hippo teeth, which this part of the river abounded in, along with some wild rubber in tight, smelly balls. But no cotton grew above the rapids, nor much in the way of oil seeds. The store functioned mainly as a transit post for goods coming down from the lake to Mandala. Once again, this was mainly ivory, but also for missionaries and hunters on their way to the lake region, or to the new Livingstonia at Bandawe, or for managers and staff at the new Company stores at the extreme north of Lake Nyasa.

In that dry season, Chindevu asked me a favour. He had to go north urgently to the new store at Karongo because Chemandala was again down with fever. So he asked me to organise the transport of a fresh supply of trade goods, new patterns of calico along with beads, axes and mirrors, from Mazaro to Katunga's and from there to Mandala. I was pleased by this proof of trust. So I travelled south in a succession of canoes to Mazaro, where the *Lady Nyasa* was waiting, and was lucky to hire Mbewe as pilot for the return journey. Apart from ensuring the piloting was managed properly, it gave us six days to catch up on our friendship.

'What happen to your Muslims?' I asked him, once we were safely in the main current of the Zambezi and he could relax.

'Selemane and Sacur? I dropped them at Mponda's. I never saw them again.'

Mponda ruled the southern end of the lake where the Shire flowed outwards. A huge man with a huge belly and a hundred wives whose main job was to take turns massaging his belly when he was drinking *pombe*. He was one of the principal slave traders, so I should have hated him. But he was always interesting to talk to and always curious about foreigners.

'What business did they have with him?'

'They talked about buying ivory and organizing a caravan to the coast near Quelimane.'

'You mean they were buying slaves?'

'I don't know for sure. They talked of a Portuguese agent there called Raposo. For slavers, they were very open about everything.'

'No palaver about illegitimate trade?'

'Except alcohol.'

We laughed again about the whisky. 'By the end of the evening at Matope, we'd finished the whole bottle, three quarters of it by the Prophet's followers.'

After we tied up at the riverbank that first evening, we were able to continue our conversation. We went ashore to escape the worst of the mosquitoes which, on that part of the Shire troubled even me. We bought a chicken and roasted it over a small fire, and then Mbewe added some lion droppings to the fire, which he said would keep off everything from hippo flies to hippos, so we would be safe sleeping there.

'They were right about Zululand,' said Mbewe, as though there was no pause in our talk. 'I feel sorry for Cetshwayo kaMphande.'

The English had reinvaded Zululand and burned Ulundi, Cetshwayo's capital. Cetshwayo himself was imprisoned in Cape Town.

Mbewe threw more of the lion droppings on the fire, and smoke billowed. It smelled slightly sweet. I wanted to ask his advice, and was considering how to approach the question.

'The first time I came to these parts was with the Bishop. He didn't want to start a colony. He wanted to find a chief he could trust by way of government, and convert people to Christianity. He also wanted to convert them to growing cotton for export. Then the slave trade would disappear. When I heard him saying these things, I volunteered.'

'I was still small,' said Mbewe. 'But I remember a time of war and then of famine.'

'Exactly. All the chiefs were fighting, and then the Bishop started fighting to protect his people, and then he died. It all got confused and the mission finished.'

'It ended right there at Katunga's,' said Mbewe. 'I remember seeing those white men, and two of them are buried there.'

'I was there myself,' I said. 'Perhaps you saw me.'

Mbewe laughed.

'You're too black. I wouldn't have noticed.'

'When I came back with Dr Laws, I studied again. They were going to stop the slave trade. But they wanted to start a colony, like another Jamaica. That prevented them fighting slavery. So I left them and travelled to Scotland with my friend Capt. Young.'

'But then you came back again?'

'Not with the mission. I came with the Company.'

'I thought they were the same?'

'They are and they aren't,' I said lamely. 'The same people are backing them, but their aims are different. The Company is a business, trying to make a profit from trade, which will replace the slave trade.'

'What about the other C.?' asked Mbewe. 'Chindevu says there are three C.s, Christianity, Commerce and Civilization.'

I couldn't help laughing.

'It has something to do with them thinking their way of life is better, and that we would be better off copying them. But I've visited Glasgow, and I don't believe it.'

'What's it like there?'

'Cold, filthy, foul air, stunted people, drunkards everywhere, and fine buildings.'

'But the people are rich?'

'Some are.'

I knew I hadn't satisfied him, but I hadn't begun to approach the question I wanted to ask him. I tried to get back to the original topic.

'I was impressed by what the Muslims said. The Company is no good at trading. I'm no good at trading, yet I'm as good as anyone in the Company.'

I spread my hands.

'You see how small this steamer is? Firewood takes up half the hold. If we make twenty-four trips a year, from Katunga's to Mazaro and back, that's two a month which is all the steamer can manage. That gives one-hundred-and-twenty tons of goods for export. Which ocean steamer is going to stop for such a tiny cargo? This isn't a commercial proposition.'

I was talking fast and, over and above the heat, was beginning to perspire on my own account. It felt as though I was resigning for a third time from a job that failed me. Not me it, it me. Mbewe was solicitous. He asked the bystanders for a gourd of *cachasu*, like lower Shire whisky, and he made me take a taste. It didn't help with the perspiration, but it calmed my nerves.

'Your Muslims were right,' I said. 'They travel by canoe, no need of firewood, and they head-load their ivory to the coast. If they sell the porters too, that is just trade.'

'No,' I added quickly. 'I don't mean that. Just that trade must follow the rules of trade. I have to re-think what I'm doing.'

I took another sip of cachasu. It began to feel like that original evening at Matope, when I was challenged about these matters.

'What I need is a crop on a plantation scale, close to the coast to make it profitable to export. The wealth will spread inland.'

I hesitated.

'Selemane asked me what I know about. What my father and grandfather knew about, the way he knows about things. My answer has to be sugar.'

Again, I sipped the cachasu. The spirit burned my throat. I was reluctant to commit myself, but unable to hold back.'

'I need some land,' I said. 'A plot or a island, close to the ocean, where I can practise what I know. I want to plant sugarcane.'

'Tomorrow', Mbewe said, without a moment's hesitation, 'Tomorrow, we'll pass *Sinyala* Maria's. We will stop to consult her. She will know.'

So that is what happened.

It amazed me to meet *Senhora* Maria. I knew the song about her, *Sina baba, Sina mama, Sina mama wakulewa naye, Mama ndiwe Mariya*. Everyone who travelled by canoe knew it. But I hadn't realised she was a real person. The missionaries, all of them from the Bishop to Dr Laws, said the song was about the Virgin Mary. They got this from Livingstone. He wrote in his book the song went back to those Jesuits from centuries ago, like the cracked mission bell he found in the ruins of Zumbo. Dr Laws at Cape MacClear made it the text of one of his most up-lifting sermons. He argued that even when failure stares you in the face, something efficacious survived from your labours.

Well, he got that wrong!

I know how easy it is for outsiders to get things wrong. For myself, being a black man from Jamaica, I assumed I would find Africa easy to understand. On my father's side, it was my great-grandfather who got sold into slavery. On my mother's, it went back a generation further. So, I was three or four generations Jamaican. But my ancestors were probably from Mandingo country in West Africa, not from the Shire valley, and what they remembered dwindled to a few stories about *anansi* the spider and some prayers we repeated without understanding the words.

So, the world I grew up in was a simple place. Sugar was all the white men knew about or cared about, beyond how to whip their slaves and help themselves to our women. And that was what we knew about too, but from the other side. It was no preparation for more complicated places, like London, or Glasgow, or Africa. But even back in Jamaica, I should have realised things weren't just black and white, slave and free. Slavery was abolished when I was one year old. But the people were just as discouraged. Because more was needed than abolishing slavery. So it led to Governor Eyre's regime and all those poor people being murdered at Morant Bay.

Now Mbewe was taking me to ask for help from the Virgin Mary, who owned thousands of slaves who sang about their devotion to her. To complicate things further, she turned out to be a frail Indian lady with crinkly white hair and dressed in a sari. I was out of my depth and glad I was in Mbewe's hands.

'She is rich in people,' he tells me, 'the African way. A little money. But mainly people. It began long ago, when she married and came here from India. She found a boy who was orphaned, and she adopted him. She took him into that compound there, and gave him food and clothes. Then another boy, then a girl, then a pair of twins. If you are orphaned, you just go to *Sinyala* Maria. For fifty years she has been doing that, forty years as a widow, and still they go to her. She is rich in so many people, not just the first but their children and their grandchildren. I couldn't count how many.'

He gestured to the man at the wheel, steering the steamer past a snag, a log only he had detected, lurking like a crocodile.

'When that is your family, there are few quarrels,' he added. 'Her real family is Matekenya. That's her son by her marriage. She detests him because he has killed so many people. But her other family, the big one, is always peaceful. If there is a quarrel, it is settled quickly.'

It sounded charming. But I was still troubled.

'Why are they called her slaves?'

'It is just a word we use. To show we respect her.'

Her house was raised on stilts to protect it from floods, like all the African houses in Chimuara. Otherwise, it was like the European houses I'd see in Quelimane, with polished wooden floors, ebony furniture and a red-tiled roof. I saw this from the steps and the doorway, for we didn't go inside. We talked to her through the upper part of a doorway with the lower part shut. As we spoke, she remained seated in the cool of her front room, but she was perfectly courteous. As he introduced me, Mbewe gave her a fathom of silk from my stock, laying it inside the doorway. She said immediately she'd heard of me from a long time back, from the time of the English Bishop. I was the West Indian cook, and it pleased her to hear I was always very gentle with the children. I was very popular with the pickneys.

How could I not smile at that? I was ready to suspect her, and found I couldn't.

Mbewe explained my problem in the Manganja she spoke better than English or Portuguese. I had no money, but I had knowledge. I knew how to grow sugarcane and needed a piece of land where I could grow it for trade.

In two sentences, he summed up what it took me three hours to explain to him.

'I will think,' she replied.

So we stood there, waiting. She gave no sign of what was turning over in her mind, and after standing in the doorway for fifteen minutes, I wondered if she had fallen asleep. I looked at Mbewe, but he motioned me to be patient.

At last, she exerted herself, and said this. 'There is a Portuguese Marquesa in Lisbon, a widow, not rich but of good family. She has never been to Africa, but she has land here. It formed part of her inheritance and she wants to keep it. With the new Lisbon politics, you can lose your land unless you are using it.'

She paused and fanned herself.

'I cannot promise, but I can try. If you grow your sugar, you must pay her the normal *foro*.'

'Of course,' said Mbewe.

'I can try. I will send for you when I hear.'

So that is how everything was fixed. *Foro* turn out to be the normal rent for a *prazo*, a tiny part of what it was really worth. The land itself was in the lower part of the Zambezi, right there in the delta and not far from Kongone. It would flood sometimes, but that would make it more fertile.

My first resolve was to do things the African way, not the Bishop's way, not Dr Laws's way, not Chindevu's way, but the local way. I asked Mbewe to accompany me when I made my first visit to the land.

It wasn't a large *prazo*, just eight miles by six, bordering the Zambezi River and the Kongone tributary, and I already knew it was not heavily populated. The slave trade had seen to that. Though the soil was fertile and well watered, you could walk for miles without seeing a village. It thrilled me, I was bringing agriculture, legitimate commerce, to a place the slave trade had ravaged. Mbewe introduced me to the headmen, the *nyakwawas*. There were just three of them, *Nyakwawa* Parose, *Nyakwawa* Msona and *Nyakwawa* Pedro. He told them I was the new *administrador*, so it was their duty to pay homage to me. But I was also a foreigner, respecting their privileges, which was why I had come to visit them.

This went down well. It meant I respected their rights, which meant they had to respect mine, which meant in practice I could do what I liked.

Obviously, I needed labourers to clear and work the land, but I was lucky here too. The Portuguese had introduced a new law, fixing a head tax on the three villages. This was the same law that got them into such fighting with Matekenya's people. Mbewe had been caught up badly in that war. But for the Kongone mouth of the Zambezi, they had installed a new custom's house, with a stockade and a flag. Lieutenant Mesquita was in command and responsible for imposing the new tax. He was just a young man with only half a dozen soldiers. He didn't have the faintest idea how to do what he was supposed to do. When I proposed to the *nykwawas* I would pay the tax for anyone who worked for me and then told Mesquita of the arrangement, both sides were delighted. There would be no need for any war, not even a tiny one.

Next thing, of course, I needed to get my hands on some sugar cane. I wanted good quality stock, not the semi-wild cane grown in the Tete region, nor the old *'Otaheite'* I knew back in Jamaica. That was too easily attacked by virus. But I'd heard of new varieties, Uba and Green Natal, fungus-resistant and already growing in Mauritius and Natal. I had heard, too, of a *prazo*-owner, *Senhor* Augusto, who ran an experimental farm, trying out new crops, including sugar cane. He was the man who got murdered by *Senhor* Raposo, who afterwards tried to marry his daughter. When I went to see *Senhor* Augusto, he was interested in my plans and freely gave me thirty ripe canes of Green Natal.

So my luck was holding, and I was ready to get started. I cut each cane at the nodes, careful to see each was budding nicely, and buried the stalks horizontal four feet apart. Some say they should be ten feet apart, but I was anxious to keep down on weeds, which in such fertile soil with a high rainfall, I considered could be a problem. I calculated in six months I would have one-hundred-and-eighty to two-hundred canes, which I could then cut up for re-planting. At the end of my first year, I would have one-thousand-two-hundred canes, plus the original two-hundred because you can leave the rattan in the ground for up to four years and it would continue bearing. After another six months, the figure would be seven-thousand-two-hundred plus the first crop of one-thousand-two-hundred and the original two-hundred, and I would be ready then to sow my first plantation.

142

There were two problems. The first was that it would take me two years before I had my first crop ready for milling. During those two years, I had to live as well as pay my labourers' taxes and, I swore on my heart, some rupees for their labour. I was not yet ready to make people work as slaves. Fortunately, there were other crops that could be harvested more quickly. I decided to devote fifty acres to maize, and fifty to sesame. I'd never studied either crop, but my workers grew them in their village gardens, and I was able to use their knowledge. The delta soil was so well watered I could get two crops of each in a single year, though I was careful to rotate the planting. The maize I could distribute to the workers as their wages, and the millet I sold to Issa Carimo in Quelimane. This proved so profitable that in later years I always maintained one-hundred-and-twenty acres of maize and sesame in addition to the sugar cane.

The second problem was I would need some means of milling the cane when my first harvest was ready. Of course, I could have used the technology of my grandfather's day—two wooden rollers for crushing the cane along with a pan for boiling the sugar. I couldn't use water buffalo as in Jamaica because of the tsetse, and I certainly wasn't using human labour as the Portuguese still did upriver in Tete. I planned to manage better than that. There were so many wrecked steamers along the banks of the Zambezi—Livingstone's original *Ma Robert*, then his *Pioneer*, then the first *Lady Nyasa*, not to mention all those Portuguese gunboats. It wasn't the engines of those ships that rotted away but their hulls, on account of something in the Zambezi water. So I was confident of finding a steam engine and boiler that could be adapted to my purpose.

I said it was my intention to do things the African way. I visited one of the *nyakwawas*, headman Parose, and I asked him to give me a wife. So he sent me Luiza. She is everything a wife should be and has already give me two sons. But I can't stop her calling herself my slave. This troubles me but, considering how we came together, it's only natural. It puts me on my guard to treat her well.

23 Maria Afonso

Afonso was the last of the three friends to set sail from Lisbon, and he felt a little chagrined that there was no one to bid him goodbye. Zé Miguel and he had given Alfredo a slap-up dinner at the Hotel Bragança the night before he embarked for Angola. They had talked of the prospects for a Republic; Alfredo, with his customary enthusiasm and wit, and Zé Miguel as a lover of Camões, whose poetry the Partido Republicano was championing as the inspiration for a rejuvenated Portugal. Afonso, as always, was non-committal, feeling that the oath of loyalty he had sworn to King Luís, on enlisting for service in Zambezia, precluded such talk. Alfredo gaily swept this aside as part of the flummery of a corrupt and out-dated system. Afonso wasn't so sure.

For Zé Miguel's departure for Mozambique, it had fallen to Afonso to provide the dinner, this time in the altogether more poetic Martinho do Arcada, under the arches of the Praça do Comércio, famous for its *bacalhau*. This time, their conversation was all about Alfredo and the brilliant future they both predicted for him—though whether as a soldier, politician, or in some branch of the professions, they could not decide.

Zé Miguel began one of his mumblings, before he ventured 'our dear friend Alfredo is not a poet,' making Afonso laugh with delight.

It was only over coffee and *aguadente* that Afonso asked what Zé Miguel was going to do back in Mozambique. His friend didn't know. His mother had sent him away to Lisbon when his father was murdered by a close neighbour. But he had been absent long enough. He was a man now, and his mother and sister Antónia needed protection. He had written to say he was planning to return, and his mother had warned him that now, more than ever, he must stay away. So he was going to Lourenço Marques to find a job there and be closer at hand. Zé Miguel was reluctant so say more, and they moved on to talk about the impending African wars concerning

144

which, for all those years at the Escola do Exército, Afonso knew he was ill-prepared.

His departure, though, was suitably warlike. It was on one of the new class of iron-clads, an armed cruiser named *Vasco da Gama*, more agile than a battleship and with a longer range. It looked a fearsome vessel, with its cannon concentrated amidships, port and starboard, in armoured citadels, with further cannon fore and aft. The plaque stating it had been built by the *Thames Iron Works* at Blackwall, London, not by any Portuguese shipyard, was a little deflating. But Afonso felt a sense of well-being as they passed down the Tagus, leaving the Torre de Belém in their wake. He recalled his first sight of Lisbon from the river, on the steamer from Cascais, when Father Anselmo brought him to enroll at the Colégio Militar. He felt that the beloved priest, whom he had bade goodbye at Mafra the previous weekend, could be proud of his adopted son.

He began murmuring Camões's lines describing the departure from Belém of Vasco da Gama's tiny fleet on its pioneer voyage to India.

> Little by little our gaze was exiled
> From the native hills we left behind;
> There remained the dear Tagus, and green Sintra,
> And on those our sight long dwelt;
> Our hearts, too, stayed behind us,
> Lodged with their griefs in the loved land…

But no, he thought suddenly. Apart from Father Anselmo, there was nothing he was leaving behind. His mother was dead. He hardly knew the sister, whose husband had vanished, as his father had done, to Brazil, perhaps also never to return. His two closest friends, concerning whom every corner of Lisbon was packed with memories, had already left before him. He would have hated not to be departing as well.

After eight hours steaming, they passed Cape St Vincent, the final tip of Portugal, and he felt further disquiet as the cruiser turned sharply to port, heading eastwards. He had taken it for granted that their route, especially on a warship named for Vasco da Gama, would be the old one, down the west African coast and round the Cape to Mozambique. Instead, here they were steaming the straits named for the English colony of Gibraltar. Plainly, their first destination was the Suez Canal, built by the French and Egyptians, but now owned by the English, who had bought it with Jewish money. Even Gladstone had said the transaction was illegal. Afonso sensed that his friend Alfredo had been right that night in Sintra. The war to which he was sailing was not about defeating African rebels to restore Portuguese authority along the Zambezi. The real war was going to be with the English.

For the English were everywhere. They were at Port Said, where the canal started. They were at Port Tawfik at Suez where the canal ended. They'd taken over in Egypt, to protect their ownership of the canal. Owning the Nile, they'd taken over in the Sudan, to protect its upper reaches. There was already talk of them advancing to protect the Nile's sources, in the lakes deep in the interior. That would inevitably lead them to control access to the interior from the east African coast, by seizing ancient Portuguese city-states like Malindi and Mombasa.

Even the Red Sea, 'crimson' (wrote Camões) with the blood of Portuguese naval victories in which he had participated, was now policed by the English from their settlement at Aden.

The latest news was they had discovered gold at Johannesburg. If that were so, there would be no stopping them.

Steaming past the date palms and ramshackle warehouses at Port Tawfik, glad to leave the sultry canal behind for the breezes of the Gulf of Suez, Afonso took a turn on the rear deck with a cigar to calm his nerves. There was young man already staring at the phosphorous of the ship's wake, and they fell into conversation. Though, like Afonso, he wore a lieutenant's insignia, he introduced himself as Engenheiro Themudo.

This confused Afonso. Themudo was not a name he could place and the man, seen in profile, could have been Indian or

African, or any mixture in between, though his Portuguese was impeccable. His reply addressed Themudo's title.

'Engineer? From the Politécnica?'

'Exactly.'

The Lisbon Polytechnic, as Afonso well knew, had been another of the Marquês Sá da Bandeira's initiatives, rivalling his creation of the Escola do Exército. Planned as the University of Lisbon, it had run into opposition from the University of Coimbra which, however moribund, opposed the creation of rival institutions. So the Instituto Politécnico de Lisboa had ended up awarding engineering degrees across the whole range of the pure and practical sciences, the social sciences, the humanities and the arts.

'And you?'

'Escola do Exército.'

'Ah.'

Themudo's superiority was established, at least in his own eyes. But he was prepared to be gracious.

'I can't believe the progress we're making. Fifteen and a half sea-miles per hour. And using the canal. When I first sailed to Portugal, it took me ten weeks via the Cape and the west coast.'

'From where? From Mozambique?'

'Yes, from Portuguese East. I was fifteen-years old and sailing to escape. Now, I'm enlisted to return. But I don't mind, I've family there.'

Afonso offered him a cigar, which was accepted with alacrity. Themudo bit the end off, spitting it into the sea, and coaxed a light from Afonso's.

'Maybe this time, it will be different.'

'Different from what"

Cigar hoisted, Themudo stared at Afonso in astonishment.

'Haven't you any idea what you're sailing to? Didn't you study these matters at the Escola?'

'I know the campaigns against Bonga were failures.'

Themudo swore.

'Failures? They were utter catastrophes.'

He ticked off on his fingers.

'1867, failure. 1868, disaster, 1869 unredeemed catastrophe. I just hope those people at Mafra have planned things better this time.'

Mafra made Afonso think only of Father Anselmo. He had forgotten the military high command operated from there.

'I spent part of my childhood in Mafra,' he said inconsequentially. 'Before I joined the Colégio Militar.'

'Ah, you were one of those,' said Themudo. 'Hello, Álvaro,' he continued, beckoning to another figure who had just come on deck.

A slim figure came towards them, girlish in his uniform despite the lieutenant's sleeve chevrons. He had a pale oval face on which a tiny beard was struggling to establish itself, and his eyes were luminous.

'Engenheiro Álvaro de Castelões Ferraz,' declared Themudo. 'I'm afraid I didn't catch your name.'

'Lieutenant Maria Afonso Teixeira Rebelo de Carvalho,' said Afonso, determined not to be outdone.'

Álvaro's pond-like eyes widened.

'Teixeira Rebelo,' he exclaimed.

'A very distant uncle,' said Afonso modestly, as he offered Álvaro a cigar.

Themudo looked distinctly put out.

'Who is this distant uncle?'

'Don't you remember?' chided Álvaro. 'We had to study his *Treatise on Artillery*. He was a distinguished Marshall, who went on to found the Colégio Militar.'

'I was never much of an academic,' muttered Themudo.

The hot, featureless desert of the canal, that for mile after mile had reached oppressively to within yards on both sides, had given way to the broad gulf, with hills rising above fishermen's settlements. A little ahead, to the port side, could be seen the dramatic rock folds of Mt Catherine, with the tip of Mt Sinai immediately behind. To starboard, the hills were sand-coloured, rising above layers of thick clay, but the rock formations opposite were brilliantly white, like repeated versions of Lot's wife turned to her pillar of salt.

It was the first time Afonso had seen such a landscape, indeed seen any landscape outside Portugal, and as it became clear the same was true of Álvaro a sympathy grew between them, from which Themudo felt further excluded.

Sensing this, Afonso was ready to be generous.

'Where in Mozambique, Portuguese East, is your home?'

'Exactly where you're going, on the bank of the Zambezi, where it's joined by the River Shire. Bonga's stockade is one hundred and fifty miles upstream on the opposite bank.'

'Can we get there by river?'

Themudo threw the butt of his cigar into the gulf.

'I hope that's what your Mafra people have planned for us. Overland, with artillery, it's a nightmare. Without artillery, we'll be wasting our time. That's my view, anyway. Without the benefit of reading your distant uncle's work.'

He marched off in the direction of the prow.

'Is he always like this?' asked Afonso.

'Not always,' said Álvaro. 'He can be tremendous fun. But he likes to be listened to, even when he's wrong. Sometimes, his colour makes him a bit prickly.'

'He's quite right about the artillery.'

'And that we'll need transport.'

24 Tony St Claire

One afternoon in October, in that exhausting heat that precedes the rains, Tony was travelling by *machila* from Namacurra to Quelimane. He hated *machila* travel, having lost that agreeable sense of being lord of the manor he had enjoyed on first arrival in central Africa. He found himself disliking the people who enjoyed it and, in any case, it was damned uncomfortable being jogged about, even by the most experienced bearers. But his leg was not yet back to normal, and he couldn't manage the six miles per hour the bearers kept up for hours.

The sun was slanting, so the shades were down and he didn't immediately see what was interrupting his journey. The bearers made a sudden diversion, swearing at someone, then slowed, and he heard a patient voice ignoring their curses and repeating that he needed to speak with the *bwana*. Drawing back the shade, he saw it was Jiwa Faz Tudo and ordered the bearers to stop.

'What is it, Jiwa?'

'You are needed, *senhor*.'

'What's happened? Is Dona Esmeralda all right?'

Jiwa said again, 'You are needed, *senhor*,' but refused to elaborate and strode off the dirt track into the scrub beneath the coconut trees.

Tony hesitated only a moment before giving the bearers fresh orders, and they set out again, this time directly into the sun's path. Night was falling as they arrived, and Tony paid them off, with extra for the diversion, and announced himself, only to find he wasn't expected.

He paused on the veranda steps, registering the fact that Dona Esmeralda was surprised to see him. When he explained about Jiwa's message, she sucked her teeth in exasperation.

'That man is becoming too cheeky.'

'I'm sorry, I seem to be intruding.'

'No, of course not.' She kissed his cheeks, clasping at her customary courtesy. But then added with a sigh, 'I'm afraid there is nothing you can do.'

150

'I hope you regard me as a friend?'

'Of course we do, but …'

That evening was dismal. Father Espirito Santo joined them, apparently by arrangement, and they dined together. But whatever was oppressing them was not discussed, and no other item of conversation took flight. Maria Antónia was not to be seen. A small plate of food was sent into her room. Evidently, she preferred not to talk. Even after dinner, when Tony and the priest sat smoking and drinking brandy on the veranda, where Tony's pallet had been set up, he could not breach the barricade of silence.

'Has there been bad news from Lisbon?' he ventured.

'No, no, everything with Zé Miguel is well. In fact, he is on his way home.'

There was a long silence, broken only by the cicadas screeching about the coming rains.

'I'm sorry for this discourtesy.' said Father Espirito Santo. 'We are not ourselves. But it is a family matter. I'm afraid there is nothing you can do.'

'Perhaps we could read some Dickens together?'

'I doubt if that will be appropriate.'

Next morning, he woke at dawn, hoping to see Maria Antónia watering her plants as usual. But she didn't appear. Dona Esmeralda brought him some bitter cocoa and half a pawpaw. Then Doto and Paulo came to see if he needed help. He said, 'Thank you, no, I'm okay now', but followed them down into the yard to take a shower. It was from the *macayayas*, the two 'houseboys', that he finally learned what was happening.

Senhor Raposo was coming that afternoon to claim Maria Antónia as his bride. Father Espirito Santo was going to officiate at their marriage, after which Raposo would take everyone to a wedding feast at his own estate house, then Maria Antónia would remain there as his new wife.

Though it took Tony no more than an instant to decide, this was not going to happen, and he could think of one sure way to prevent it. Towelling himself furiously, he considered the various aspects of the situation.

'One step at a time,' he muttered. 'The rest can wait.'

He stormed back to the veranda with his lame leg, confronting Father Espirito Santo as he emerged from the dining room.

'I know what you're plotting. How can you possibly be complicit in this? I thought you were a good friend of this family.'

The priest winced under this assault.

'I am, and I hope ever to be. I have no power in this matter.'

'How many wives does this man have already?'

'His one legal wife is dead. I've looked into all that. There is no impediment I can raise.'

'We'll see about that,' said Tony, and continued into the dining room, where he found Dona Esmeralda distraught.

'Please, don't,' she said. 'I'm a widow and I'm helpless.'

Tony took a deep breath and spoke more quietly.

'Please ask Maria Antónia to join us.'

The summons wasn't necessary. Maria Antónia had heard everything. After a moment, she emerged slowly, pale and red-eyed but determined.

'Let us sit down together, all of us, round this table.'

Everyone accepted that he had taken charge. If indeed, he had a solution, they were prepared to listen. They sat facing him, Maria António between her mother and the priest.

Tony addressed her directly in a gentle voice.

'Maria Antónia, we have known each other for perhaps eight months, and almost half that time I was an invalid. We have not ...'

He hesitated.

'We have not so much as danced with together. You should see me dance.'

She smiled faintly.

'This is not how I would have chosen to do things. I would have taken more time, I would have courted you properly. But this is an emergency. Maria Antónia, I love you. Will you do me the honour of consenting to be my wife?'

She couldn't utter a word, but her face spoke for her. Tony reached across the table and clasped her right hand.

'But is this possible?' exclaimed Dona Esmeralda.

'Father Espirito Santo has made all the arrangements for a wedding. If he marries us within the hour, we will be man and wife by midday.'

'But *Senhor* Raposo …'

'There will be nothing he can do. He will have lost his chance.'

'He will be furious.'

'I will deal with the fox.'

For the moment, everyone seemed too overwhelmed to speak.

Then, in a faint voice, Maria Antónia ventured, 'It is necessary, is it not so, that I say, Yes.'

'It is indeed,' said Tony.

'Then yes,' she said, and for the first time smiled broadly.

'I'm afraid it is not possible,' said Father Espirito Santo. 'You are a heretic.'

'I belong to the communion of the Church of England.'

'Precisely, you are a heretic.'

Tony sawed the air furiously.

'If you are concerned with this girl's soul, who is most likely to endanger it? Me? Or Raposo?'

'It is not a pastoral matter. It is the law. I cannot marry a good Catholic woman to a heretic.'

Maria Antónia gave a sudden wail, and Dona Esmeralda reached round the priest to embrace her.

'Father Espirito Santo,' said Tony, 'if you will perform this wedding today, I pledge you my word of honour, as true as my pledge to Maria Antónia, that I will place myself under your instruction and, when you judge that I am ready, I will be baptised as a true Catholic.'

The priest hesitated.

'There is a rite of initiation for inquirers,' he said slowly.

Maria Antónia gazed at him pleadingly.

The priest stood up and went out to the veranda. They could hear him pacing up and down between Maria Antónia's potted plants. But the battle between love and doctrine could not be prolonged. After a few minutes, he returned and stood in the doorway to the dining room.

'So be it,' he said. 'There is scope in canonical law. Let the wedding be at noon.'

They had had three hours to prepare. Dona Esmeralda and Maria Antónia disappeared into her bedroom, and talked long and loud, until some sort of agreement led to a lot of activity with the sewing machine at the far end of veranda. There wasn't much Tony could do. He asked Paulo to polish his boots, and Paulo ventured the information that Doto knew how to cut *muzungu* hair. He used to cut, in fact, the hair of the *patrão*. So Tony sat in the yard for half an hour with a towel round his shoulders as Doto washed his hair, shaved him, and gave him a careful trim.

Returning to the veranda, looking distinctly neater, he found Father Espirito Santo hovering.

'My son,' he said, and Tony noted this new form of address. 'Might I ask if you are familiar with the Apostles's Creed?'

'I am indeed, Father. We said it every morning at school. Would you like me to recite it.'

'I will ask you to recite it before you take communion.'

Evidently, his conscience was still troubling him.

'In your English version, how does it end?'

'I believe,' said Tony, 'in the Holy Ghost, the holy Catholic Church, The Communion of Saints, the Forgiveness of sins, the –'

'Extraordinary,' said Father Espirito Santo. 'The holy Catholic Church. That is the phrase?'

'Yes, Father.'

'You English are a constant surprise. I am delighted. This will be a fine marriage.'

Time dragged. There was still an hour or so to go. The sewing machine whirred. From somewhere, a seamstress had been found, and items were exchanged between veranda and bedroom with increasing urgency. Tony heard Maria Antónia worrying whether her hair would dry in time, and smiled to himself at the thought of her in her curlers.

Suddenly, quite out of the blue, Consul Doveton arrived, 'Mr Consul' as Tony thought of him.

'Ah, good,' he said to Tony. 'You're here. Your witchdoctor sent a message there is some sort of crisis.'

'There was, but it's being resolved. I'm delighted that you've come. I'm in need of a best man.'

'What the devil?'

Tony led him down the front steps, along the citrus-lined drive, well out of earshot, and explained all that had happened.

'But you're crazy,' said Doveton. 'They're a good family and she's a pretty girl. But she's totally unfitted to be the wife of an Englishman like yourself.'

'Careful,' said Tony.

'I'm advising you to be careful. Oh, I know being young Lochinvar appeals to you, and I agree Raposo is a reptile. But think of your career!'

'I have done,' said Tony.

As a matter of fact, he hadn't. But now that he did so, he knew it would make no difference.

'I'm not cut out to be a diplomat. There's a life for me here. Anyway, it's getting late. Are you ready to be my best man?'

Doveton sighed theatrically.

'Your signature as witness will be very useful when I confront Raposo.'

Doveton's eyes widened.

'When's he coming?'

'Late this afternoon.'

'I'll sign with all the majesty I can muster. I'll even give it an official stamp.'

Late that afternoon, Tony was sitting on the veranda, from which he could see two hundred yards down the approaching drive. Opposite him, alongside the veranda's entrance, he had positioned an empty chair. Behind, out of sight in the dining room doorway, Father Espirito Santo was also seated, holding a loaded Martini-Henry rifle. Since the wedding, which he had conducted with enormous zest, he had become a veritable Knight Templar in his zeal to protect the young couple. Behind the window that looked out over the sewing machine, this time brandishing an elephant gun, sat *Senhor* Pombo with his trim white beard and intense blue eyes. Alongside him, holding a Winchester, was *Senhor* Rato, the notary. He had arrived panting just as the ceremony was to begin, embracing Tony with enthusiasm and chagrined he had not had time to bring a present worthy of the occasion.

'But I will—you will see!'

Now that warmth was transformed into an equal passion to protect.

Doto and Paulo, simple shotguns in hand, were positioned at either end of the veranda, Doto behind Tony's pallet bed and Paulo crouching next to the bougainvillea. Meanwhile, concealed in the citrus lining the drive to left and right, were one hundred and three men armed with whatever firearms they could lay their hands on, ancient flintlocks, Arab trade muskets and the odd shot gun, all under the command of Jiwa Faz Tudo.

Tony was astounded by the transformation in his position. It began at the lunch following the ceremony, when he found himself being treated with bewildering deference. As guests there were, of course, Father Espirito Santo and Consul Doveton. But *Senhor* Pombo had also arrived for the ceremony and, of course, stayed for the wedding breakfast, along with *Senhor* Rato, and two neighbours Tony had not previously met, whom he was secretly amused to learn were *Senhor* Formiga (ant) and *Senhor* and *Senhora* Barata (cockroach). Two convent friends of Maria Antónia's had also appeared, Ana Filipa and Isabel Margarida, and were instantly recruited as bridesmaids.

This seemed in itself remarkable. How was it possible for news to travel so fast and yet remain a family secret? But Dona Esmeralda had also done wonders in combining dressmaking with preparing a feast—*sopa da pedra*, then boiled prawns with slices of avocado, or fried baby pigeons, served with chilled white wine from the Douro, then roasted guinea fowl with rice and a rich, red Dão, and finally a fresh fruit salad of pawpaw, oranges and mango, followed by Aliança brandy.

The bride, of course, was the centre of attention, looking suddenly mature and very lovely, in a dress that turned out to be Dona Esmeralda's own wedding gown. It was the respect accorded Tony that surprised him. Hitherto, he'd been 'Tónio' or 'o inglês'. Suddenly, he was *'Senhor,'* even to Dona Esmeralda. He wanted to protest but got only as far as a quizzical glance at Doveton, who took advantage of a burst of laughter to whisper in his ear.

'I told you. Descent here is in the female line. You're now the lord of the manor.'

As the lunch ended, Tony had further proof of his new status. Dona Esmeralda whispered he should show himself in the yard, where he discovered a crowd of three hundred men, women and children assembled to greet him, with smiles and small presents of a pawpaw or a coconut, but mostly with congratulations and good wishes on the prospect of many sons and daughters. They were from the villages closest to the estate house. Their pleasure was in having 'o Inglês' as their new *patrão*, not Raposo and, as proof, most of the men had brought guns, ready for the confrontation they knew to be inevitable.

'I wish you luck,' said Doveton seriously. 'But if you are going to start a war, I think I had better not be present.'

Tony understood immediately.

'Should I resign now? Or will a letter in the coming days suffice?'

'Oh, a week or so will do. It may make Raposo think twice.'

'You mean killing me wouldn't just be murder. It'd be a diplomatic incident?'

Doveton pulled a face.

'He's a killer, but he's not stupid. You've pipped him at the post, and it looks as though you're well protected. I reckon he'll just swallow it.'

Raposo's nuptial procession could be heard long before it came into sight, with frenzied drumming, tubas blaring, repeated blasts on a trumpet and ululating women, combining in a cacophony audible half a mile off. At last, they appeared at the end of the drive and, at walking pace, approached the veranda. The women and the tuba players were in the lead, but they divided to allow Raposo's *machila*, instantly recognizable from its carvings and the four parrots perched on the corners, to draw close. Behind him was a second, less ostentatious *machila*, which proved to contain the military governor, *Senhor* Corvo. The two men disembarked, Raposo climbing the steps swiftly, despite his bulk, and Corvo lumbering behind him.

Raposo stopped in surprise at the sight of Tony, who had also risen to his feet. He had shaved off the stubble he wore on his last visit, presumably in deference to the occasion. On his heavy body, his shirt and trousers looked too tight, but his boots shone and looked expensive.

'*Senhor* Raposo, *Senhor* Corvo, you are welcome to this house.'

Raposo's close-set eyes glanced about him, suspecting some trick. Where the devil was Dona Esmeralda?

'By what right do you give the orders in this house? Where is the mistress?'

Suddenly, he caught sight of the gun barrel pointing at him through the dining room door, but couldn't make out who was holding it.

'I have come to claim my bride. This was agreed. You have no business interfering like this.'

'Especially as a foreigner,' said Corvo, in a threatening tone. 'No better than a spy.'

'*Senhor* Raposo,' said Tony. 'I advise you to take great care. There are five guns pointing at you at this moment. There are one hundred armed men concealed in the trees either side of the drive. Your party is outnumbered and outgunned.'

Corvo became agitated, his stomach straining the thick leather belt of his *capitão-mor's* uniform. Tony feared he might snatch his pistol from the holster dangling to the right, but the moment passed.

'This is an insurrection,' he said, 'tantamount to a foreign invasion, and you are nothing less than an English pirate.'

'No,' said Tony, 'I am nothing more than a husband protecting my family. The laws of all civilised countries permit that.'

He saw light dawning in Raposo's eyes.

'Husband?'

'Maria Antónia has done me the honour of becoming my wife. We were married at noon today.'

'By whom?'

'It was my doing,' said Father Espirito Santo, pushing the door open without lowering the rifle. 'You are a corrupt and evil man, Raposo. Praise God, the little one has been saved from your clutches.'

'The priest?' exclaimed Corvo. 'This cannot be legal.'

Senhor Rato spoke, from the window by the sewing machine, his Winchester held steady.

'The documents are all in order, correctly signed and witnessed. The groom's witness was Consul Doveton.'

'An insurrection, an invasion, an international outrage,' spluttered Corvo. 'The Governor will deal with this.'

'No,' said Tony calmly. 'Mr Doveton bore witness as my friend, not in his official capacity. This will become an diplomatic incident only if you make it so. My concern is to protect my family.'

He had confused them. The wedding party, stranded on the drive, was still drumming and ululating, and a fresh blast on the trumpet irritated Raposo.

'Stop that noise,' he shouted.

Gradually, the crowd fell silent. For the first time, they realised something was wrong. The women were still dancing, but they ceased ululating. Tony saw there were about forty men bearing arms. One of them raised his musket and fired into the air.

'Stop that,' shouted Raposo again.

He turned back to Tony, and said 'How do we know you are not bluffing?'

Tony raised his left arm and fifty men emerged from the cover of the citrus trees to the left of the drive, some knelt, some remained standing, all aimed their weapons at the wedding party. Then he raised his right arm, and the same manoeuvre was performed by another fifty men to the right of the drive. The wedding party fell completely silent. Then two of Raposo's men threw down their weapons and ran back along the drive. Seeing they had been allowed to escape, others followed, first in twos and threes, then as a mass of men, women and children, until the space before the veranda was empty. Only the *machila* bearers remained.

It was time for Tony's armed supporters to celebrate and they did so, leaping up and down and firing their weapons into the air. As the pandemonium died down, Tony seized the initiative.

'*Senhor* Raposo, you have had many wives, and a man like you will enjoy many more. Why should it matter that a girl one third your age has set her heart elsewhere?'

He knew very well that it was the land that was at issue, that Raposo's plan all along had been to double the size of his estate. But it suited both men to talk only of Maria Antónia.

'*Senhor*, we are now neighbours, and it is my intention to be a good neighbour. I can be of service to you.'

'You have made a fool of me.'

With that confession, Tony knew he had won.

'There will be a little laughter. Once it has died away, you will laugh yourself at the foolish Englishman.'

Corvo was not satisfied.

'This is a foreigner intervening in our internal affairs. An Englishman holding a Portuguese official at gunpoint!'

Raposo sighed.

'They are married. What can be done about that?'

'We will tell the governor. He will inform the king. The king will appeal to the Pope.'

Even Raposo smiled at that.

'We will all be dead, my friend.'

'I am not detaining you, *Senhor* Corvo,' said Tony. 'You are free to leave whenever you choose.'

'No, I will have no part of this. And you, you devil Priest, you will suffer. I will have you arrested. I will have you de-frocked.'

He lumbered back into his *machila*, and gave loud instructions to the bearers.

'Take me away from this place.'

Raposo turned again to Tony.

'How can you possibly be of service to me?'

25 Maria Afonso

Lieutenant Maria Afonso Rebelo kicked moodily at one of the two rusting cannons half buried on Baramwana hill overlooking the town of Sena, and felt an overwhelming sense of desolation.

Half his young life, since he had talked with Serpa Pinto at the Colégio Militar, he had looked forward to this moment with a religious curiosity. He wanted to see for himself the ancient city that formed the first of three stages of Portugal's line of advance along the Zambezi valley. Three cities, Sena, Tete, and Zumbo, with Sena the most prestigious. He wanted to pace the battlements of the Praça São Marçal, feeling beneath his boots the stonework worn by the boots of so many of his fellow countrymen down the centuries. He wanted to pray in the ruins of the four churches and convents, scene of such heroic missionary endeavour. He longed to visit the municipal graveyard, reading for himself the catalogue of discovery, conquest and settlement.

There were no battlements, no ruins, no graveyard. What lay before him was a mud-brick slum, extending two hundred yards from the foot of Baramwana to a backwater of the Zambezi. A stone arch, once the entrance to the town, lay to his left, with a dirt road curving towards half a dozen houses in what once may have been the city centre. The four dirt roads linking them looked like an obscure hieroglyphic, or perhaps some Arab inscription, stamped in the mud. There were no graves, no fort, no holy precinct. Buildings constructed of water-worn pebbles, stuck together with mud and coated with plaster, are no match for African rains. When the Zambezi floods, as it must every thirty years or so, it sweeps all before it.

'There are more baboons than people', he muttered.

A pack of baboons was indeed scampering up the widest of the tracks, extending from the foot of the hill to a house at the edge of the backwater, snatching figs, bananas and mealie cobs at will. Someone invisible shouted, but without effect. A black man emerged with a muzzle-loader, firing randomly, and they scurried away.

Some of the one-storey houses had corner-stones, and there was a cattle kraal with stone foundations, looted from the ancient fort. The priorities of survival. After a flood, you needed to be able to establish where your house had been, and cattle, along with family, were the most secure form of wealth.

Disillusioned, he lit a cigar rolled of local tobacco, puffing a cloud of acrid smoke to dispel mosquitoes. The effort made him cough, but he felt calmer.

His disillusion had begun at Quelimane, where he landed from the frigate. He was well aware it was still a slave port, despite the Lisbon reforms. What surprised him was the number of Indian traders, dealing in ivory and oil seeds, bringing what prosperity existed in the mean streets of the town. The Moors, as he thought of them, were back again.

In 1571, Francisco Barreto had massacred all the Muslims of Sena, claiming the town for Portugal in the true spirit of King Afonso the Great, the king who had expelled the Moors from Portugal. But they were back, and there seemed no getting rid of them.

Then there was the river. Vasco da Gama had christened it the River of Good Signs, because it was here he first heard reliable news of India. Afonso had imagined a fast-flowing stream like the Tagus at Belem, but fringed by coconut palms. Between the town and the estuary was a wide mudflat, with twisted mangrove instead of coconuts, at low tide extending several hundred yards. He had spent a whole morning on a wooden jetty, first staring disconsolately and then with fascination, at millions of mud-skippers and fiddler crabs for whom the exposed, stinking marsh was home. The crabs lived in holes, brandishing one large claw at the entrance, to catch food and for protection. The mud-skippers seemed neither fish nor slugs but some sort of intermediate creature, and he couldn't decide whether they could breath in or out of water, or somehow both.

Only at dusk when the tide was full and the temperature bearable, was he able to conjure a sense of pride, as he paced the promenade in front of the squat cathedral with its twin baroque towers. From mid-stream would come a sudden flash of pink as a flock of flamingos veered in the dying light. But darkness dropped quickly, and mosquitoes drove him to the shelter of the *quartel*. The traders, in their flowing robes and turbans, didn't seem to mind the mosquitoes. They stayed on the river bank, smoking and chatting in tiny groups, until quite late.

In the local language, the river was called the Kwa Kwa. It was the principal route to the interior but was navigable only by canoes. He and his company spent six weeks travelling a mere hundred miles. It was so narrow in parts that their canoes had to proceed in single file, and where it widened, on the curves of its sinuous twisting, it became so shallow the canoes had to be unloaded and carried to the next deep water. This meant hiring carriers in addition to the canoe men, from the headmen of the villages they passed. They were supposed to be Portuguese subjects, but they behaved like independent chiefs, levying their own taxes and duties.

The villainous Dombe and Sangalaze he remembered with especial hatred. Their villages were on opposite banks, and they cooperated in their exactions. Dombe said he was anxious to help, but Sangalaze would object. Sangalaze took the opposite line. In the end, they both had to be paid off. They had previously been jailed for four years after an earlier bout of rebellion. But it had not changed their exactions. Afonso could scarcely credit that an armed Portuguese company was helpless before such insolence. But experience had shown how many warriors Sangalaze could muster, and how vulnerable the Portuguese canoes were to ambush.

Eventually, they had reached Mazaro, the fort on the Zambezi. From there, they could travel upriver by steamer as far as Tete or, depending on the season, to Chicoa. While their baggage and equipment were being loaded, he was allowed a day off to make a small pilgrimage. Mopeia was within walking distance. This was where Major Caldas Xavier, the man who had embraced him, had fought off the screaming hoards. He wanted to visit this site of heroism in the true Portuguese tradition.

But at Mopeia, nothing remained. On the hill, the former administrator's house was intact. On the plain, there remained no evidence of heroism, nor of endeavour—no fields, no ditches, no flood defenses, not even the stone foundations of the block house where Caldas Xavier had individually kept the rebels at bay. Last year's flood had swept all before it. Were those mango trees, or perhaps that Bahia orange, planted by the Opium Company's manager? Who could say? The 'hero of Mopeia' had no other memorial.

Back at Mazaro, his depression turned to a fever. He was forced to stay behind, in the captain's house, while his company embarked for Tete. Of the next three days, he remembered nothing. On the fourth morning, an African woman brought him a hot infusion. It stank. He tried to wave it away, but she insisted this was what he had been drinking the three previous days and the medicine had worked.

'I have quinine,' he protested.

'It will make you vomit,' she said. 'This is better.'

He drank it, shuddering at the taste. But indeed he felt better and suddenly very hungry.

'I will bring.'

She paused to adjust some bunches of leaves hanging in the doorway, then poured out some liquid on the threshold. A few minutes later, she returned with two baby pigeons, fried in sesame oil.

'This first,' she said. 'If your belly holds, you will eat more after.'

He ate them swiftly licking his fingers with relish, and promptly fell asleep. It was late afternoon when he arose and dressed, a little unsteady on his feet, and went out to a low veranda. The captain was squatting, cleaning a rifle he recognised as his own.

'You must excuse me,' said Captain Mesquita. 'There was a lion troubling us, and we don't have guns as good as this one.'

'Did you shoot him?'

The two men shook hands.

'I think he's fatally wounded. But he ran off. We shall try tracking him tomorrow. I will need your gun again.'

'I need to join my company'.

'Not tomorrow. It is too soon. The fever will return. Maybe three days. Isadora will decide. She understands these things.'

'Isadora?'

'*Sinyala* Isadora. My wife. She has been nursing you.'

Afonso grimaced.

'Her medicine has an awful taste.'

'Ah, but it works. Either what you drank, or what she poured round the doorway. I gave up arguing about these things long ago.'

'What is this *Sinyala*?'

'It is what they say here for *Senhora*.'

Afonso stared at a large grass-walled compound below the veranda. There were chickens, Muscovy ducks, guinea-fowl, several geese, a pigeon house—evidently the origin of his snack—and a large white turkey displaying its tail so that its rump was quite naked. Once again, he felt hungry.

'Choose what you like', said Mesquita. 'My wife will get it prepared for you.'

'I've never eaten guinea-fowl. Are they good?'

'Couzinheiro', shouted Mesquita, and a young African poked his head though a window at the end of the veranda.

'Nkanga,' Mesquita added, pointing at the compound.

The man jumped down and chased one of the squawking birds round the pigeon house, past the well, past a stack of firewood and, diving full length, managed to grab one of its legs.

'It's always good to have a guest,' said Mesquita. 'We shall eat well.'

'*Sinyala* Isadora,' said Afonso. 'She is *senhora* because she is your wife?'

'Ah, no. She is *senhora* in her own right. She was adopted by a great lady in these parts. Her estate is at Mutarara, across the river from Sena. Everyone calls her *Sinyala* Maria.'

Afonso frowned, trying to remember.

'The canoe men at Dombe's. They had a song '*Sinyala* Maria is my mother'.

'*Sina mama, sina baba, sina mama*', said Mesquita, humming a few lines. 'They're her slaves.'

Feudalism, thought Afonso. He remembered Caldas Xavier writing it had been the feudal lords of the Zambezi valley who instigated the revolt against the opium company. They didn't like the new commercial order.

'She has hundreds, and all well cared for.'

Feudalism, thought Afonso. And superstition. No wonder everything was in such decay.

26 Tony St Claire

At Tony's request, they were rounding off the day reading *Great Expectations*. He chose the description of Wemmick's marriage to Miss Skiffins as appropriate to the day's events.

Pip was speaking, as always.

Punctual to my appointment, I rang at the castle gate on the Monday morning, and was received by Wemmick himself: who struck me as looking tighter than usual, and having a sleeker hat on. The Aged must have been stirring with the lark, for, glancing into the perspective of his bedroom, I observed that his bed was empty.

When we were going out for the walk, I was considerably surprised to see Wemmick take up a fishing-rod, and put it over his shoulder. 'Why, we are not going fishing?' said I. 'No,' returned Wemmick, but I like to walk with one.'

I thought this odd: however I said nothing, and we set off. We went towards Camberwell Green, and when we were thereabouts, Wemmick said suddenly:

'Halloa! Here's a church!'

There was nothing very surprising in that. But again, I was rather surprised, when he said, as if animated by a brilliant idea:

'Let's go in!'

We went in, Wemmick leaving his fishing-rod in the porch, and looked all round. Wemmick was diving into his coat pockets, and getting something out of paper there.

'Halloa!' said he. 'Here's a couple of pair of gloves! Let's put 'em on.'

As the gloves were white kid gloves, and as the post-office was widened to its utmost extent, I now began to have my strong suspicions. There were strengthened into certainty when I beheld the Aged enter a side-door, escorting a lady.

Halloa!' said Wemmick. 'Here's Miss Skiffins! Let's have a wedding.'

Tony glanced up from the magazine to confirm what he suspected. His audience was not with him. Dickens's grotesque humour matched his own mood, but not theirs. Maria Antónia was smiling, but her eyes were full of tears. Her long day had begun in despair, moved through ecstasy to a terrible fear, and now she felt exhausted in her relief.

He set the magazine down and took a sip of the white Port wine Dona Esmeralda had served for each of them, along with dry biscuits.

'The English always like to make a joke,' said Father Espirito Santo, shaking his head.

'My husband was the same,' said Dona Esmeralda. 'It is an attitude to the world.'

Tony felt a little abashed. His habit was always to take things lightly and move on. But for this family, the day had been momentous and his intervention a miracle. He had to learn to accept that, along with his new responsibilities.

'What we don't know,' said Father Espirito Santo, 'what still concerns us, is how you managed to satisfy Raposo. Is that the end of the matter?'

After Corvo's departure, Tony had asked for all the guns to be lowered and withdrawn and had invited Raposo to sit in the chair opposite him, the one arranged at the veranda's entrance. Their talk had been entirely private. Tony had informed him of the report that had been submitted to the Anti-Slavery Commission about his slave-trading activities. Some of it went back years, based in part on information provided by *Senhor* Augusto, Dona Esmeralda's husband, whom Raposo was reliably believed to have murdered. Some of it was very recent, such as details of the consignment he had received from Selemane Abdullah and Sacur Latif, which had been secretly exported from a creek within sight of his own estate house. One hundred twenty-three men had featured in that transaction. Tony stated he knew the report, which he omitted to mention he had drafted himself, had been dispatched to Natal, where the court, established by international agreements to which Portugal was a signatory, had its headquarters. *Senhor* Raposo could expect to be summoned for trial there. If convicted, and the evidence against him was strong, he would serve time in jail, probably in Natal, and the lease on his *prazo* would be automatically terminated.

Senhor Raposo listened impassively until Tony had finished. Some of it, he said, was false. The killing of *Senhor* Augusto for instance, he had not been directly involved in that. Some was half true, and he was secretly appalled at the wealth of detail and the number of witnesses ranged against him.

'So how can you be of service to me?'

'The presiding judge in Natal is my uncle,' said Tony.

Raposo's mouth fell open. This was doing business the way he understood. That the English understood it too was a surprise.

'I am prepared to testify that much of this belongs to the past, and that the most recent transactions were conducted without your knowledge. After all, your *prazo* is a vast one, and you can't know everything that is going on. I will write that you wish to cooperate in the suppression of the slave trade. This testimony will be offered as that of a neighbour willing to vouch for your future conduct. I know my uncle well, and I believe he will, at the very least, adjourn the case indefinitely. Of course, if anything were subsequently to happen to me …'

Raposo nodded in full understanding. He even took Tony's hand at departure.

'You will write all this?'

'I will write tomorrow.'

'Basically', said Tony, in response to Father Espirito Santo, 'I blackmailed him. It is better the details should remain a secret. But they involved his past and recent activities and the Anti-Slavery Commission.'

'So he cannot touch you?'

'He will lose everything if he does.'

27 Lorenzo

Dr Nogeira Rato brought news of the wedding to Lorenzo Johnston in his prison cell only to find he had already heard. It was the talk of the district and even Luiza had been excited.

'I don't know the man,' said Lorenzo. 'Or the girl. The father gave me sugarcane for planting. Afterwards, I was sorry he was murdered.'

'The murderer was Raposo,' said Dr Rato, 'who then tried to marry the girl.'

'So, it's a happy ending. I'm glad for them.'

On the other hand, he was going to remain in prison for some time. The wedding had angered local officials, and relations between Portugal and Britain were worsening. There was talk of a Portuguese expedition to strengthen Portugal's claim to this part of Africa. The outline of Lorenzo's defence had not changed. But this was not an auspicious time to press for a hearing on a matter involving guns for the missionaries.

I'm not going to give too many details about the gun-smuggling, wrote Lorenzo after his lawyer had gone. Other people were involved, and I'm not going to play Judas. Let me say just that Mr Consul had nothing to do with it. Nor Mr Acting-Consul who is now in jail at Mozambique, charged with the same offence. It surprised me that the Portuguese should do this, because although he works for the Company, he is still Vice-Consul. They are playing with fire because England is a powerful nation.

I'm just going to explain my motives, and then explain what I did.

I was still working at Matope when Chemandala established the station at Karonga, at the far north of Lake Nyasa. Chindevu asked me if I would go there as agent. It would have been a promotion since the ivory trade there was already bigger than at Matope, but I'd made my own plans by then. I didn't tell him that. I just said I didn't speak the languages of the area, so there was no advantage in appointing me.

Karonga was about ivory. Mr Rhodes, that's Herbert Rhodes, the brother of Cecil Rhodes who is now the big man in Johannesburg, Mr Herbert saw hundreds of elephants when he was visiting there. Afterwards, he died in a fire at Ramakukan's. He was drinking rum and set himself on fire. So the Company took over and established the station with Mr Fotheringham and Mr Nicoll.

At the same time, Arab traders set up their own stations in the area to catch the same elephants. Mlozi settled at Mpata, twelve miles west of Karonga, and Kopa Kopa and Msalemo build stockades close by. Afterwards, especially in Scotland, they called this a competition between legitimate trade and the slave trade. Once the war started, that was all you heard. Honest businessmen fighting slavers. But I knew this was false. From the start, the Company was buying Arab ivory, and the war began when the Arabs got impatient for their money. It ended with me smuggling the big Armstrong Mountain gun to the Company, along with rifles and ammunition. So the Portuguese put me on trial. But the war was never about trade. It was about taking over the country. Faced with that choice, I made the same choice as Mbewe. I threw in my lot with the British.

At first, Mr Fotheringham and Mlozi got along very well. They weren't rivals. There were plenty of elephants, and for the Arabs it was easier to sell their ivory at Karonga than to carry it all the way to the coast. That way, they didn't even have to raid for slaves to carry the ivory. They just used the *Ilala*. What went wrong was the old problem. The *Ilala* was too small for the job, especially sailing on the lake where firewood is hard to come by, and they needed a reserve supply in case of storms. So there was never enough calico in the store at Karonga to pay for the ivory the Arabs brought in. That meant they had to wait for payment until the *Ilala* made its next round trip. That meant they had to settle nearby, with all their elephant hunters and retinue. That meant, in turn, they started raiding the villagers of the Ngonde people for food and for women, until the Company could pay them.

I don't know the Ngonde like I know the Manganja and the Yao, but I you could push them too far. When a quarrel near Mpata ended with a headman called Mwini-Ntete getting killed, the warriors killed some of Mlozi's people, including several of his wives. So Mlozi took revenge, burning Karonga where the Company's station was located. The Ngonde responded by asking the Company to protect them. That was in October.

Mr Fotheringham owed the Arabs too much for them to attack the Company straightaway. But when he went to negotiate with Mlozi about the villagers, he was told Mlozi had declared himself Sultan. Any negotiations had to start from there. So the war wasn't about trade. It became a war about who the land belonged to.

I learned this from Mbewe. After I started my plantation, I rarely saw Chindevu or anyone from the Company. But Mbewe had a friend call Kolembo who had been with him at the Blantyre Mission school. Kolembo, like Mbewe, could read and write good English. But the only employment he could find was as a porter for the missionaries, carrying a new steamer to be launched on Lake Tanganyika, far to the north. It annoyed Mbewe that learning to read and write brought no benefit. For himself, he had gone back to being a pilot, since that paid better than being a *catequist*. The river was his trade, just as sugar was mine.

This same Kolembo was at Karonga, working as a carrier, when the war started. So, he kept Mbewe informed, in letters that made him laugh. It was Kolembo who wrote that the war was about who owned the land. If Mlozi was Sultan and the Company no longer existed, the slave trade would start again because Mlozi would need to get his ivory to the coast..

Early November, the *Ilala* arrived with goods to settle the debt with the Arabs. It also brought four *azungu*, including Mr O'Neill, the new Consul for Mozambique. But it brought no weapons and very little ammunition to add to the thirteen rifles in the Company store, so the moment was dangerous. As soon as the Arabs were paid, they attacked. The Karonga station was fired on from stockades the Arabs built, fifty yards back along three sides, while the Ngonde hid in trenches on the beach. This went on for five days, for the *azungu* had just enough ammunition to hold out, but nothing more. On the sixth day, Mr Nicol arrived with five-thousand Nyakusa fighters he had recruited from chiefs along the new road to Tanganyika. As news spread that they were on their way, the Arabs withdrew. That was the first battle. It ended with the Karonga station being abandoned.

That's when I became involved. The Portuguese had begun to make trouble on their own part. They tried to insist that the Company's new steamer, the *James Stevenson*, should be registered as Portuguese and carry a Portuguese crew. This, after the Company had paid for it. Next they forbad the importation of guns and ammunition through Quelimane. Lord Salisbury, the British Prime Minister, declared the Zambezi River was a international waterway and that guns could pass perfectly legally through the Kongone mouth of the Zambezi. When my trial begins, I intend to call Lord Salisbury as my first witness.

So I was approached. My estate was right there on the Kongone. I was sent one-hundred Chassepot rifles and ammunition, smuggled by bumboat from a East Indian steamer, and I hid them behind sacks of brown sugar until I could transport them by canoe to Katunga's. This happened in February, and by March Chindevu felt he had enough weapons to re-open the Karonga station.

In May, Captain Lugard arrived. I can name him because the part he played is well known. For the first time, a proper soldier was in charge. He'd served in Afghanistan, the Sudan and Burma, and he knew his profession. When the *azungu* asked him to take command of the war against Mlozi, he had his own reasons to agree. I never knew why, but the rumours said a woman was involved. He brought some discipline to the station at Karonga—separating the Tonga, the Yao and the Nyakusa into companies, and digging proper latrines downwind of the station.

Kolembo's letter describing this was funny beyond belief. He described Captain Lugard's outrage at finding Chindevu sitting, smoking his pipe, right there on a box of gunpowder.

In June, Captain Lugard launched his big attack. But he was doing what Mlozi's men had already tried at Karonga. Attacking a stockade with rifles doesn't work. The defenders have all the advantage. Chindevu tried to climb the stockade fence and fell back with his right arm shattered. Lugard was shot through both arms and chest. Back at Karonga, he declared they needed to bring up some artillery. Chemandala left at once for Quelimane, to ask the British Navy for a field gun from the naval anti-slavery patrol. Captain Lugard went to recuperate at Mandala, and Chindevu left for Scotland to have his arm patched up.

I learned these details in October, when they brought the gun for me to hide at Kongone. It was a 6lb Armstrong mountain gun, less heavy, they said, than a field gun, so ideal for the purpose. All the same it was heavy. It weighed a full three hundred-weight, so it took five strong men to carry it. Six months passed before I saw it actually mounted, but I realised immediately that transporting the separate parts, two wrought-iron wheels, a wrought-iron gun-carriage and wrought-iron tube, all inlaid with the wood of European trees, was going be a botheration.

A month after the separate parts and the boxes of shells were delivered to me at Kongone, they set up their scheme. Two ship's boats brought a memorial sculpture to Shupanga on the Zambezi. It was sent by admirers in Scotland to be erected on the grave of Mary Livingstone, who died there in 1862. Of course, it was the Glasgow statue, with my face carved in the Arab slaver, that inspired this, but it helped deceive the Portuguese. It was arranged that the same ship's boats would carry the gun parts as far as the first wooding station on the River Shire, where the *James Stevenson* would pick them up.

Mbewe was pilot from that point, and I travelled with him to Katunga's. I was mindful of how Captain Young managed to transport the *Ilala* the length of the rapids without losing a single bolt or rivet and was determined to supervise the task myself. No one challenged me on this. No one wanted to be caught with the gun until well beyond Portuguese territory which, since the war with Matekenya's people, extended to the Ruo junction with the Shire. Once I reached Matope, the *Ilala* was able to pick up the various boxes.

It was January when the Armstrong finally reached Karonga and I saw it mounted. It looked a fearsome weapon, especially when Captain Lugard surveyed it. He'd returned to Karonga, more or less recovered from his wounds.

It was my big moment. I had fought Arab slavers, on and off, for thirty years. Finally, I had delivered the gun that would put paid to them. Captain Lugard thanked me personally, and even Chemandala eyed me with a new respect. On 21 February, the Armstrong was positioned in front of Msalemo's stockade, with a dozen *azungu* and five hundred Africans ready to storm it once the walls were breached. But when the shell was fired, it passed straight through the palisade, cutting a hole twelve inches across, then out the other side, cutting another neat hole, before it exploded against some rocks half a mile off.

They tried again and a second shell made a small hole in both stockade walls without exploding.

'God damn it, the bugger's not worth a tinker's cuss,' said Captain Lugard in exasperation.

I'd never heard the phrase before, and it turned Chemandala bright red.

'We won't prevail if we use profane language.'

'We're not going to prevail anyway,' said Captain Lugard. 'This is a high-velocity gun. I used it on the North-West Frontier against proper forts. Not these mud-and-wattle affairs.'

So that was the end of that. We withdrew once more to Karonga, and Captain Lugard left next day for England. The Company and the Arabs maintained an armed stalemate for the next six years, but without resuming their trade.

But this wasn't quite the end. The Armstrong was on loan from the British Navy, and it had to be returned. I was the one who'd brought it, so I was asked to smuggle it back. Chemandala let me use the *Ilala* as far as Matope and lent me carriers for the section to Katunga's. From there, I had a problem. By then, the Portuguese had twice ordered the *James Stevenson* to stop and be searched at their new military post at Mpassu, and though the British Government protested about this, the Company didn't want to be caught with a powerful gun.

I hired the two biggest canoes I could find at Katunga's, lashing them together with the gun wheels straddling the sides, hidden under oil palm branches and the tube and the carriage in the bodies of the canoes. It was hard to steer them, especially through Dambinyi and in the fast water at the Ruo junction. Just opposite Mpassu, I ran aground on the inside of a bend. Even then, I could have got away clean, but while I was searching for a pole to refloat the canoes I disturbed one of the Portuguese sentries in the reeds with an African woman, and he raised the alarm.

I was arrested, of course, and charged with smuggling arms. My lawyer, Dr Rato, likes to joke, it's the first time anyone have been accused of smuggling guns out of Africa. As for the Armstrong, the Portuguese confiscated it, along with the remaining shells.

28 Maria Afonso

Next morning, Afonso felt well enough to walk the few hundred yards to the bank of the Zambezi River, which he now viewed for the first time. 'God's highway,' Livingstone had called it. He didn't like Livingstone, who had been treated with great generosity by the Portuguese and had repaid his hosts with libels. But he was right about the highway, whether God's or the Devil's.

The river was miles wide at this point, but only the fringe of sepia-coloured palms on the opposite shore made it possible to distinguish the many islands from the mainland. It was fast-flowing, pewter-coloured with little boiling eddies. Floating islands of reeds and papyrus were being whirled downstream. Two thirds of the vista was taken up by the vast dome of pale blue sky.

He knew the history well enough. Years of drought seven decades earlier had destroyed the existing colony. Slave-trading had provided an alternative mode of living, and the valley had been taken over by warlords, most of them of mixed Indian and African origin, operating from huge stockades from which they fought against each other for the diminishing supplies of slaves and ivory. To retain any semblance of metropolitan authority, the Portuguese had been forced into humiliating alliances, offering government appointments to some in the hope of defeating others, so that Zambezia became a by-word for officially-sanctioned brutality and corruption.

Efforts to stop slave-trading had only made matters worse. Instead of being exported, the slaves had been dragooned into the warlords' private armies, making them all-but invincible. The humiliation of making alliances with such people was nothing compared to the humiliation of seeing modern Portuguese armies repulsed by them. Four expeditions had been sent again Bonga between 1867 and 1869, all of them defeated. The skulls of Portuguese soldiers still decorated the outer walls of his stockade at Massangano, which controlled the river beyond Tete.

Yet it should have been and would become a highway. The river was wide and full of water. The main current looked deep. The whole valley was fertile. Caldas Xavier's poppies had grown well, but the descendants of one of the warlords had destroyed the opium enterprise. Sugar had always grown along the valley, but the technology of manufacture was primitive. Oil seeds, too, were a profitable crop. He had witnessed that in the prosperity of the Indian traders at Quelimane. There was coal at Tete and wild rubber in the interior. The river was the key. But first, it had to be opened, with the defeat of the last warlords and the economy brought under Portuguese control.

That was why he was here. Or rather, since he was not given to self-dramatization, this was the enterprise in which he hoped to play a useful part.

That evening, Mesquita returned his rifle, cleaned and oiled after use.

'We got him,' he said. 'But only after he killed my best tracker. He was the very devil.'

Isadora, who was serving them wine, spat angrily.

'You have destroyed a spirit.'

She marched off, leaving the demijohn behind. Mesquita moved it into the shade of his hammock.

'What does she mean?'

'The chiefs who used to rule here, before we Portuguese came, when they were defeated and killed by our armies, returned as lions to take their revenge. Every time a lion turns to man-eating, they say, 'That is Inhacatundu, protecting us.''

'Even when he eats an African?'

'The man was working for me.'

Afonso studied Captain Mesquita, who spoke excellent Portuguese. He was a Goan, from Portuguese India. He was very dark, with high cheek bones, slim wrists and a neat athletic way of moving. His hair and moustache showed he took care of his appearance, but not excessively so.

'How long have you been in command here?'

'Here in Mazaro? Eleven years since I married Isadora. It was her mother got me the appointment.'

Feudalism again!

'What brought you to Zambezia? Were you born here?'

'I came for the war with Bonga. With the Goan regiments.'

'1869?'

'The disaster of 1869. After the disaster of 1868. And the two disasters of 1867.'

Captain Mesquita spoke without bitterness. He had made his peace with the country. His command was meaningless. He had ten black soldiers under him and their pay was months in arrears. The fort was safe because it was defenceless. It posed no threat to anybody. But through his wife he lived well off the land. In addition to the chickens and guinea fowl, he had goats and pigs, orchards of orange, lemon, mango and pawpaw, and several hectares of maize, millet, beans and pumpkins.

'How could a man like Bonga defeat modern armies with modern weapons? Didn't you have artillery?'

'Twelve-pounders, yes. We had mules but they all died of tsetse. We dragged those guns overland. Seven months, from May to November. I don't know how many men died, of fever and exhaustion And when we got to Massangano, they were useless.'

'*Por amor de Deus*, why?'

'Have you seen the stockades they build here? I don't mean this hovel at Mazaro. I mean the big ones, Shamo, Muchena, Massangano. They're not stone works. Further up at Monopatapa's, they're built of stone with massive outer walls. But Massangano has wooden stakes driven into the ground. The wood is green, so they take root. In a few years they're trees, thick as this mahogany here, planted so close together you can't pass between them. Then they weave other poles between the trees and reinforce the outside wall with ditches and mud escarpments. You can fire cannon at them all day and not make a proper breach.'

Mesquita offered him the demijohn and then refilled his own stone mug.

'Is there no higher ground?'

'Ha! You are Escola do Exército, not so? You think clearly. Yes, there is a hill overlooking Massangano. We had guns there and guns on the riverbank. But we couldn't make a breach.

179

Our lines were overstretched. We couldn't bring up supplies. Bonga had so many men outside the stockade, we were the ones being besieged. All the time we were losing men, from fever as much as the fighting. When at last we retreated, Bonga's men ambushed us, and it became a rout. I'm sure you know the story.'

'An army of eight-hundred and fifty men, and you came back in twos and threes.'

'Those that came back, yes. No one really knows how many. I meet Goans here sometimes—Ignácio, Chico, Joaquim from Caia, Frasinho from Missongue—and I recognise men I was with that I didn't know were still alive.'

'What are they doing now?'

'Surviving, like me. But the ones I know are in trade.'

Afonso couldn't quite believe what he was hearing. He was aware that European armies were not impregnable. The Zulus had dealt disaster to the English at Isandhlwana. They had studied that defeat at the Escola. Lord Chelmsford, the commander, was to blame, not the troops, and the English had quickly returned to the field and conquered Zululand. It was almost twenty years since Bonga had routed a Portuguese army, and still he held on in his Massangano stronghold.

'There was revolt here, four years ago.'

Mesquita groaned.

'Matekenya's people. Yes, those days were terrible.'

'Do you remember Major Caldas Xavier?'

'That popinjay? Yes, we all do.'

'He is my friend and a great soldier.'

Mesquita slapped his forehead, exclaiming, 'I am a clown and a wastrel. You should pay no attention to what a man like me says.'

Afonso took this as an apology.

'Did you go to the Major's assistance? I mean, when he was besieged in Mopiea?'

'With what? With these men? They haven't been paid in months. I can't even shoot a lion without borrowing your gun.'

'But weren't you afraid of being attacked, like Sena and Chironje?'

'They never reached Sena, and they would never attack us here. Not *Sinyala* Isadora's place.'

'Why not?'

'Don't you know? *Sinyala* Maria was Matekenya's auntie. We're all family here.'

Mesquita took the demijohn, and poured a small libation on the ground beneath the hammock.

'In any case, the English soon sorted things out.'

'The English?'

'The foreign traders from Quelimane. English, French, Dutch, Germans, Swiss—I can't remember who exactly. Some Indian traders were in the column. British Indians, I mean. They knew their fellow countrymen were in danger. Anyway, they marched straight to the rebels and drove them back. That was the end of the war. My men weren't needed.'

So, the hero of Mopeia had been saved by the English, helped by British Indian shopkeepers. Afonso's disillusion was complete.

Four days later and fully recovered, Afonso arrived at Sena by canoe. His company had already proceeded upriver. His bitter instructions were to remain at Sena, taking charge of the supplies left there for when the company returned, presumably victorious.

An inglorious task. If he anything went missing, he would be responsible. If he kept the goods intact, the achievement would be passed over.

He found the crates in army tents guarded by Sergeant Malaca, who was much relieved to hand over responsibility.

'This is too much goods, *senhor*. Too much rice, too much flour, too much wine, too much guns. These Sena people is thieves.'

'We have three enemies,' said Afonso. 'The people, the climate and the ants. I must find somewhere secure.'

It was then that he climbed Baramwana Hill, kicking moodily at one of the rusting cannon, and began to form a plan.

He would not beg any of the Sena settlers to accommodate him in guarding the supplies—part here, part there, in their scattered houses. He certainly wasn't going to ask any of the Indian traders. Instead, using his authority as the senior military officer in town, he would commandeer twenty slaves from the settlers, along with three carpenters.

At the entrance to where the Sena fort should have been was a magnificent arch of carved freestone, shipped from Lisbon in 1704. It straddled the main path into the town, half-hidden by thorn trees and overgrown with sand vines. Barefoot women speaking not a word of Portuguese walked daily between its embossed pillars, water pots on their heads. The huge keystone loomed high above them. Above that, a pediment bore the royal coat of arms and an inscription declared that Dom João Fernandes de Almeida, then Captain-General of the Sena Rivers, had erected the gateway in 1704.

The carpenters would fit a sturdy doorway inside Almeida's arch, once it had been cleared of undergrowth. The slaves would use mud bricks from the derelict houses to construct an attached warehouse, large enough to contain all the supplies entrusted to his care. The goods would be stacked on wooden planks, raised above the ground on metal spikes, and each spike would stand in a clay pot of water to be replenished daily. Ants would be repelled, the mud wall would have openings for ventilation and the thatched roof would be thick enough to keep out the rains.

Afonso derived a grim satisfaction from this plan. It was like a satire on his youthful dreams of the ancient city with its battlements and convent.

Part Two

29 Shire

Perhaps I'd become too used to being a god. The people who build their villages on my banks call me a god, as did the short brown people who lived here before them. I provide them with water, for drinking and cooking and to irrigate their gardens. Reeds and bamboo grow on my banks, which they use to build their houses and to make fish traps. So I feed, water and house them, and I accepted their worship as no more than my due. When the present people drove away the brown people, there was a god-ship issue they had to address. But it was nothing to do with me. I was just god or, if you prefer, the river. Today, they leave little sacrifices of millet and millet beer to the brown people they dispossessed.

Then these *azungu*—they're called white though they're a sort of hairy, grey pink—these new people called me 'God's Highway to the Interior'. Not a god, but their god's instrument. I heard they had things called locks and dams and canals in their own country, and I worried what their plans for me might be.

But it's true I've learned from them. Until they came, I never knew I was one river, like the famous Thames. I was different rivers—the one connecting Lake Nyasa with Lake Palombe, the long curve from Lake Palombe to the cataracts, then a dozen separate waterfalls, then the broad stream to the Dambinyi marsh—and so on, all the way to the River Zambezi. Each bit separate and each with its own name. Even the waterfalls had different names—Kapichira, Mpatamanga, Nkulu, Khorombizo near Matope.

Not my names, you see. They were the names given me by the people who live on my banks. They spoke a rainbow of languages, each merging with the next one, so the people who were near neighbours could always understand each other, but with accumulating changes until the language of Lake Palombe was different from the language beyond Chief Tengani's.

Did I ever have a language of my own?

I'm fluid and formless. I take the shape of my banks. If they're straight and narrow, I flow fast. If they're curved, I am deepest on the outside of the bend, while the opposite bank is thick with papyrus. Where there are no banks, as at Dambinyi or Ndindi, I spread out over hundreds of square miles and my channels are a mystery even to myself.

I'm transparent, which means I'm never without colour. Blue, of course, from the sky, but also golden, grey and every possible variety of green. I reflect what's around me on my travels, and I pick up their accents.

For the most part, I'm earth-bound. Three quarters of any of my vistas are pure sky, except for the cataracts, when huge black boulders loom above me and the sky is a narrow blue slit.

There are seasons when I take control—when, brown and foaming, I burst my banks and forage over the countryside, destroying and re-shaping. But I can't keep this up for long. I subside into my new course, bounded by and reflecting new river banks. Then I hear people saying, 'this child saw the light in the year of the Ndombo flood', or 'my child's husband the year after Muali', and I know I've made my mark. I take my history from them.

Occasionally, long after midnight when hippos go ashore and the other animals come down to drink, or when the full moon is reflected in one of my calm stretches, I have a sense there are depths to me which their different languages can't fathom. But I can't put words to it. I've only their words, which keep changing.

This present language is the one spoken by the *azungu* who first showed me I was one river, Shire, all the way from Lake Nyasa to the Zambezi. The man they called 'living stone', *mwala ali ndi moyo*, was the first to do this. When I heard this name shouted from the steamer, I thought it was some new kind of fetish. But it was just a man, a *muzungu*, though different from the Portuguese *azungu*. He was jeering at Chief Tengani who had tried to stop him sailing upstream. The steamer chugged on regardless, and Living Stone shouted so the chief would remember his name.

Until then, no one had tried to voyage very far on me. Chief Tengani and before him Chief Nyampindiku had always stopped the Portuguese coming with their canoes to take slaves. If the people further north went travelling, for adventure or for trade, they made straight for the east coast where the Arabs and the Portuguese had their trading posts. There was no point using my stream to sail south. Overland to Angoche or Kilwa was much nearer. They crossed me where Lake Nyasa ends or above the waterfalls with their cargoes of ivory, and afterwards slaves. This was always in the dry season. Four months afterwards, they re-crossed me with sacks of salt and bales of calico and bundles of axes and iron hoes.

Then Living Stone sailed up with his iron boat belching clouds of smoke, showing me my course at far as Kapichira. He walked past the cataracts and hired canoes at Matope to take him to the lake.

So my whole length was exposed.

That rainy season I was in flood, and the people downstream called it the *vapori* flood and named their children's birthdays after the vapours belching from the steamer.

After that, so many different strangers came with their steamers and ship's boats and sometimes just dugout canoes —English, Scots, Indians, Jews, Portuguese, Arabs, so many missionaries, so many traders, so many hunters, so many planters and then suddenly soldiers and administrators. All came to be reflected in my sliding surface with their Babel of languages:

'*Graças à Deus.*'

'I make a good price, isn't it?'

'I say, old chap, how can I help you?'

'I vow by the god of Abraham.'

'You'll nay get a better offer. Not from here to Sauchiehall St.'

'*Esta bandeira*—that Union Jack—is not recognised *em território portugês.*'

'There is one god and Allah is his prophet.'

'The returns are 25%. 15% guaranteed.'

'I have rupees. I have shillings. I have mil-reis. I have whisky.'

'The natives are treacherous fighters and are too cowardly to come within range of our guns.'

That last dialect was the one that prevailed. But now they've built the railway, I'm back to my old peace and quiet. They got tired of complaining about my sandbanks and the unpredictability of my currents. I'd stopped being God's highway. I'd become shallow and stinking and mosquito-ridden. So they built a railway along my right bank, crossing to the left by an iron bridge at Chiromo, and climbing past the cataracts to the highlands. So for the most part the *azungu* leave me alone. Sometimes, just for the pleasure of it, I wash away the track south of Tengani's or wreck one of the trestles crossing my tributaries. But it doesn't take them more than a day or two to make repairs, and I wouldn't want to do lasting damage. Else they'd re-launch their steamboats that are still beached, decaying along my banks.

So I'm no longer a god. Not even a god's highway. Just a witness.

Did I notice in the old days the kingfisher reflected in my surface, perched on an upturned dugout canoe? Did I see the heron standing on one leg, or flopping lazily about its double, mirrored in my surface?

I must have done, but I don't remember. The words I use are not the old words. I use the language of my whole watershed, the dialect backed by gunboats.

That word *mirror*. It was Bwana Chemandala who first brought the mirrors here. Until then, the women could catch a glimpse of their faces as they filled their water pots. But the crocodiles took anyone who stopped to admire themselves, and no one knew as well as me what they really looked like. Then they began to have mirrors and they knew what I knew, even as I was forgetting it.

But of course I noticed. The people living on my banks still speak the old languages. They have their own words for heron and kingfisher. Yet the noticing is different.

These birds live by fishing, and people admire them for the way they go about their work. The heron's patience—perching on one leg for an hour until the fish are deceived by their shadow and take shelter there. Then *pchiu*! And the heron flops away with a small *chambo* in his beak.

Surprise is also the kingfisher's weapon. Hovering high above the surface, then again *pchiu!* Like an arrow with bright feathers.

Their own methods are different. They fashion traps out of reeds or split bamboo and moor them in the current, the mouth facing downstream. They weave circular nets, with stones tied to the circumference then, standing in their dugout canoes, spin them like reed mats until they clasp the water and close around their prey.

They construct dams—you see! I knew that word after all —forming shallow backwaters, safe from crocodiles, where schools of tiny *usipa* swarm and can be caught in cupped hands.

Sometimes, like the kingfishers, they wait and throw their spears, *pchiu*!

So the noticing is different, because I'm making comparisons. I give the people their living, and it's their living they take good note of. My clay is for water pots and cooking pots and for brick making. My reeds are for sleeping mats, grain bins and for baskets woven so tight they're are beer-proof. My river-side grasses provide them with salt and with waterproof thatch for their houses. My ebony trees are for carving, for the best chairs and stools and for mortars and pestles which will last a lifetime, to be inherited by a woman's granddaughter. My giant fig trees provide the hard wood for dugout canoes and for the slats of xylophones with their resonator gourds dangling like udders.

When they look, they see resources, the world they survive in. They know my value.

The *azungu* are different. Even their food they bring in tins, labeled Fortnum and Mason. Their drinks are in demijohns with thick corks, or in bottles with screw tops. They have their own snuff and tobacco.

They worship killing. If a fish eagle circles overhead, they can't just leave it alone. They take a potshot at it. If a hippo surfaces with a snuffle and a pink yawn, they blast away. Killing elephants for their ivory or kudu for their meat I can understand. The native hunters do this, though they have strict rules about killing and sharing the spoils, and they say a prayer for the animal's soul. But killing just for pleasure! That was the first thing we wondered about these new *azungu*. It was as though my river, which they didn't need for survival, existed for sport. Or had to be tamed.

They absorbed me in other ways. I remember a lady, Chendevu's wife, reading aloud on deck from a diary she was keeping. It was below Liwonde, where the banks are level and I make a wide curve between the village gardens. My main current, hugging the curve, is strong and deep, but there's nothing to show this apart from duckweed spinning in little black eddies. The pewter surface slides as if motionless, and the whole curve is like a placid pond.

She described the duckweed. She described the heat and the stillness, the tendrils of water hyacinth extending from the reeds with red-legged waders splashing from one leaf pad to the next. She saw the exploding heads of papyrus with the nests of red-beaked bee-eaters, and two elephantine baobab trees, looking as though they had been planted upside down with their roots in the air. She saw two dugout canoes on a sandy beach next to an anthill, crowned by a monstrous hippo skull protecting the villagers' gardens. And she saw a fever tree with a dozen storks' nests, its shimmering yellow bark ghastly with guano.

'I should like to have painted it,' she read aloud. 'But even writing is difficult when the sweat from my wrists smudges the page, and the steamer chugs on regardless.'

She had a nice voice, very even and melodious, quite different from the barking of the men. Listening to her, I began to see myself differently.

30 Shire

Something I do well is detect sounds. In my depths, I can hear something long before I hear the same sound on my surface. Through the rocks, or through the piled earth my banks, I hear things even faster. I don't know why this is so, but it is so.

Paddles, for instance. I can hear canoe men paddling minutes before I hear them talking among themselves. I can hear the weights of the net they have twirled hitting the water, and know which fish they've caught, before the sound of their jubilation reaches me.

Paddle steamers I can hear even further off. The first I ever heard was the *Ma Robert*, the one belonging to Living Stone, and it puzzled me as much as it alarmed the crocodiles and hippos. The people on my banks heard the whistle and saw the belching smoke as it approached. But long before them, I had heard the twin paddles slapping the water like deranged war drums not quite synchronised. Now, of course, I'm used to the steamers and can distinguish between them. I can tell that's the *Lady Nyasa*, or the *James Bowie*, or the big new *James Stepherson* with its single rear wheel, an hour before they trundle round the green bend.

The War of the *Azungu* started with another new sound, heard this time through my river banks. It came from far away, down in my delta where I begin to exhaust myself in the Zambezi. The sound was a regular thumping, like women pounding maize. When women are doing that, they often sing, and when I strained my ears I could indeed hear distant singing, but men's voices.

Eventually, I could detect three different sounds. There was the singing, of course, but the thudding was of two types. One was heavy and spaced, very like the women's mortars. The other was more like the *James Stephenson's* paddle, a fast but regular slapping. Sometimes I heard the one, sometimes the other, sometimes both together, though it was the faster rhythm that was accompanied by singing.

By the time I learned from the talk of canoe men what was happening, the faster rhythm had stopped for the moment.

But the other sound, like the women's mortars, remained. It was the sound of Portuguese soldiers marching in their boots.

I'd seen boots, of course. All the *azungu* wore them, the explorers, the ivory hunters, the traders, the missionaries. Chindevu used to say his were made of hippo-hide, right up to his crotch, and that no black mamba could ever harm him. He also had heels to make him look taller, because he was a very short man. But never before had I heard the *azungu* marching, thump, thump, thump, with—as I saw later—a black boy marching with them, beating a tin drum.

There were sixty-four of them. I say they were Portuguese because they all wore boots and a uniform, but only six of them were *azungu*. The rest were Africans, speaking a language I had never heard before, from the other side of the continent in a country called Angola. The old Kololo chiefs, Ramakukan, Katunga, Mulilima, and Chipatula who was killed by Piri-Piri, they used to talk about Angola because they had been there with Living Stone, walking all the way there and back, without boots. That was before they came to build their villages on my banks. These new Angolans, the soldiers, had come by steamer all the way to Quelimane and then up the Zambezi to my delta at Chimuara.

Chimuara was where *Sinyala* Maria lived, the same *sinyala mariya* all the canoemen used to sing about, and it is true she owned a lot of slaves. I never saw the lady myself and I don't think the canoe men did either. She kept to her house, dressed always in bright silks from India. But everybody important who was passing by on the river felt obliged to call on her, and the leader of the Portuguese soldiers did so. I soon found out his name was Major Serpa Pinto, and that I had seen him before. Almost twenty years before, when little more than a boy, he had been with the disastrous expedition against Bonga's *arringa* at Massangano and had barely escaped with his life, hiding on the island in my delta until he was rescued by *Sinyala* Maria's slaves.

This time, when he called on the *Sinyala*, he told her his expedition was peaceful and scientific. First, the old lady laughed at him, and then she became angry.

'If your expedition is peaceful,' she said in her very bad Portuguese, 'why have you brought the big guns back?'

It was true. His men had unloaded a big iron cannon with iron wheels as tall as the major. I had seen this gun before. Mbewe's friend, the Jamaican, had been arrested at Mpassu while carrying its parts downstream in two canoes. It was called an Armstrong mountain gun, and now the Portuguese were going to use it in their own war.

'And why have you brought the Landeens back?'

The Landeens were the other sound I had heard, the regular slapping like a paddle wheel. They were Zulus from the far south, who had quarrelled with other Zulus and founded their own kingdom. For as long as I could remember, they had sent their *impi* up to the Zambezi, and across to the people living on my banks, demanding women and tribute. They struck with incredible speed, running with great loping strides and covering forty miles in a day, and they fought hand-to-hand with shields and assegais in a way our own people couldn't withstand. Even when the Kololo came with guns they had bought from the Arabs, it made no difference, for the Landeens' cowhide shields were strong enough to stop musket balls.

That was why *Sinyala* Maria's nephew Marianno, whom they called Matekenya, the one who makes people tremble, set up his own kingdom on my left bank, below where the Ruo river joins me. He wanted to be safe from the Landeens, but he had to fight the Kololo chiefs, who ruled this land, and afterwards he had to fight the Portuguese who destroyed him. First of all, of course, he had to fight the real owners of the land, the ancestors of the people who were now the slaves of the Kololo and the Portuguese.

I said perhaps I'd become too used to being a god. But the god was never me. The river god was a python called Mbona, who of all living creatures was most like me, being long and sinuous and muddy-green in colour, with large blotches like sandbanks. Mbona lived with a wife, or with a series of wives who had to be replaced each time one wife died, and her job was to maintain his shrine at Khulubvi. People went there to pray to the ancestors, asking them to pray to Mbona, especially when they had hoed their gardens and were waiting for the rains.

When Matekenya came, he couldn't destroy the python because Mbona was a god. But he destroyed the shrine and raped Mbona's wife. Mbona got his revenge, by sending a drought. For three years, there were no rains. Thousands of people perished of hunger, and two of the white missionaries who came with the Bishop went mad before they died. So Matekenya had to re-build the shrine and find Mbona a new wife. In those days, being a god still mattered.

Now Matekenya was dead, and Portuguese were bringing the Landeens back. *Senhora* Maria was furious with the Portuguese major.

'Why are you bringing the Landeens back? It will make everyone here want to fight you.'

So Major Serpa Pinto had to find some other soldiers. In fact, he kept the Landeens, as well as the Angolans. But he dispatched them ahead to establish a camp at Mpassu, where they would be beyond local quarrels, under the command of a young engineer called Álvaro de Castellões Ferraz, assisted by Amaral Themudo, who was *Sinyala* Maria's grandson. He also recruited irregulars from the *prazos*—two hundred from Boror near Quelimane, two hundred and fifty from *prazo* Manganja aquem Shire on the left side of my delta, and two hundred dog-eaters from across the Zambezi at Gwengwe.

Two hundred armed men came from a tiny *prazo* south of Quelimane called Maindo. These were led by a tiny Goan with a pale moustache called Zé Miguel. Another two hundred, known as Raposo's men, turned out to be from a *prazo* that bordered on Prazo Maindo. The biggest group, however, were a thousand irregulars from Sena. Except for the men from Boror, who spoke Chuabo, the rest could understand each other. When Serpa Pinto's army advanced, the thousand men from Sena marched up my right bank, and the mixed army of just over a thousand marched up the opposite side.

You must be wondering how I know these numbers. Of course, I didn't know at the time. Everything was confused, and the irregulars didn't move in formation like the Landeens. There was just a mass surge of men, milling around like a disturbed nest of black ants. It was after the battle at Chiromo, when *Muzungu Nkulu* was pacing the deck, that I heard about the numbers. 'Big Man', for that's what the name they gave him means, was Azevedo Coutinho, the captain of the *Chirem*, a rear-wheeled steamer with terrible guns, and he had just been told by Serpa Pinto that he was now in command of the whole expedition. That's when he started calculating how many men he had at his disposal, counting aloud on the fingers of both hands. He was a very young man, not yet married, so I could understand why he was anxious.

I said the two armies advanced up both my banks. But I'm a river, not a road. I'm shaped like Mbona the python, and you never saw a python resting in a straight line. He coils himself, as I do—especially towards the delta where my valley widens and the fields are flat. Moreover, there are no roads. The widest path is just after Pinda, where a Portuguese flag and three borassus palm trees mark the route the Indian traders follow to Sena. It's quicker that way than following the wide curve I make before joining the Zambezi. It brings them out to the bank opposite Sena, where they can hire canoes to get across. That's how the thousand men from Sena must have come, crossing the Zambezi in those big canoes the fishermen have, able to carry twenty-five men. But once they reached my right bank, that was the end of any roadway.

Of course, there are tracks everywhere, but they're narrow, and they lead between the villages which, of course, are nearly always built close to me, their river. They have to be close because they depend on me. This means that the tracks that connect the villages follow the river banks. If my stream makes a wide curve, the tracks follow the curve. If you try to take a short cut, in a straight line, you soon find yourself in dense forest, having to cut your way through thorn trees and razor-sharp elephant grass.

Sometimes, when the two armies were on the move, they would be travelling in opposite directions, jeering at each other from different sides of the curve, and especially at those going backwards. I don't know why the armies didn't just travel upstream by canoe, the way everybody else did. I suppose they reckoned it would cost too much, because they couldn't just seize the canoes. They needed paddlers and experienced pilots, men you can't just commandeer.

I said the tracks are narrow, usually intended for a man and maybe two wives. The man always walks in front, of course, with his hands free to cope with any danger. The women follow in line, carrying baskets on their heads, or hoes. They're not wide enough for armies, and in addition to linking the villages, they make detours round creeks or tributaries, leading to where fording the stream is easiest, or where a fallen tree acts as a bridge. Sometimes, to find these tracks, they needed local guides, and when the guides pointed them in the wrong direction, they got lost.

The guides did this because the villagers were angry. There was always disturbance when an army passed through. It had happened just a few years before when Matekenya's people attacked the Portuguese, and then the Portuguese came up river in revenge. But when that happened, people could flee to the opposite bank. Their huts were spoiled, or even burned to the ground, and their granaries were raided. But they found safety in the reeds of the other bank. This time, there were armies on both banks, and the only place to hide was the forest or on Morumbala mountain.

The armies stole food and commandeered people's homes. But the men, hundreds of them, also wanted women.

Men travelling up and down my river, in traders' canoes or working as crew on the paddle steamers, had always wanted women. It was dangerous to travel at night, even at the full moon, because though my main current is fast it's not easy to track it among the shoals and sandbanks, even with the best pilots like Mbewe, and there are many islands and backwaters to negotiate. So the steamers would halt for the night, and the crew would look for women. Usually a few women were available, in return for half a dozen coconuts brought up from the delta. You would see them negotiating as the steamer passed, standing on the bank cupping their bare breasts and beckoning while the men on the steamer laughed and shouted promises. Often, it was just a joke, but these travelling men were popular.

The men in the armies were different. They weren't interested in paying and although some had their own women with them, there were never enough women to satisfy everyone. When they dragged a poor woman from the reeds or from the forest, no matter how young or how old, they simply raped her right there on my bank, sometimes ten of them at a time. When they were finished, they would pick her up and fling her into the river. So many times, I heard the screams and sobbing and moans, and when the body hit the water crocodiles would rush from the depths and fight over it, pulling away an arm or a leg or a hunk of the torso as the blood ran in my current as a slowly fading stain.

The men also fought between themselves. Some of them, the ones recruited in the *prazo* next to the delta, the one called Manganja, had relatives in these villages and attacked the men who were raping their nieces and aunties and grandmothers. Then it was men's bodies that were tossed into my stream, sometimes local men, sometimes the invaders.

There were also terrible quarrels between the men from Prazo Maindo and Raposo's men. This wasn't anything to do with the war. It was based on where they came from, in neighbouring *prazos* south of Quelimane. Alfred José Miguel, the little Goan with the faint moustache, was furious about the behaviour of the men from the other group. He used to mumble to himself before he actually spoke, but when the words came out they were bitter and to the point.

'Your slaves are no better than baboons,' he told Raposo, after one especially brutal mass rape.

Raposo told him to mind his own business.

Zé Miguel mumbled again. I could see he was nervous, but furious at the same time.

'It is my business. We need these people to welcome our rule. Otherwise, we have no right being here.'

I said the men stole food. The first thing they did when they entered a village and were sure there were no women left behind was to empty the granaries and check the houses for pots of beer. They would set the women they had brought with them to collect firewood to cook millet flour and anything else they had managed to plunder. These were men with guns, and though most of the game had been frightened away, there were plenty of waterfowl. So the day's march could be a short one, often ending at noon, depending on what resources they encountered.

Sometimes, it was two or three days before they marched on. One dawn as they were setting off from Masaopa, the men from Manganja disturbed a hippo returning to the river from the villagers' gardens. The villagers placed huge hippo skulls in the papyrus next to the tracks the hippos used, and normally they would beat drums at night at frighten them off. But, of course, that previous night they had run away into the forest. So when the hippos came, they could forage where they liked because the soldiers were too drunk to chase them off.

One of them, however, returning to the river that morning, ran under a trap they villagers had set. It was a beam of mahogany, six-feet long with a metal spike, covered with poison and suspended from a pole, and held in place by a rope of plaited reeds, so arranged that when the hippo disturbed it, the beam dropped and the spike drove into the animal's flesh between the shoulder blades. This didn't kill the hippo immediately, but the men knew it had been fatally wounded and if they watched the riverbank long enough, its carcass would float to the surface. So that day they waited, and the next three they feasted, for there was ample meat for two hundred men, followed by days of resting while they cleared their heads. That was just the men from Manganja. The men from Boror wouldn't touch hippo meat, which they called filthy, and those from Gwengwe would only eat dogs.

With all this, it took the armies three weeks to get as far as Megaza, and beyond Megaza lay the Ndindi marsh.

31 Shire

People called this the *War of the Azungu*. But I never saw more than a dozen Portuguese taking part, including little Zé Miguel who looked Goan, and Themudo, the *Sinyala's* grandson who, though he was called Portuguese, was of mixed descent. As for the English, none of them, from the Company or from the missions, once showed their faces. The *War of the Azungu* was mostly between Africans on both sides.

I don't understand why people are like this. Rivers like me never divide, except very briefly to encircle an island or because a big rock lies in our path. Our policy is to join together, becoming stronger and stronger in the process. When I flow out of Lake Nyasa, through Lake Chirwa (this is what I learned when Living Stone first sailed my whole length), I begin to be joined by other streams—the Mwaza, the Mombasi, the Mkombedzi-wa Fodya, the Mucurumadzi, the Lisangwe, and many others. None of them is as big as the Ruo River which boasts of its source in the mighty Mlanje Mountain, but even when I am nearing my delta, little streams tumble down from Morumbala, and I embrace them gladly.

As for my marshes, Ndindi and Dambinyi, when I get almost completely lost, I suppose that's when I most resemble human beings, and it takes a master pilot like Mbewe to understand me.

While the African armies were marching, Serpa Pinto was still back in Chamo. He had two officers with him, a naval doctor called Rolão Preto, and a young lieutenant called Maria Afonso de Rebelo. Chamo, on my left bank just where I join the Zambezi, had been the first of Matekenya's stockades. He lived there very comfortably until he was driven north and started fighting the Kololo. That was when he destroyed Mbona's shrine, causing the drought, and it from there his people made the war against the Portuguese a few years back. But Chamo was still a very comfortable place. There was a brick house with Portuguese furniture, a storehouse, an arsenal and dozens of separate huts, all surrounded by a double line of stakes. which had grown into trees, and earthworks with holes for musket fire.

Serpa Pinto had done a lot of African travelling. Like Living Stone, he'd crossed from Angola, so he knew all about sleeping in smoky huts, full of lice and rats and even snakes in the rafters. A brick house with comfortable facilities and protective earthworks was not a headquarters to abandon in a hurry. Until he heard his army was in place and ready to attack, there was no point in joining the march, and raping women and eating hippo meat were not much to his taste. The hippo meat I'm sure about. As for the women, who can say?

While at Chamo, he kept up the pretence that his expedition was purely scientific. I would see him pacing my left bank, collecting what he called specimens, usually bits of grass pressed between sheets of paper, and sometimes small insects, which he sealed in containers carried for him by Lieutenant Afonso. The lieutenant was with him constantly, just a few paces behind, big boned and slightly clumsy in his movements, and breathless with admiration. It turned out they were from the same part of Portugal, from different sides of the River Douro, and the Major had attended the same Colegio Militar in Lisbon, though more than twenty years earlier than Afonso. The lieutenant used to say things I don't understand, like '*Zacatraz*' when they found a new type of plant. The first time he said it, the major burst into delighted laughter, so he kept on saying it. Whatever the joke was, it soon turned stale. Another thing he liked to say was 'You have printed the *mapa rosa* with your feet.' Whatever it meant, Serpa Pinto didn't get tired of hearing that one. When the major was invited to dine with Themudo's grandmother at Chimuara, to enjoy one of the *Sinyala's* curries, I could see the lieutenant torn between chagrin at being left behind, and pride at being left temporarily in command. For all his size, he was still a boy, as fresh as one of my tiny tributaries.

It turned out the major was waiting for two gunboats to help in his 'scientific expedition'. They had been ordered from England from a town called Jarrow, and were delayed because Jarrow had sent only two workmen to assemble them at Quelimane. This was another strange thing about the *War of the Azungu.* What were the English doing, selling gunboats to the Portuguese to be used against them? Meanwhile, there was nothing for him to do but enjoy the *Sinyala's* curry and collect specimens.

Ndindi Marsh was where the first terrible event happened.

As I said, it's part of my course where I get lost, not as thoroughly as in Dambinyi, but confusing enough. There's just one low hill, five miles back from my right bank, with a wide mudbank where people make their *dambo* gardens. But all other directions are flat and featureless and it's twenty miles back to the first village across the other side. There are lakes and pools where bits of my river emerge and disappear again, and lots of small islands. But the rest is water plants—cabbage, hyacinths, lilies with great spreading leaf pads, along with patches of reeds, and papyrus and clumps of fever trees where my water is shallowest.

It's a place where the river steamers are completely dependent on pilots like Mbewe, even the canoeists carrying Indian traders need to shout to the fishermen for advice. As for the fishermen, they know the bit of the marsh where they lay their traps, or the lagoons where they cast their nets. If they intrude on their neighbour's fishing grounds, there's trouble. So, they know their own bit of the Ndindi but not much more. They also know the paths and fords connecting the temporary huts, where they stay, a week at a time, making their catch, then drying the fish they have caught before returning to their villages. But there's no path going all the way across Ndindi. To get past, you have to make a wide detour—not so wide on the right bank, but at least three days' journey on the left, unless you do the sensible thing and travel by canoe.

I say all this to explain what happened. The men from Sena, travelling up my right bank, could get round Ndindi without much too much trouble. Their only obstacle was the lush *dambo* gardens, with their pumpkins and melons and fresh green *mapira manga*, the delicious 'foreign millet' which was the local name for maize, a crop the ancestors didn't know. The men from Sena, feasting in this land they were passing through, were careful that the libations they poured to the

201

ancestors of the people whose gardens they had just raided were of millet beer.

The other side of the marsh, the men from the different *prazos* encountered similar gardens but on a wide arc that, if they stopped at every village, threatened to delay their progress for weeks. So, when men from Kakawa offered to guide them through the marsh, some of them accepted.

Is there a path through? If there is, I don't know it.

The men from Kakawa made their offer because they wanted revenge. Some of the soldiers from the *prazos*, including the dog-eaters from Gwengwe, had been there before, with the Portuguese army that had burned village after village in reprisal for Matekenya's war. Now these men were back, further upriver than the tracks they knew, and dealing with men who swore they could guide them.

Of course, not all the army was present when they made this offer, just the dribs and drabs that had reached their village. There were men who liked the idea of making the wide detour, enjoying the women and other pleasures of the journey. There were men, too, who looked at Ndindi and drew back in fear. My marsh was not for the faint-hearted.

But two hundred and eight irregulars agreed to try the marsh, hoping to arrive at fresh plunder before their fellows.

One hundred and ninety-seven perished.

I could see what the three guides were doing, leading the men by winding underwater paths that were only accessible when my waters were low, before the rains. It was tough going because the paths were narrow and slippery, especially for the men at the rear, who were walking in mud churned up by those before them. Some became impatient and tried to overtake only to find themselves waist deep in marshland that bubbled with gases as their companions pulled them clear. Every few hundred yards, they crossed islands thick with reeds. They would have liked to have paused, but the guides urged them on, pointing to the sun now high overhead and talking of how far they had to go. So they plunged again into the shallow water covering the invisible tracks. It took them four hours to cover nine miles, and then the guides disappeared.

Slowly, it began to sink in that they had been betrayed,.

They were on an island, with reeds stretching as far as they could see in every direction, making the low hill to the west completely invisible. There was obviously no going forward. But they quickly discovered there was no going back. They could see where two hundred men had scrambled up through the mud on to the island, pulling at the reeds to climb up. Beyond that point, their route had been too circuitous for anyone to recall. Underwater tracks are quickly invisible as the disturbed sediment settles. In any case, they had been staring at the path ahead, and there were no landmarks anyone could identify.

The island had two abandoned fishermen's huts, which gave them hope they could summon help, first by shouting and then by firing their guns into the air. This sent the swamp birds spiralling, shrieking in protest, but otherwise it was a waste of time. The few fishermen in the vicinity knew very well what was going on, and in any case the guns would have made them keep their distance.

By this time, it was mid-afternoon and they began to be frightened. But they made a plan. They cut the thickest of the reeds, and tried leaving the island single-file, prodding at the water with the reed-poles to locate the path. When the first had managed to proceed a few yards, the second followed, and then the third. Each time the path took a turn, a reed was planted to mark the spot. But it was slow going. After an hour, the first man had covered less than a mile, and the two hundred and seven others were strung out at intervals behind him. They realised it was too late in the day. They would have to return to the island and try again early next morning.

As they turned back, the first crocodile struck. It happened with astonishing speed, with a splash like a wave breaking and a scream, then they saw their companion's right leg kicking the air as the creature pulled him into deeper water. Some stood where they were, firing their guns uselessly at the water. Others, in sudden panic, pushed past them to regain the island. A second crocodile struck, then a third, and the return became a mad scramble, with men losing the path and sinking into the mud, shouting desperately for help as they disappeared, horribly.

Forty-nine men died that afternoon. The rest huddled all night on the island, periodically firing their guns to keep the crocodiles at bay. The moon was in its third quarter, casting indeterminate shadows, which intensified their fears. There was a further panic just after midnight when one group found themselves sharing their refuge with a huge python. By the time they had killed it, it had bitten three of them. It was still hanging by its fangs from the thigh of the third man while blood spurted in a fountain from his artery. He was dead in minutes, and by then the men from Manganja, who knew all about Mbona, the python god, knew that they themselves were doomed.

Next morning, they set out early and covered the first mile quickly, retracing their steps from the previous day. But from then on, it was slow going and as the crocodiles became evident it was hard to maintain their discipline. How many drowned and how many were eaten, I doubt even the river god knows. No one made it to the shore on foot, but one small group of eleven men were lucky to encounter two fishermen's canoes beached next to a hut on an island. It was late afternoon when they reached Panyathwa village, whose very name means 'place of suffering'. There they rejoined their fellow irregulars and told their story.

The three guides, of course, were nowhere to be found, and the villagers, too, had already fled the invading army. The men took their revenge on everything in sight, huts and their contents, granaries, gardens, even the mango and banana trees, leaving a wasteland to mark their passage and vowing to do worse on their return.

32 Shire

Serpa Pinto's first news of this disaster was that a thousand men had died, and it was a relief when it turned out to be less than two hundred. His army, both armies, were close to Mpassu, where Álvaro de Castellões with the Landeens had established their camp. That was the last point on my right bank where the Portuguese flag flew, but he was still awaiting news of the gunboats the two Englishmen were assembling at Quelimane. The delay was making him suspicious, and he was uncertain whether to move on to Mpassu or to return to Quelimane to remonstrate.

Before he could decide, a fresh *muzungu* arrived, an Englishman, who turned out to be very important. At first, I hardly noticed him. He entered my stream in a tiny ship's boat, not the way for a big man to travel. Then, at Morumbala, he boarded the *James Stevenson*, so I thought he was just another trader. He was a short, thin man, with a small head like a lizard, the kind of man who is perpetually looking upwards because everyone around him is taller. It was hard to think of him as having authority. He had been paddled in the ship's boat past Serpa Pinto's camp, and it was only after he had boarded the steamer that the major learned he was the new Mr Consul, far more important than the Mr Consul who had negotiated with Mphetomwanyama and Ramakukan. This was a bigger Mr Consul, the English Queen's messenger to the whole region.

When Serpa Pinto learned this, he sent a message asking for a meeting. So the *James Stevenson* came back down the river and anchored. For a while, the two men stared at each other, the one from the river bank, the other from on deck, neither wanting to be the first to move. Serpa Pinto said he had refreshments, tangerines from *Sinyala* Maria's and, if Mr Johnston was interested, for that was Mr Consul's name, two bottles of excellent Portuguese wine from the *Dão* region. So Mr Johnston stepped ashore.

I was interested that the two men were exactly the same size. For an instant, each stared over the other's head, until Mr

Johnston held out his hand and the major shook it. I had got used to *azungu* being as tall as Landeens, but these were the size of people from the highlands. Despite their talk, they didn't look very warlike.

Serpa Pinto put on a pained expression. He said his mission was entirely peaceful, one of scientific exploration, but the Kololo chiefs were refusing to let him pass. This was an unfriendly act, and he believed the English, who were supposed to be Portugal's ally, were responsible. Mr Johnston asked why a scientific mission needed to be backed by cannon and two thousand warriors. The major denied this. His men numbered only seven hundred and thirty-one. This made Mr Johnston snort in derision, and the meeting turned nastier. The bottles of wine were forgotten. Mr Johnston said he had just returned from Lisbon. It was common knowledge there that King Luís had instructed the Serpa Pinto to 'secure our dominion on the west bank of Lake Nyasa *by any means necessary*'. He placed special emphasis on the last four words. It was well known, too, that Engineer Álvaro de Castro Ferraz, and Lieutenant Amaral Fernando, alias Themudo, engineers in the major's company, had been instructed by the King to conduct a survey establishing communications between Chibisa and Matope, that is, between the first and last of the rapids on the River Shire.

'Do you still maintain your purpose is scientific?'

The major blushed a little at this, but declared he intended to advance up the Shire valley. Mr Johnston said the Kololo chiefs would resist. The major replied that would be an insult, which the Portuguese would have to punish. That would mean war, said Mr Johnston, a threat to British lives and property and an end to freedom of navigation on the Shire. It was the major's turn to snort. Was freedom of navigation only for the British? All he wanted was freedom for his expedition to proceed.

These two little men glared at each other. The flag on the *James Stevenson* was British, the flag next to the table where they were sitting, Portuguese. Then the major made a proposal. Two of his officers, Lieutenant Afonso and Engineer Álvaro, would travel with Mr Johnston on the steamer to negotiate free passage with the Kololo chiefs. That way the scientific expedition could proceed and war be avoided. To this Mr Johnston replied that he would negotiate with the Kololo on the major's behalf. With this proposal, which even I knew was dishonest, the two parted.

I never understood this business of flags. The *azungu*, all kinds of them, have this belief that putting a piece of coloured cloth at the end of a pole proves the land is theirs. But owning the land is more complicated. It's not enough just to send in your army. You have to have the consent of the people who live there. As, for instance, when hunters present the right hind leg of any animal they have killed to the chief of the land where they hunted it. Or one of the tusks of a dead elephant. It's a recognition of mutual rights and duties, the chief's duty being to protect and sustain his people. You also have to have the consent of the ancestors, as Matekenya found when he destroyed Mbona's shrine and the ancestors refused to send rain. Sticking a head on a pole, as Chipatula's people did to Piri-Piri, makes a serious statement. Sticking a flag on a pole is just a joke. Mponda, who has his village where I flow out of Lake Nyasa, has two flags which he keeps in a bag. When his messengers tell him who is approaching, English or Portuguese, he hoists the one that will please them. It's just a game the *azungu* play.

Except, of course, that they play it seriously. They use big guns to defend these flags, and they don't care whether the crops are growing or not.

Did that flag at Mpassu turn the people into Portuguese? Did they start wearing tight trousers with shiny black boots? Did they grow little moustaches, curled up at the ends? Did they start eating out of tins? When I flowed past Mpassu the morning after the flag was raised, in that loop with the two lagoons just before making one of my spectacular white-water zigzags, I'd hardly time for reflection. But I didn't notice that the people were any different.

Even the Kololo, upstream at Chiromo, Mitengo and Ramakukan's, even those people who made such a fuss about being 'Anglesi', never looked any different to me. They had

English flags, all of them except Mlauri, but when it suited they weren't 'Anglesi' at all.

Suddenly, there was the business about treaties. A Portuguese expedition would arrive in a village and ask the chief to accept one of their flags, making all sort of promises about protection. They would produce a piece of paper with words like sovereignty and submission, and the chief would be asked to sign it. Except, of course, that he couldn't sign. So he made what they called his 'mark', a little wavery cross, which they then surrounded with their own signatures, adding the date. Once this started, the Company and the Scottish missionaries began doing the same.

For the Kololo chiefs, this was a complicated matter. After Ramakukan's death, they couldn't agree as before. Mlauri, who had been just one of his headmen, tried to take over as paramount chief. But the other chiefs didn't accept him. Katunga and Mulilima, who lived close to my first cataract, refused to obey him, and Chitaonga, who now ruled at Chiromo over Chipatula's former people, was in open rebellion. So when the *azungu* came with their treaties, they couldn't agree among themselves what best to do.

There was a big *mirandu* at Katunga's. Mulilima was there, and Masea. Chemandala was present, along with Mr Johnston, the new big Mr Consul who had just arrived from his meeting with Serpa Pinto. There was also another man called Acting Consul, Mr Buchanan, the planter, who did most of the talking. Mphetomwanyama was there, Ramakukan's old messenger, since he was used to talking to the English Queen's messenger, and his advice was valued. But Mlauri refused to attend. Chitaonga sent his brother Chikusi, but with instructions he should say nothing. Mbewe was summoned from Chiromo to act as interpreter, though in fact to be Chitaonga's spy. Mbewe was no longer regarded as an enemy. He had studied at the mission school, like the other boys who had run away after Chipatula's death, and his hair was cut like theirs, with a straight line down the middle. But anything Mbewe said could be denied afterwards. He was still only a slave.

I always liked Mbewe. Of all the pilots, he was the one who knew me best and treated me with respect. I could always tell when a steamer approached with Mbewe as pilot. Coming upriver, he could steam twenty miles further on a single load of firewood than anyone else. All the other pilots made a point of steering directly into the main current. It ensured they didn't get lost in my various backwaters. Mbewe avoided this, keeping to the slack water on the inside of a bend, taking advantage of the backwash when the current was baulked by an obstacle, knowing exactly when to cross the current to the other side, or when he could risk treading the dead water between a string of islands. Usually, these days, he would be piloting the *James Stevenson*. First, I could tell that was the steamer approaching, long before it came in sight with its huge rear wheel, Immediately afterwards, I would know from the course steered it was Mbewe in charge.

He also knew how to steer his way through an argument.

After Katunga had greeted everyone, and asked Mbewe to interpret, Mbewe interrupted with a speech of his own.

'My father Chitaonga has asked me to tell you,' he began, 'this is a dangerous matter. We have six wars here.'

It was not his place to speak, but he had already caught their attention.

'The Portuguese are making war with the English. They say this is their territory. Matekenya's men are coming back with the Portuguese. They have made their own peace. That is three wars. The Portuguese, with the English, Matekenya's men with the Kololo, and so the Portuguese with the Kololo.'

It was a skilful way of putting things. No one at Katunga's knew much about the Portuguese who had never been there. But they knew about Matekenya, even though he had died years back.

'But now Mlauri wants to fight the English, and we Kololo are fighting each other.'

He didn't mention the sixth war, and didn't need to. Everyone present knew what Chemandala kept repeating, that the Kololo chiefs and the Manganja people spoke with different voices.

'My father says it is better', concluded Mbewe, 'to sign the Englishman's paper. That will protect us.'

But would it? That, of course, was the issue. Mulilima was the first to respond, asking Mphetomwanyama to speak for him, who in turn asked Mbewe to translate for the Anglesi.

'If we sign the paper, will the English Queen protect us?'

Mr Acting Consul replied, 'We will ask the Queen to protect you. Then we must wait for the Queen to answer whether she will have your country or not.'

When this was translated, the chiefs and headmen looked at each other, repeating the words, some of them quoting fragments of the English, 'must wait' and 'have your country'. Then they shook their heads, and Masea laughed out loud.

Mphetomwanyama asked, 'What will happen if we do not sign?'

'There will be strained relations with the Foreign Office.'

Mbewe struggled to do his best with this, but Mphetomwanyama interrupted.

'The Queen is a woman. The Portuguese King is a man. He has many soldiers at Mpassu. How many soldiers does the Queen have?'

Before Mbewe could translate this, Chemandala intervened. He spoke in Manganja.

'You all know Ramakukan was my friend. When Ramakukan's messenger here spoke with the Queen's messenger, there was always peace and good will. Do I speak truly?'

The chiefs and headmen looked again at each other. Some of them remembered the dispute about ivory. But the Queen's messenger had resolved that.

'Last time there was war, the English fought against Matekenya's people. When the Portuguese came, the English stopped them at Mpassu. So the Kololo were safe. Do I speak truly?'

This time, the chiefs and headman nodded and agreed, Chemandala spoke truly. Some of them clapped their hands gently. Women at the fringe of the meeting began to ululate, and were told to be quiet.

'Now there is war again. But there are not six wars,' he said, nodding towards Mbewe. 'There is only one war, the Portuguese against the Kololo. They are bringing Matekenya's people, but they want the country for themselves. Mlauri talks of fighting the English, but Mlauri is nothing, he is a fool. The only question is, do you want the English to help you?'

I could see the chiefs were not convinced. If the Portuguese were coming, of course they wanted the English to help them. But Ramakukan had dealt with the English Queen on equal terms. Now they couldn't say 'no' because they were supposed to be friends, though they suspected the English also wanted to take over the country. Why else were they being asked to sign a piece of paper?

'All the paper says,' explained Chemandala, 'is that you will not sign any other paper without the Queen's agreement.'

This was getting to be like a riddle, which the chiefs usually enjoyed. What is 'Going they talk much, coming back they keep silent'? Or what is the answer to 'a little child removed the chief from his throne'? Or what causes 'the bending-bending that even white men do'? Do you give up? The first is water pots, taken to be filled at the river. The second is a bed bug. The third is a doorway.

But 'the paper you sign not to sign another paper'?

Impatiently, Mr Acting-Consul asked Mbewe to translate word for word what was actually on the document.

'We the undersigned agree,' read Mbewe slowly, 'not to enter into any Agreement, Treaty, or Arrangement with any Foreign Government except through and with the consent of the Government of Her Majesty the Queen of England.'

There was a long silence while they absorbed the implications.

'It means,' said Masea, 'we can't do anything without the Queen's permission.'

'No,' replied Katunga, 'it means we can't make treaties without the Queen's consent. But we don't intend to anyway. So what's the harm in signing? It's not a treaty.'

'A treaty would mean we were partners,' said Masea. 'This paper says the Queen is our new ruler.'

'It doesn't ask us to pay taxes to the Queen.'

With that, it was clear Katunga had won the argument. He repeated that since they didn't intend to sign any treaties with the Portuguese ('because that's who we're talking about'), there was no harm in promising not to. After all, they wanted the English to remain their friends. It wouldn't be sensible to cause offence.

So they signed the piece of paper. Or at least, they made their marks with little spindly Xs, while Mr Acting Consul wrote that these were the authentic signatures of Katunga and Mulilima. Masea was still unhappy, saying his ancestors didn't like him holding a pen. So Mr Acting Consul made his mark for him and then signed that it was his authentic signature. Mr Johnston, the new big Mr Consul, and Chemandala also signed as witnesses, and the meeting ended with everyone shaking hands in the English manner.

33 Shire

Serpa Pinto's army, two thousand strong, less two hundred dead in Ndindi Marsh, was at last in place, and news came that his gunboats were ready and about to sail from Quelimane. Rather than wait for them at Chamo, he decided to advance to Mpassu. He commandeered an ancient rusty steamer belonging to the French trading company, overriding the manager's protests by telling Herr Gubler, in excellent French, that he was privileged to be doing business in a Portuguese territory and that he should never have assumed that the Shire, meaning me, was an international waterway.

The steamer was the *John Bowie*, and I remembered one of the missionaries calling it a 'sardine tin'. I'd seen them eating these fish, bright silver things like *usipa*, out of flat tins with round edges, digging with their fingers into the recesses, and the *John Bowie* was exactly like that, even down to how it smelt, oily, smoky and fishy. It was also one of the slowest steamers on the river. Three days after Themudo, travelling downstream by canoe, had brought him news of the disaster at Ndindi, he embarked with the doctor Rolão Preto, and engineer Themudo, with Lieutenant Afonso in charge of the Armstrong mountain gun, and a day's supply of firewood. Themudo brought other news. Mr Acting Consul had declared the whole Shire valley a British Protectorate.

'It makes no difference,' said Serpa Pinto. 'My expedition is purely in the interests of science.'

The voyage began badly. Themudo insisted, as *Sinyala* Maria's grandchild, that he had known this river since his childhood. He had played here with his nurse, fished, hunted, and chased black girls through those reeds. It was ridiculous to say they needed a pilot. When they ran aground, he apologised and said he had mistaken this section for another further on. When they hit the second sandbank, he said he had never known me so low. When the anchor had to be lowered to winch the steamer off the third obstruction, Serpa Pinto lost his temper. Themudo was sent ashore in search of a pilot and ordered not to come back without one.

I wasn't surprised he was gone several hours. With the passing of the two armies, the whole population had fled. The few who had returned briefly to salvage what might be left of their crops kept well out of sight when they saw a man in a Portuguese uniform approaching. Eventually, he returned with an old man with just one leg, hobbling behind him on two makeshift crutches. It turned out he'd been mauled by a leopard and had been unable to flee with the rest. For three weeks he'd been hiding in his hut with nothing to eat but dry maize cobs, and nowhere to drink but the local stream. It was hunger that brought him to the door when he heard Themudo outside, and hunger that made him offer to be their pilot.

'For food,' he said, 'I will take you to Ramakukan's.'

'Ramakukan's?' asked Serpa Pinto.

'The Kololo chief's capital,' said Themudo. 'That's how hungry he is.'

In fact, Ramakukan had already joined the ancestors. The pilot was willing to go further than Themudo thought.

'Feed him well,' said the major. 'But no alcohol.'

They had only got as far as Pinda, where palm trees marked the track to Sena, and by the time their lame pilot had eaten it was too late to continue that first day. Sleeping on the *John Bowie* was impossible. There was only one tiny cabin and no mosquito nets, so they slept ashore in three abandoned huts, lighting a fire to brew some tea and eating corned beef from a large tin labeled *Sutherland Brand J & A Carpenter*. Themudo managed to find some elephant dung and showed them how to burn it to repel mosquitos.

'If this was lion dung,' he said, 'it would keep everything away. Even spirits.'

Next morning, they tried again. My stream at this point is deep and fast-flowing, so the steamer captains don't normally complain. But I was a bit too fast for the *John Bowie*, whose engines struggled against my current, and my loops and bends irritated the major. When he saw Morumbala on his left, when he reckoned it should have been on his right, he was tempted to stop the steamer and walk, but when lieutenant Afonso pointed to the wheels and carriage of the Armstrong gun, stored in the prow, he pronounced a single 'Merde' and returned to pacing the small deck.

He had another cause for irritation. He was dependent, I heard him telling Dr. Rolão Preto, on daily doses of magnesia. Without the medicine, he was liable to lose control, and he was amazed the doctor had neglected to bring supplies. The doctor had heard of this trait in the hero but hadn't taken it seriously. Now, he was not allowed to forget it. He had his own cause for complaint. He applauded Serpa Pinto's ban on alcohol for the pilot and the crew. He hadn't realised it would extend to himself. The memory of last night eating ship's biscuits and corned beef with only tea to wash the meal down rankled. He was a naval doctor and entitled to some *digestivo*.

As they approached Bompona, he made a discovery that gave him pleasure. The *John Bowie* was smelly and filthy and, having been beached at Chamo for over a year, was crawling with wildlife. Engineer Manuel Joaquim almost had a heart attack when he found a black mamba in the firebox, and he became used to slapping scorpions with a *palmatoria*, used normally for punishing laziness in the crew. But, as the doctor noticed that morning on the rusting bridge connecting the paddle houses, it was spiders that terrified Major Serpa Pinto.

One with a black abdomen, shiny like a beetle, with eight spindly legs, thin as needles, was clinging to the rail. There was nothing menacing about it and, so far as Dr Preto knew, it was not in the least poisonous. But the major went pale and froze where he stood, breathing heavily as beads of sweat appeared on his forehead.

'Lieutenant Afonso,' shouted the doctor. 'A specimen. Hurry.'

Afonso rushed to the bridge, clutching a small box. Seeing the spider, he tapped it with his baton and sealed the container, turning to Sera Pinto with an exultant *'Alcatraz!'*, then hastily withdrew as he observed the scarlet flush spreading across his hero's face.

'Idiot,' muttered Serpa Pinto, relaxing his clenched fists and breathing deeply. 'I can't stand those things.'

'It's called arachnophobia,' said the doctor pleasantly.

'I know very well what it's called. What earthly difference does it make naming things?'

'An interesting philosophical question. I imagine we shall be naming quite a few things before this campaign is over.'

The remark did not improve their relationship. But Serpa Pinto cheered up when he realised he was passing one of the Company's wooding stations. He could assert Portuguese sovereignty, while saving himself the delay of cutting wood, by helping himself to the supply of logs piled there. This made him feel in command, and he paced the small bridge, tapping his left palm with his baton. But no sooner had they loaded a day's supply and resumed their voyage than the *John Bowie* shuddered and lurched violently to the left.

This wasn't the pilot's fault, Themudo explained. The left paddle had become choked with water hyacinth, the long tendrils winding round the axle and dragging up the roots. It was one of the things that happened with side-wheel steamers. The rear wheels, like those on the steamers they were expecting from Quelimane, operated in the wake already created by the steamer's course and were much less likely to become entangled.

The major waved such matters aside.

'How long is this going to take?' he demanded.

'The rest of the day.'

Serpa Pinto swore again in French. Then added, 'What are you standing there for? Get on with it.'

'The men need to go in the water,' said Themudo. 'To cut the wheel free.'

'So?'

'It's dangerous work. There are crocodiles.'

That impressed the major, who had already lost two hundred men to crocodiles. He organised a cordon, some on deck, some on shore, with instructions to fire a fusillade into the river at five minute intervals to protect the men cutting the weeds from the wheel, standing guard himself to shoot at any movement in the water that looked dangerous. The operation was successful, and when they retired for the night in the Company's warehouse, he felt a sense of accomplishment.

But they were still two days' steaming from Mpassu.

34 Shire

From the time of Living Stone and the first missionaries, I'd seen lots of *azungu*, and they were all strange, but strange in different ways. Living Stone was two different men. One of them was always taking notes, about dates and names and places and plants and animals, like a man who wanted to be sure of his facts. The other believed what he wanted to believe, about my river being a broad highway and about my fevers being harmless. He seemed to have no need for women, which surprised me because most of the men I've seen have needed women. Even the Scotsmen who came after him, the missionaries, needed their women. Not African women, they were too high-minded for that. But they wanted their women from Scotland. One of them was so eager he brought his wife, big with child, all the way from Scotland, so she could give birth at midnight in the middle of Dambinyi marsh. I remember her screams. Only the little daughter survived.

But Engineer Álvaro was different again. Like the other Lieutenant Afonso de Rebelo, he was still a boy. They were very good friends, more at ease with each other than either was with Themudo. But Afonso was big-boned with broad shoulders, and his dark hair showed through his cheeks no matter how often he shaved. He was a boy only in being so eager to please. His eyes, when he looked at the Major, were like a new wife's, adoring and timid. Álvaro was more like a virgin, slender with an oval face ending in the merest tuft of a beard that looked as though it struggled to grow. His eyes were like the gazelles that come at night to drink at my inlets, soft and brown and full of yearning when he stared after the girls. They soon noticed him doing it and would burst into happy giggles. Some were ready to be kind to him had he done anything more than staring, but he never made a move.

The day he arrived at Mpassu, he actually started the war because that's when the first shots were fired. He arrived in a canoe, with all the equipment to pitch camp carried in other canoes, while the Landeens marched along my right bank.

Near Mpassu, there was a small Kololo village belonging to Balalika, a sub-chief of the dead Chipatula. It was a mile off, huddled between a low cliff and a small creek that drained into my river, and Álvaro went out to talk—to parley, as he called it, taking four Landeens with him and an interpreter called Chingasala.

It was strange to see this slim Portuguese boy talking to elders as though they were unimportant and he was already in charge, especially since he couldn't speak Manganja and they didn't understand anything he was saying.

He told the Kololo he didn't want war. Chingasala translated this as 'these men are too powerful.' He told them he they had passed five villages on his way, without doing violence or harming anyone. Chingasala said, 'They have already destroyed five and will destroy you.' He explained he simply wanted to pass upriver with his men and his baggage. Chingasala turned this into, 'They will advance like a bushfire through the whole country.' One of the villagers opened fire with a musket loaded with pebbles. Álvaro and the Landeens fired back with their Martini-Henries, killing six before advancing into the village and using a barrel of gunpowder they found there to blow everything up.

Satisfied he had avenged an insult, Álvaro returned to Mpassu to be warned that he had started the war too soon. The news was that Mlauri, Ramakukan, Katungu and all of Chipatula's sons would attack. Just then, the *Lady Nyasa* arrived heading down river, carrying two English traders. Their news was that Mlauri had six thousand rifles, three thousand of them Martini-Henries, just like the one Álvaro was brandishing.

Dismissing this as a blatant lie that only confirmed the English were in league with the Kololo, Álvaro decided nevertheless it was too early to advance upriver and that he should fortify his position. A small fort already existed, of course, with a Portuguese flag. To that he added a palisade at a distance of five hundred yards, and a trench along the side of the creek flowing into my stream from the tiny lake. He also built for himself a comfortable, rectangular house with an overhung veranda for relaxation. It was as though he expected to stay at Mpassu a long time.

While he was supervising this, he used to pace up and down on my riverbank, and I would hear him chanting:

I adore these paths
where the two of us cling
in the shade of trees
where nightingales sing.

What on earth was this? I knew the canoe men had songs, like *Sina Mama* about *Sinyala* Maria, and other songs about women that they wouldn't have wanted their wives to hear.

The missionaries had songs, too. They would sing something that went 'All people that on earth do dwell, Sing to the Lord with cheerful voice.' It was very heavy and doleful, not at all cheerful, so I thought at first it must be a funeral song, especially the way they dragged out the words *with che-er fo-ol vo-ice*. But they sang it when they were pleased about something, so I had to assume they were being happy in their own way. What Álvaro's song was about I had no idea, though he didn't sing it. It was more like a speech made by one of the elders, with a good deal of waving of hands.

His fortifications weren't very impressive. They faced north, and it was hard to see why the Kololo couldn't attack from the east and south, or even from across me to the west. From the left bank, their guns would easily reach the fort, without there being any chance Álvaro's men could chase them off. So the attackers began to think of themselves as defenders. Apart from the Landeens, who feared no one so far from their own country, Álvaro's men were the same as had welcomed the Portuguese into their country to protect them from the Kololo. That was the only reason the Portuguese flag was flying at Mpassu. But if the Portuguese couldn't protect them, they had little choice but to flee.

Álvaro responded with an angry speech no translator could misinterpret. He called them cowards, poltroons, wretches, and traitors. He vowed if he was the last man remaining, he would die beneath this flag which was his country's pact with them. Honour and truth required no less. But they would not fail, if they stood their ground. They had Portugal on their side, and the Portuguese were a match for any—at this point, he hesitated. I think he was about to say baboons, or some such word. He changed tactics, appealing to them as allies, and abruptly left the podium where he had been waving his arms.

Yet half an hour later, he was pacing my bank alone with another of his strange chants:

> I hail you, broad and deep river
> reflecting the profound blue of the sky
> in your bosom of limpid silver.
> You are for us the road of discovery.
> I hail you, unknown frontier,
>   O Portuguese Shire.

This one was even weirder than the first. He seemed to be talking to me, as though I could answer him back. At the same time, he didn't expect me to answer back because I was like a woman, with a bosom. I was 'unknown' and yet I belonged to him. Or, at least, I belonged to the Portuguese. Living Stone and the missionaries and traders had never spoken to me like this. It made me feel very strange.

Just in time, the *John Bowie* dropped anchor at Mpassu. Just in time, that is, if you belonged to the Portuguese, as Álvaro's chant said I did. Mlauri had missed his chance.

Afterwards, everybody said Ramakukan would have done things differently. If he was going to attack, he wouldn't have waited until the whole Portuguese army was in place. He'd have overrun Álvaro's little fortifications and ambushed the two armies on the move. However, he probably wouldn't have attacked. As Ramakukan said, he wasn't afraid of the governor of Quelimane, but he was afraid of the King in Portugal, and wouldn't have done anything to provoke him.

The mystery was why Mlauri attacked Mpassu at all. He was no friend of the English, as the Portuguese claimed. He seems to have thought the English had invited the Portuguese to come and protect them from him. It's hard to follow the thinking of a man like that.

His attack came far too late. But even I could see there were other things wrong about it. My stream has mirrored a lot of wars, especially since Living Stone sailed through the blockade mounted by Chief Tengani, showing the way for all kinds of scoundrels—Matekenya, Bonga, Nhaude, Belchior, even men from *prazo* Gwengwe sent by Dona Luisa to capture women, the same dog-eaters who were now with Serpa Pinto's army. They were very noisy affairs, with lots of guns being fired, and they usually ended with captives being led away as slaves. But not many people were killed.

It used to happen like this. The men would arrive at the place to be attacked, and would spend an hour or so shouting and beating drums and firing their guns into the air. The defenders would put on a similar show, and that was usually how things were decided. One side would give way. The attackers would decide it was hopeless and desist, or the defenders would run away. A successful attack found Chipatula's or Matekenya's capitals deserted. It would be burned to the ground, of course, and some stray refugees would be captured. But there weren't many deaths.

The *azungu* changed all that. They came with better guns, not just bigger and noisier but more accurate. But they were also strict with their ammunition, and when they took aim they were careful not to miss. Until the *azungu* came, I hadn't seen wars where so many died, and died at such distances from the point of fire. They did it just as if they were shooting game.

Mlauri got some things right. The Kololo were divided among themselves, but he managed to bring men from Katunga's and Maseya's and Mulilima's, together with Chipatula's sons. He ignored Álvaro's palisade and attacked from both banks, east and west. He even attacked from the river, using a beached wooden steamer that used to belong to some Jesuit missionaries. The Landeens, who lay in the trench next to the creek, were actually taken from behind, but soon re-grouped themselves beside the fort. But all the noise Mlauri raised from three sides was not going to make the *azungu* retreat. That was not how they fought their wars.

As I say, they had better guns, and they aimed to kill. But the battle was decided by lieutenant Afonso's mountain gun.

I'd never seen a gun like this before. When it was loaded on the *John Bowie* at Chamo, I didn't even know it was a gun. It was in three parts. First, there were two huge wheels. I say that, but in those days I didn't know what wheels were. They were two iron circles, with twelve spokes like the rafters of a hut. There was a kind of bed, like a metal *machila* and finally a tube looking as though it was also made of iron. Lieutenant Afonso was in charge of these things, and when the *John Bowie* reached Mpassu, the night before the battle, he fixed them together like the men who had assembled the steamers.

When he fired it, it seemed I stopped in my course. It was like an earthquake, the explosion booming through my bank while my surface rippled with the shock waves. But it wasn't easy to see what had happened. It turned out only four men were killed. But they weren't killed so much as cease to exist. The shell passed through them, leaving only scattered bits behind, continued on its path until it exploded against the cliff face behind Balalika village. In some ways, this was the most frightening thing of all, that the big explosion occurred almost a mile behind the attackers. They hadn't even seen the flash, so it was like a thunderbolt falling from the skies, nothing to do with the battle they were waging.

It took several minutes to reload the gun, which Lieutenant Afonso did somehow from the back, not by the barrel as I would have expected. They wheeled it round to face the men in the reeds on the west bank and I saw clearly the orange flash as my mirror rippled a second time. Again, the shell obliterated men in its path before travelling a good two miles to explode against a boulder.

It happened a third time, but there was really no need as Mlauri's men knew they were defeated. They melted away, quarrelling between themselves and cursing Mlauri for leading them into this trap. They knew this was not the end of the matter. Mlauri himself fled across the river to Thyolo mountain. What to do next was up to Chipatula's sons.

35 Shire

What did happen next was that the two new gunboats arrived from Quelimane. Of course, I heard they were coming. I thought at first it was the *James Stevenson*, because that was the only rear-wheeled steamer on my river. Then I realised there were two of them, beating my current powerfully as they progressed. They took a long time about it, sailing only during the hours of daylight and blaming me, as all the *azungu* did, for winding in my course and not having much water in my main channel this time of year—as if I was responsible. They eventually arrived at Mpassu two days after the battle.

You will wonder why I didn't know about them earlier. After all, I'm a mirror. I reflect everything my whole length simultaneously. Of course, I saw the new steamers, the *Chirem* and the *Maravi*, as soon as they entered my river below Chamo. But I find when I reflect on what I'm reflecting, I get confined to specific places and times. It wasn't so when I was several different rivers. But since I was taught I was one river, from the lake to the Zambezi, like human beings I find my attention confined.

I worked out some time ago it's thinking stops them seeing. Now it was happening to me.

This was important to me because the *azungu* are so hard to understand. They keep themselves completely covered, except for their face and hands, and even their faces are hidden by so much hair. I can tell half a mile off when one of the Kololo is angry. His whole body declares it. But with the *azungu* you have to wait until you hear them speaking. That's when you know how angry they are. When their faces are red, it could be just the sun. The missionaries go around all the time with scarlet complexions.

It's partly that they spend so little time in my company. They believe in something called bad air, or malaria, and blame my breezes for giving them fever. So they run away from me, up into the highlands, as quickly as they can manage. When their steamers get stuck, as Living Stone's always did, they get very angry. But they all agree in blaming me, so I don't discover much else about them individually.

But the week after the battle, several Portuguese camped on my right bank and I had a chance to take a good look. There was Serpa Pinto, of course, the Major in command. There was his constant shadow, Lieutenant Afonso. There were the two other lieutenants, Álvaro Castelhões with his strange chants, and Themudo, *Sinyala* Maria's grandson. There was the naval doctor Rolão Preto, and there was Zé Miguel in command of the men from the *Prazo* Maindo.

The quarrel between him and Raposo's men had taken a fresh turn. Zé Miguel was summoned one evening to Serpa Pinto's tent. The major was slouched on a bunk bed, but Zé Miguel saluted all the same.

'I'm told you're an English spy,' said the Major.

The little Goan was unable to speak. He began mumbling, but the Major overrode him.

'You have an English name. Your sister is married to an Englishman, who used to be in the consular service and who is a friend of Ramakukan, our main enemy.'

Zé Miguel didn't know where to begin. His head was spinning and he fastened on the last fact.

'Ramakukan is dead,' he said.

The Major frowned, taking in this information.

'And how do you know that? You must be a spy.'

'No, no, no, sir. I am no spy. It is true my brother-in-law told me. But I am a loyal Portuguese, and my sister's husband does not support the English in this affair.'

'But he was in the Queen's service. Are you telling me he is a traitor to his Queen and country?'

Zé Miguel began again to mumble. This time Serpa Pinto waited him out.

'He is resolved to be neutral, sir. He is not impressed with the missionaries. He is not impressed with the traders at Mandala. He thinks the Portuguese have a better claim to this region historically. Also, he is loyal to my sister and to me. That is what he told me to say if anyone asked about him.'

The major waited again.

'That is why he allowed me to bring the men from the *prazo*.'

'Ha! And where did you learn soldiering?'

'In Lisbon. At the Escola do Exército.'

'What?'

Serpa Pinto could not credit what he was hearing. This *colono*, in charge of a bunch of irregulars from an obscure *prazo*, was a metropolitan-trained officer.

'What rank do you hold?'

'I graduated as second-lieutenant, sir. Lieutenant Maria Afonso de Rebelo was my class mate.'

Serpa Pinto strode to the entrance of the tent and shouted to the orderly outside.

'Summon Lieutenant Afonso.'

Afonso came in a few minutes, wondering what he had done wrong. Standing to attention and saluting the major, he didn't see little Zé Miguel at first.

'Do you vouch for this man?'

As Afonso turned to follow the major's gaze, his mouth fell open in astonishment. He hadn't realised his friend had joined the campaign. It was obvious from their expressions that, but for the major's presence, they would have embraced.

Afonso smiled broadly.

'Like my own brother, sir.'

So that episode ended happily. Afonso was ordered to take Zé Miguel and his two hundred men under his personal command, with special responsibility for transporting the Armstrong the length of the Shire valley, my valley.

The last to arrive were the captains of the two gunboats, with their respective crews—engineers, stokers and helmsmen. The first was captain of the *Chirem*, which he explained was the original name for my river. I never knew this, but then I never knew I was called *Shire* until Living Stone sailed my whole length. He was called Azevedo Coutinho. But after his destruction of Chiromo, he was named *Muzungo Nkulu or* 'big man', so that is what I'll call him. Despite that name, he was very young, like Álvaro and Afonso in being little more than a boy. But he had a confident, friendly face, and made a point of chatting to everybody, especially if he was in a position to be giving them orders. He talked constantly about being proud of his crew, especially the Africans. The other, called Salter de Sousa, was captain of the *Maravi*, which was supposed to be the original name of the people who lived on my banks before the Kololo came. He, too, was a boy and I could see he was very shy. He made up for it by staring constantly into the distance, past the head of the person he was speaking to, as though his mind was on horizons.

The new arrivals greeted Álvaro and Themudo with hugs and kisses, and it turned out they, too, had been fellow students, this time at a college called the Politécnica in Lisbon. Strangely, they called each other engineers, though they weren't anything like the engineers on the *Lady Nyassa* or the *James Stevenson*, who spoke with strong Scottish accents and were always covered in oil. They weren't even like Manuel Joaquim, in charge of the *Chirem*'s engines, who was short and fat with a gleaming bald head. These engineers wore smart uniforms, with polished leather boots and belts, and their moustaches were neatly trimmed with upturned points. Somehow, they were more important than Major Serpa Pinto and Lieutenant Afonso, who had attended the Colégio Militar, even though the Major was in command and had printed the *mapa rosa* with his own feet. It was a bit like the difference between Mr Consul and Chemandala, who could talk together in the same language but not sit down to eat at the same table.

Because that's what happened. Both captains, *Muzungo Nkulu* and de Sousa, opted to sleep on my bank, on hammocks strung between the poles of a hut. That way they could use fires, fueled with animal dung, to ward off mosquitos, something they couldn't do on board the steamers. But at first light, they went back on board, drew hot water from the boiler, and bathed more lavishly than I'd ever seen an *azungu* do. They are, I found out, pale all over, but otherwise exactly like other people, and their shit smells just the same.

After they were bathed, shaved and dressed and perfumed, they sat down to breakfast. That is, *Muzungo Nkulu*, Captain de Sousa, Engineer Álvaro, Themudo and the naval doctor, Rolão Preto. Not the major, not Lieutenant Afonso or Zé Miguel who were now inseparable, nor the oily engineers, the stokers or the helmsmen. The *Chirem* was more luxurious than any of the Scottish steamers, and Rolão Preto expressed his delight in eating with silver knives and forks, off porcelain plates instead of tin and, above all in having a glass of cognac as a digestive to round things off.

After breakfast, everyone was assiduous in reporting for duty and obeying orders promptly. This made Serpa Pinto suspicious, but he had his own concerns about rumours of a fresh attack by the Kololo. These men were fellow students, so he overlooked their high spirits. The second day, he looked more closely, and the third morning he ordered Afonso to join the breakfast party on board the *Chirem*. Warned by the doctor, *Muzungo Nkulu* and his friends entertained the lieutenant lavishly, but omitted the cognac from their repast.

Meanwhile, the major had sent out two men as spies and they returned with the news that the Kololo were gathering at Chipatula's old village at the Ruo junction, where his son Chitaonga was now chief. Mlauri was still sulking on Mount Thyolo. Many of his warriors had deserted him and joined Chitaonga instead. More men were arriving daily, so they would not attack immediately. But an attack would happen soon, and this time they would be better armed.

Wishing to discuss this with the two captains, next morning the major intruded on their breakfast. They didn't have time to hide the bottle, and when the major saw it his temper broke.

'This is contrary to my express orders,' he shouted.

Seizing the bottle, he flung it over the side. As it sank, I felt a faint burning sensation and saw that the label read *Courvoisier*.

The young men expected to be disciplined. Instead, Serpa Pinto left them abruptly. An hour later, when *Muzungo Nkulu* and Álvaro approached the hut where the major had his headquarters, they were told by a guard he was not to be disturbed.

That afternoon, the season's first rains arrived, with a series of thunderstorms that drove all humans to take shelter. My surface was pitted like the hulls of the first paddle steamers when they were beached for inspection, and turned white at each flash of lightening. Water poured in a torrent from the decks of the paddle steamers, and the creek where Álvaro had dug his line of defence became a foaming river that would have stopped any army. Water poured past the huts and only those on stilts or with raised verandas escaped flooding.

At daybreak when the skies cleared, the annual miracle of termites rising with wings from their nests occurred, millions of them in a silver mist, to mate in flight before falling to the earth. It was a time of great excitement for the soldiers and the villagers alike, the war forgotten as they rushed around collecting the creatures, now wingless, termites in clay pots. This was obviously something the *azungu* had never witnessed. When they were offered fried *ngumbi* to eat, they turned away their faces in disgust.

Muzungo Nkulu and Álvaro tried calling on the major again. This time they were told he had a fever.

'I doubt it's fever,' said Dr. Preto, 'He has these attacks. He reckons he needs daily doses of magnesia. Without them he loses control. As you saw.'

'I think I may have some magnesia,' said *Muzungo Nkulu*.

He went below deck to the steamer's medicine chest and returned with a blue bottle sealed with a thick cork. The label had a picture of a unicorn with Magnesium Tablets in black letters.

'Efficacious in preventing Depression, Dizziness, Stress, Muscle Spasms,' read *Muzungo Nkulu*. 'Does he suffer from any of these?'

'He's afraid of spiders,' said the doctor maliciously.

On shore, people were still chasing termites, though most had finished swarming and their discarded gauze wings littered the wet earth.

Muzungo Nkulu shouted to one of them.

'Call Lieutenant Afonso.'

To his guests on the steamer, he added 'We mustn't forget that this is a very distinguished man.'

Afonso arrived carrying a small specimen jar in which he had been collecting termites, thin brown grubs three-quarters of an inch long. Some had shed their wings after being captured, and these stuck to the sides of the jar.

'Ugh,' said the doctor. 'What are you going to do with those?'

'Eat them,' said Temudu.

'What?'

'Why not? They're delicious. I used to love them as a child.'

'They're specimens,' said Afonso stiffly. 'Have you forgotten this is a scientific expedition.'

'Quite correct,' said *Muzungo Nkulu*.

He handed him the blue bottle of magnesium tablets.

'Would you be kind enough to give these to the major with my compliments. Would you please say that Doctor Preto is anxious to be of service to him professionally.'

The tactic worked.

Half an hour later, Serpa Pinto emerged from his headquarters looking fresh and purposeful. Whatever the medical benefits of magnesia, the tablets had restored his good-humour. Stepping aboard the *Chirem*, he asked, without a hint of suspicion, if they had breakfasted well.

Then he delivered his instructions. Next day at first light, the *Chirem* under Captain *Muzungo Nkulu* was to proceed cautiously upstream with sufficient wood for three days. Themudo would accompany him, along with the one-legged pilot from the *John Bowie*. Six sailors would man the guns and he would carry thirty-four Landeens armed with rifles. The purpose was purely reconnaissance. They should check the Kololo position at the Ruo junction, their numbers and disposition, and report back. However, if they were attacked, they should use every weapon at their disposal in self-defence.

Muzungo Nkulu asked permission to take three stokers to ensure maximum efficiency, and the request was approved. Major and Captain exchanged salutes, and the major returned to his hut.

'Back to his cognac,' muttered Doctor Preto as soon as he was out of ear-shot.

'What?'

'He's got a bottle of Hennessy under his bed. That's what his fever was all about.'

The young men stared, and fell about laughing.

36 Shire

The Ruo River is the largest of my tributaries, almost a companion. Its source is on Mount Mulanje, a huge plateau, which I can see from my banks, rising in the west like a vision of ice and sunlight. The waters of this river are cold and fresh and when they join mine, as I emerge from the stink and sweat of Dambinyi Marsh, I feel as refreshed as if I'd just leapt down another series of cataracts.

From there down to Mpassu, or from Mpassu paddling north as the *Chirem* was doing, is the part of my river where my banks are most heavily populated. I like that English word. Populated because they're popular. People like my clean stream, which is always there, even in the driest of dry seasons. The current is slow, which is good for fishing, and it's deep, which means the fish are large. One *chambo* or catfish can feed a family. The soil is good, and the banks are high enough to contain most floods. Even the islands, and I own many, are thick with acacia trees because they have been established for many generations—not like the islands in my delta, which can change with the seasons, and are treeless. Some of the islands, especially above Mulolo, have whole villages on them, with crops of beans and millet and the new millet they call maize. There are places where my stream divides into so many channels I resemble an inland delta. But I gather them together again, like an *azungu* woman combing her hair, and I never lose sight of my course, as happens in the marshes.

The *Chirem* was the fastest paddle-steamer I had seen, and though the rains had started my current was still slow. For once, the people running along the bank couldn't keep pace with a boat that drove upstream as fast as the *John Bowie* went down river. They were alarmed, of course, by the Portuguese flag. The large villages on my right bank, like Tengani's and Nyamula's, were used to living free of the Portuguese—except for raids by Matekenya's people from the other side. But they were no friends of the Kololo, and they knew that was where the steamer was heading.

I had watched the two armies on my right and left banks take four weeks to travel from Chamo to Mpassu. I had seen the *John Bowie* take four days making the same journey. Now the *Chirem* travelled an equivalent distance in just seven hours, taking the Kololo completely by surprise since there hadn't been time for Chitaonga's spies to give warning.

His capital was on the left bank, just above my confluence with the Ruo. It was a large village, swelled by deserters from Mlauri, who had come to rejoin battle. But by now it was mid-afternoon, and the active part of the day was past. The women had returned from the fields, where yesterday's rain had drawn them to begin planting the next season's crops. The groups of men were well into their second gourd of millet beer. People sat in circles on the shady verandas of their houses. Nobody was prepared for fighting, nor in the mood for it.

Muzungo Nkulu's orders were only to make a reconnaissance. He was to fire only if attacked first.

The captain was young and very cautious. Immediately opposite the village, my river is narrow, making a sharp curve to the left under a high bank. But a little downstream of this position is a group of islands, and the *Chirem* passed between them, edging forward slowly until the village could be seen clearly without the steamer being fully visible. For a long time, nothing happened. *Muzungo Nkulu* was standing on the bridge counting the houses and taking note of the village's slightly elevated position, when a group of youths on the right bank threw some stones, following them up with sling shots. Some of the stones clattered on the deck and provoked one of the Landeens into firing warning shots.

At this, the village was aroused from its languor. Men grabbed their weapons from their huts and raced like columns of ants to positions just short of the river bank where, it soon became clear, were pre-dug trenches, like the ones Álvaro had prepared in Mpassu. Within minutes, the steamer was swept by musket fire, and a fresh fusillade began from the opposite bank. The shots were mainly small stones, but *Muzungo Nkulu* was wounded in the left hand along with two of the Landeens, and two blades of the huge paddle were dented.

And so it happened, the most terrible event I have ever reflected. I can barely credit what the Portuguese did.

The *Chirem* had two guns, fore and aft. I had thought they were some kind of navigation equipment, but now that *Muzungo Nkulu* ordered them unwrapped, I could see the one before the bridge had twelve rifle-like barrels, arranged in a line and mounted on what looked like a capstan screwed to the deck. The other, to the rear, had five larger barrels arranged in a circle, again mounted on a structure that held it steady while it was swiveled to take aim. Each gun had six men in attendance. I saw both pointed to face the village while the steamer edged forward clear of the islands. Then the first gun fired.

I have heard the missionaries reading from their Holy Book, *'I will show wonders in heaven above and signs in the earth beneath: blood, and fire, and vapour of smoke: the sun shall be turned into darkness and the moon into blood.'* It puzzled me that they enjoyed these words, but now I knew what they meant.

It was as though my current flowed backwards so that, although I was appalled and confused, at the same time I mirrored exactly what was happening. From the first gun, it was as if a thousand Martini-Henries had fired at once, then fired again and again, a horizontal hail of lead pellets, without pausing. The second gun was like the cannon at Mpassu, but five of them, as the barrels revolved, hurling thousands of balls the size of goose eggs into the village.

The harvest of death was over in three minutes. When the guns paused for re-loading, there was absolute silence. The very baobabs seemed stunned. Then a terrible wailing arose, from dogs, chickens, women, babies and old men who had little idea what had happened but knew catastrophe had struck. It arose from the village, as the pigeons rose in spirals, followed by spirals of smoke as fire spread through the huts. People who could flee did so in panic, leaving behind the dead and horribly wounded. At first, they ran in widening circles, then they made for the forest as they realised the enemy was on my river. How many hundreds were blown to pieces I shall never know. The battle was over in those three minutes. When the guns were swiveled to train on the right bank, where the young men had first started throwing stones, there was no one to be seen.

Muzungo Nkulu had been on the bridge all this time, with a rag wrapped round his left hand, squinting though a long tube. As I say, he was little more than a boy, and he wasn't sure what to do next. He had been attacked and the enemy was routed, that much was obvious. But should he go in pursuit? He seemed as stunned as they were. He had powerful guns, but his force was a tiny one. He had six sailors, three stokers and thirty-four Landeens whom he didn't entirely trust. But sitting in the middle of the stream when the enemy had fled seemed unheroic, and he was anxious to be a hero.

He ordered the steamer forward, approaching the bank on the Chiromo side, and landed with four sailors and twenty-eight of the Landeens. They found the trenches filled with bodies, and bodies everywhere on the approaches to the village. There were scattered body parts and much blood. The village itself was abandoned but, in the thick forest half a mile off, survivors had taken refuge, carrying their wounded. Suddenly, standing there with his small company, between the inhabited forest and the river, he felt vulnerable. With night approaching, he ordered a retreat. Five prisoners were captured, and on the Company flagpole on the promontory between my river and my tributary, he hoisted a Portuguese flag. Then he withdrew to the *Chirem* with his men, reversed to the safety of the islands midstream, mounting an all-night guard on the guns.

Next morning, Serpa Pinta arrived in the *Maravi* to resolve his doubts. The battle of Chiromo had been a great victory. Four thousand Kololo, armed by the English with Martini-Henries and other high-velocity guns, had been repulsed with the loss of just two mercenaries and two Portuguese wounded, including their brave commander. That the Portuguese flag was flying above the town was sufficient proof. Chiromo was officially re-christened Vila Coutinho, and a great feast was ordained.

The main part of the army was still advancing from Mpassu, but news of the feasting gave them wings. They occupied Chitaonga's village where they found goats and chickens in abundance, along with maize flour and millet beer, and even two crates of whisky. Chitaonga shared his father's taste for the drink that had led to his death. Of course there was dancing, and for the first time I saw the Landeens doing their war dance, advancing in new moon formation, banging their assegais on their tall shields and stamping as they sang *Muzungo Nkulu's* praises, calling him the new M'pezene, after their own war chief in the south. Compared to this, the *likuba* drums of the men from Sena and the *madudu* drums from Manganja, were less intimidating.

Meanwhile, Serpa Pinto and *Muzungo Nkulu*, together with Engineer Álvaro and Lieutenants Afonso, Zé Miguel, Themudu and the doctor Rolão Preto, were squeezed round the table on the *Chirem* eating a celebratory dinner of corned beef with *nsima*. They were in high spirits, thrilled and a little envious at what the *Muzungo Nkulu* had achieved. Even the lack of a *digestivo*, following Serpa Pinto's orders, did not spoil their mood.

Then a canoe drew up alongside the *Chirem*, bearing a messenger with a telegram. It was marked *com urgencia* and addressed to Serpa Pinto.

Opening it, the major turned very pale but said not a word. He rose to his feet, laid the telegram on the table, and went ashore, secluding himself in his hut until the following morning. Álvaro was nearest. Glancing at the telegram, he read its content aloud, his high-pitched voice choking. King Luís of Portugal was dead. He had passed away four weeks earlier on October the 19th.

In the shocked silence, Afonso was the first to recover.

'He was the popular. He was the good. We shall never see his like'.

He had never met the king or even seen him. But he had been named after the *Infante,* and he was accurately quoting the common opinion.

Rolão Preto located another bottle of Corvoissier in the depths of the steamer, and they solemnly drank a succession of toasts to the dead king and his successor.

37 Shire

The events of the next two months were the hardest of all for me to mirror and reflect on. I'm used to seeing people do strange things and the *azungu* strangest of all, like singing a funeral song when they're happy and thinking a loin cloth on a pole makes them owner of the land. I'd just watched death on a scale I'd never before imagined, worse than even the biggest of my floods, worse than an earthquake. But the folly upon folly of what happened next stirred my mirror to its depths.

At dawn next morning, to the sound of a bugle, *Muzungo Nkulu* was raising the Portuguese flag when he stopped at half-mast, something I'd never seen before. After he saluted, he was summoned to the major's hut. The major was leaving for consultations with the Governor at Mozambique Island. In his absence, *Muzungo Nkulu* was appointed as Military Governor of Chire with the responsibility 'to occupy this large region'. It was a declaration of war, even at the moment he was leaving the battlefield. I never saw him again.

I said before how strange it was to me that the English should have built the gunboats the Portuguese were using to attack them. Now, in the middle of the war, the English and other steamers continued to sail up and down my river without hindrance. It seemed war and trade were different things. Once the *Lady Nyassa* was stopped at gunpoint but, just as it looked as though things were turning nasty, *Muzungu Nkulu* explained he was carrying some mail for Chemandala and asked for it to be delivered safely. Then the *James Stevenson* was stopped while *Muzungo Nkulu* claimed it should be flying a Portuguese flag. The flag was lowered just to please him, but as soon as the steamer was round the next bend it was raised again. Mbewe, as always, was piloting.

Chitaonga had refused to join the attack on Mpassu, and when Mlauri fled to Thyolo Mountain, he re-occupied his father's old capital, half way through Dambinyi Marsh on my right bank. It was there, as the *James Stevenson* continued upstream, that Mbewe took the news of the Portuguese king´s death. Chitaonga's people were overjoyed. The English Queen had won, despite being a woman. The Kololo assumed there would be forty days of mourning with no one in control, as had happened when Ramakukan died. The further news that the Portuguese major had gone away, leaving a mere boy in charge, confirmed this. For the time being, there would be no war.

Mbewe's next message, ten days later, was that *Muzungo Nkulu* was preparing to invade. At this, Chitaonga and his brother Chikusi were panic-stricken. They took it for granted *Muzungo Nkulu* was already steaming upriver through the marsh with his big guns, and that they were going to suffer the same fate as those at Chiromo. No plans were made to resist, only to evacuate the village as soon as the sentinels gave news of the steamer's approach.

Why that didn't happen is a mystery to this day. *Muzungo Nkulu* had the whole river at the mercy of those two guns, the one with its twelve rifle-like barrels, arranged in a line, the other with its five larger barrels arranged in a circle. What stopped him, I don't know. Perhaps it was the memory of how exposed he felt when he went ashore after the battle at Chiromo. Surveying the ditches and raising the flag with just a handful of men, some of whom he didn't trust, had felt dangerous. He had been relieved to get back on board the Chirem and retreat to a safe distance. He had been even more relieved when Serpa Pinto arrived next morning and, soon afterwards, the main army. Winning a battle was one thing, securing the territory another.

Another perhaps is that he was fixated on my river. Every bit as much as Engineer Álvaro with his strange chants, he had this notion that I belonged to Portugal and that the English were trying to steal me. His instructions were 'to occupy both banks of the Chire' and he took that literally. It never struck him that in Dambinyi I had no banks. He could so easily have gone round, staying on firm ground the whole way and capturing Ramakukan's original capital, which would have made him master of the region. But no, he decided he had to follow my course, even when I myself had little idea what my course was, and without the help of his steamer with its big guns.

A further mystery is why he chose to follow my right bank, as he called it. His first target was Mitengo, Chipatula's old capital, now owned by Chitaonga who was his main enemy. But Mitengo is on the left bank, on a bluff some twenty-five miles north of Chiromo. To attack Chitaonga, his whole army was going to have to find a way across my river. There were two other rivers to be crossed, two of my tributaries called the Mkombedzi-wa-Fodya and the Mwanza, in the language of the people who now live there. He could have avoided all this by following the edge of the marsh on the opposite side, using Thyolo mountain to guide him, and attacking Mitengo from dry land.

So there you have it. This handsome, cheerful man, barely out of his teens, decided to invade Dambinyi Marsh with eight Portuguese at the head of an army of eighteen hundred men. The Portuguese included Engineers Álvaro and Themudo, along with Lieutenants Afonso and Zé Miguel, together in charge of the Armstrong that had won the battle for Mpassu. There was an elderly captain called Augusto Brito, who had heart problems, and three white sergeants. Lieutenant Salter de Sousa of the *Maravi* was instructed to follow with ammunition and supplies. I told you I had heard *Muzungo Nkulu* pacing the deck of the *Chirem* and calculating how many men he had—a thousand men from Sena, two hundred from Boror near Quelimane, two hundred and fifty from Maganja next to my river delta, plus two hundred dog-eaters from across the Zambezi at Gwengwe, two hundred from Maindo under Zé Miguel, and two hundred under Raposo. All these men, less the one hundred and ninety-eight who had died in Ndindi, he elected to lead on foot into the vast wilderness of Dambinyi, the marsh where even I lose my sense of direction.

I said he wasn't sure he trusted them. Nor were they sure they trusted him. Even the Landeens, who had called him the new M'pezene, had their doubts. They were used to marching in columns, covering up to forty miles a day with their regular pacing. Hacking their way through a swamp was not their style. As for the men from Sena, they knew what had happened to their fellow countrymen in Ndindi.

Dambinyi is nine times the size of Ndindi. I'm the same river but, spread out over so much swampland, Dambinyi is shallower. You don't drown in Dambinyi simply by missing the path, though you can drown in one of my streams. On the other hand, there are no obvious paths, certainly none leading from the south to the north. There are fishermen's paths, but they come in from the right bank or the left bank to the stream where they do their fishing. They're short, and they're useless for armies trying to do what *Muzungo Nkulu* was trying to do. As for those streams, well, they're simply where there are signs of a current. They're not my course. But there is a certain brown current, with swirling cabbage plants and floating islands of papyrus. Sometimes it's a mile across and shallow, sometimes a mere fifty yards and deep, and never the same from one season to another. Pilots like Mbewe can spot it, and that's how he makes his living from my river that at times doesn't know what I'm doing.

Muzungo Nkulu's army had to find its way through the reeds. The reeds were evidence of solid ground, not dry but passable a foot or so down. Every now and then, he would reach an island and pass more freely, but then plunge back into the reeds, keeping as close as possible to the drifting brown current. He had secured three guides, promising to pay them but also taking the precaution of seizing their wives and children as hostages back at Chiromo. There was to be no repetition of the events at Ndindi. He had also recruited a team to cut the reeds, supplying them with machetes of a quality they had never seen before. However, a path two yards wide and knee deep in water only allowed three men to pass at a time. Before long, his army of eighteen hundred was strung out over two miles.

That army was carrying all the goods needed for an invasion—rifles, ammunition, sacks of flour, with tinned meat for the *azungu*. But *Muzungo Nkulu* had also brought the Armstrong mountain gun, which had to be carried by Zé Miguel's men in three parts, the two wheels needing five men each, the carriage a further four, and the barrel three men. Such heavy loads made them sink thigh deep in the slime. Each step became a process of hauling one leg from the sucking mud as the other became embedded, at times it took an hour to progress a hundred yards. Meanwhile, it rained incessantly. When the march was halted at dusk, the different groups of the divided army made their own arrangements for surviving the night, looking for islands and building reed shelters in the absence of trees. The leading party of *azungu*— *Muzungo Nkulu*, Álvaro and Afonso—cowered in a fisherman's hurt, eating maize meal and tinned beef, while clouds of mosquitos and hippo flies made their night a misery.

That first day, Chitaonga and his headmen couldn't believe the folly they were witnessing. Their warriors wanted to attack, but the chief restrained them, suspecting some trick. Next morning, spies reported that the *Chirem* and the *Maravi* were still anchored at Chiromo. So, by mid-morning, when *Muzungo Nkulu's* army was strung out even further, the Kololo began their skirmishing. They knew Dambinyi intimately, advancing down known paths to ambush the stragglers. Attacking the rear of the column, they thinned out *Muzungo Nkulu's* army without him even knowing what was happening. Dozens were killed silently, by spear or poisoned arrow, while dozens more fled down the same paths their attackers had used for their approach. By dusk on that second day, *Muzungo Nkulu* had already lost a further three hundred men.

I say 'further' because men had died, too, at the column's head. Two of the men bearing the bronze barrel of the cannon had been seized during the night by crocodiles when answering the call of nature. Three of the reed cutters had been bitten by green mambas, and one had died during the night while the others remained helpless. This was a danger impossible to avoid. As the men hacked with their machetes at the base of the reeds or the papyrus grass, whatever was lodged in them fell towards them, and the snakes were so camouflaged as to be invisible.

That third morning, while the attacks to the rear continued, the advance party encountered other problems. Hacking through the reeds in the torrential rain, and climbing gladly to yet another island with a fisherman's hut for temporary shelter, they found themselves surrounded by elephants. This couldn't have happened in Ndindi but

Dambinyi, as I remarked, is shallower, and herds of elephants sometimes intrude to feast on water chestnuts or hyacinth roots. Normally, this wouldn't have been a problem. The elephants would have retreated as humans approached. But *Muzungo Nkulu* couldn't resist taking a potshot, and he happened to wound an adult tusker who became enraged. Trumpeting his fury, he charged the island, trampling the hut and killing two more of the cannon-bearers, before a fusillade from Sena men, who were professional elephant hunters, laid him low. The result was a day's delay as they cut up the meat and prepared a feast, joined by more and more as the straggling army began to catch up. *Muzungo Nkulu* appointed four bearers to carry the tusks back to Chiromo.

So the fifth morning began with the army once again united, though some four hundred men short and only half way towards their first destination at Mitengo. As *Muzungo Nkulu* began his march, the problems recurred. After couple of hours, the column was strung out as before, the men at the rear waiting their turn to use the narrow track cut between the reeds, and resenting their vulnerability to ambush. For each man felled by a silent spear from the papyrus, three more opted to desert. Chitaonga's warriors were smart enough not to harass them once they had thrown down their weapons, so the steady attrition continued.

That afternoon, disaster struck. The advance party of Zé Miguel's men was crossing a creek when one of the group carrying the gun's left wheel slipped. The little Goan slithered forward to stop it as, agonizingly slowly, it rolled to the edge of the bank and toppled into the mud on top of him, wedging itself at an angle, axle deep in the sucking slime. Five men jumped into the creek trying to free him. They grabbed his legs, which were thrashing wildly, but the upper part of his body was wedged fast. Others took hold of the rim of the wheel, but lifting it where there was no secure foothold and no room for more hands, was impossible.

Afonso rushed up and plunged into the creek, pulling frantically at Zé Miguel's limbs, trying to coordinate the men to raise the side of the wheel that was pinning his friend. He and *Muzungo Nkulu* were supposed to be engineers. Had one of the steamers been close by, they would have all the lifting equipment they needed. But in Dambinyi in the pouring rain, with only their bare hands and rifles, they felt as helpless as children as little Zé Miguel's kicking gradually slowed and then ceased.

'Oh Holy Mary!' wept Afonso in despair, crossing himself.

'We have the flagpole', said *Muzungo Nkulu* eventually.

One of the items the bearers were carrying was a white-painted flagpole, to be erected at the head of the valley to mark their conquest. The pole was brought forward and Afonso thrust one end through the spokes of the wheel.

'It might take the weight', said *Muzungo Nkulu*. 'But we've no fulcrum'.

The word was new to me. Gradually I realised they were looking for a boulder or a tree trunk to wedge beneath the pole. But, of course, in Dambinyi, there are no rocks or trees.

'There was a canoe,' said Afonso, 'next to that last island we crossed.'

'Bring it,' ordered *Muzungo Nkulu*.

Two hours later, a dozen men returned, carrying a small dugout canoe. Being the kind of canoe the fishermen use in Dambinyi, it came with the long stinkwood pole used for controlling canoes where the water is too shallow for paddles. The canoe was laid up side down parallel to the wheel, and the second pole inserted through the spokes. Both poles were wedged against the canoe and, with men in the water to help with the lifting, the wheel was levered clear.

It was far too late for Zé MIguel. There was not a mark on his body as Afonso knelt beside it, weeping helplessly.

All they could do was to bury him there in Dambinyi, in the highest ground they could find. They wiped as much of the clinging mud as they could from his uniform, being careful to cover his face with a Portuguese flag. Afonso recited as much of the burial service as he could remember from his days as an altar boy, and fashioned a rough cross from the stinkwood pole.

38 Shire

It seems beyond belief that the Company's steamers were still passing up and down my river, but when the *James Stevenson* arrived at Mitengo, Chitaonga seized the chance to send Mbewe and Mphetomwanyama to speak with Mr Consul at Mandala.

His message was that he had put his mark on Mr Acting Consul's piece of paper, along with Katunga, Mulilima and Masea, to ensure that the English Queen would protect him from the Portuguese. Now, even though the Portuguese king was dead, Portuguese guns had destroyed his capital at Chiromo and driven him and his people to live like wild animals in the bush. Was the English Queen sleeping? Was she drunk on millet beer?

On their return, Mphetomwanyama was insistent. As Chitaonga's messenger, he had spoken with the Queen's messenger, with Mbewe acting as his interpreter. Mbewe would now convey to Chitaonga what the Queen's messenger had said and he, Mphetomwanyama, would translate.

Mbewe said, 'Mr Acting Consul says the treaty declared that you agreed not to enter into any Agreement, Treaty, or Arrangement with any Foreign Government except through and with the consent of the Government of Her Majesty the Queen of England. That is all.'

Mphetomwanyama translated, 'The paper said we wouldn't sign any other paper. That is all.'

'However, Mr Acting Consul says he has declared this country a British Protectorate.'

Mphetomwanyama interpreted this as, 'We now belong to the English.'

'But,' said Mbewe, 'first the Queen must say whether or not she wants your country.'

'We will all be dead before the English help us,' translated Mphetomwanyama.

'Mr Acting Consul says that, as the Queen's loyal subjects, we should fight against the Portuguese invasion.'

'We will all be dead before the English help us,' repeated Mphetomwanyama.

Surrounded by his elders, Chitaonga considered their situation. The riddle of the treaties he dismissed as foolishness. It seemed all the English were drunk on millet beer.

To this, the elders assented with some laughter.

'Mr Acting Consul says I am the Queen's loyal subject. You are my loyal subjects, as are all the people of Mitengo, and the refugees from Chiromo. You pay me tribute, and I give you my protection. Is that not so?'

Again, the elders assented. That was how society worked.

'Whether the people of Katunga, Mulilima and Masea are my subjects, or the subjects of Katunga, Mulilima and Masea, is a matter to be decided. Since Ramakukan died, some things are uncertain. But the people of Katunga, Mulilima and Masea pay their taxes to their chiefs and are protected, in war, and in famine. Do I speak truly?'

There was no denying, this was supposed to be how things happened.

'I am not the Queen's subject. I pay no taxes to the Queen. She may agree to protect us, she may not. Either she is confused, or Mr Acting Consul is confused. The matter is, once again, foolishness.'

The elders exchanged nervous glances. The argument was undeniable, but what conclusion was looming?

'The Portuguese are just across the river. They have left their big guns in Chiromo. Their army is stretched out in a country they do not understand. They are at our mercy.'

Chitaonga paused till he had their full attention. He knew his authority was at stake, not just in Mitengo but for the whole of Kololo territory.

'We shall attack them at cockcrow. The *mirandu* is over.'

For *Muzungo Nkulu* and his men, the fifth night of the campaign was miserable. Afonso was inconsolable, telling *Muzungu Nkulu* and Álvaro about all his dealings with Zé Miguel—about their days at the Escola, about the trip to Sintra and Mafra where Father Anselmo had blessed the little Goan and his friend Alfredo, about his regret that he hadn't visited Zé Miguel's family home in Maindo, he just hadn't realised it was so close, about how, if only they had moved the wheel quicker, his life might have been saved. For all three young men, it was the first time they had lost a companion in a campaign.

Then the night turned to terror. The creek by which they had camped, the one where Zé Miguel drowned, was a path used by hippos emerging from my river to forage in the villagers' *dambo* gardens, before returning at first light.

I like hippos. They appreciate me. On land, they're huge, lumbering creatures, as dangerous as elephants, but the moment they re-enter my stream, they become tame and even elegant, floating in groups or making graceful underwater leaps in slow motion. Unlike fish, which take me completely for granted and whose memories seem to last about five seconds, hippos know when they're at home, making little snuffles of delight. It's always a pleasure when I emerge from cataracts or a stretch of rapids to round a placid, green curve and find a dozen of them, with their pink ears and noses, and the bull hippo yawning as though he's ready to swallow a baobab.

But, of course, for *Muzungo Nkulu's* men, it wasn't like that. They were camped right next to the hippos' track, and hippos don't like to be diverted. Worse, they can run faster than men, and with their short, stumpy legs they don't slither about in the mud. So, after banging pots and pans and firing their rifles in the air, there was nothing for the Portuguese to do but to run for it, abandoning their supplies and munitions and leaving the parts of the Armstrong to be trampled into the mud. That was before midnight. Before dawn, when they thought they were safe, the same hippo stampede was repeated in reverse.

As they reassembled and prepared to resume their march, it seemed Chitaonga might be right. This didn't look like a victorious army. *Muzungo Nkulu* could only guess how many men were still strung out behind him. Even the Landeens, whom he trusted, though not entirely, looked bedraggled. This wasn't their kind of warfare. Of the thousand men from Sena, only some two hundred and fifty, mostly experienced elephant hunters, were still near the head of the column. As for the *azungu*, their arms and faces swollen with mosquito bites, they were beginning to bicker. I'd seen it happen before. Even the closest of friends, even brothers like Living Stone and his younger brother, Charles, would become moody and quarrelsome in the steamy heat of my valley, and I would recognise the symptoms of fever.

Engineer Álvaro, with his gloomy chants, was the first to fall ill. His colleagues were used to his solitary ramblings, so paid no attention when he kept to himself, muttering away. But I heard him. His grumblings actually made good sense, but he was not the man to challenge his superiors or question their thoughts and actions, so I knew he was not himself. This march through the swamp was pointless. They were on the wrong side of the river to attack their main target, and if they tried to cross it in canoes they would be massacred. As for carrying the parts of that murderous Armstrong, what was the point when they had modern guns on the steamers? Where was the *Maravi*, which was supposed to have joined them by now? There was nothing glorious in bad tactics, nothing Portuguese about folly.

> I curse you, foul, stinking river
> With your mosquitoes and crocodiles,
> The *terra ignota* of fever:
> You are for us an endless ordeal,
> I curse your impassable marshes
>   O Portuguese Shire.

That day, as he stumbled some fifty yards in the rear, watched impassively by a group of Landeens who knew when a man was at breaking point, his grumblings were given point. They reached the Mkombedzi-wa-Fodya river, one of my larger tributaries, which barred their passage. There was nothing for it but to turn upstream, following its course until *Muzungo Nkulu* and his men actually left Dambinyi behind, reaching the solid ground of the first *dambo* gardens, where the river could be forded. From there, of course, they could easily have continued overland to capture Ramakukan's old village in the north. But no, having crossed the river, *Muzungo Nkulu* elected to re-enter the marsh, with the aim of attacking Mitengo.

First, though, they enjoyed the luxury of spending one night on dry land, sleeping in huts they had commandeered and cooking over open fires. For once, the mosquitos and jiggers seemed bearable. Álvaro, though, had a sweaty night, and when they moved on next morning, he had to be carried in a *machila*, the risk of abandoning him, even under armed guard, being too great. This time, using fishermen's paths, their journey was easier, so shortly after midday, the army was able to make camp immediately opposite Mitengo, and *Muzungo Nkulu* summoned his officers to explain his strategy.

Obviously, they had to cross the river. He reckoned, however, that by raking the opposite bank with shells from the Armstrong, while posting groups of men with high-velocity rifles at vantage points, they could provide cover for sufficient men to cross in canoes and establish a beach-head, which would then provide cover for the rest of the army to cross. This seemed sensible, and Álvaro who had insisted on being present, shivering in a blanket, felt ashamed of his doubts. Afonso began planning where to position his artillery.

It was Capitão Brito who raised a difficulty.

'There are no canoes.'

'What? There are always canoes'.

'None that I can find.'

It was true. Chitaonga had ordered all the fishermen's canoes to be drawn up on my left bank.

Muzungo Nkulu's army had seen several canoes in their slow march through the swamp. But they were tiny affairs, managed with a pole, holding three fishermen at most. In any case, they were back across the Mkombedzi-wa-Fodya river, a day's march behind them.

Muzungo Nkulu stared at my broad and deep water, reflecting the profound blue of the sky in my bosom of limpid silver. How to get across? Swimming was too dangerous. There were crocodiles. There were no trees to build rafts. I was too wide for a rope bridge, and in any case, how could the far side be protected? Sending men to search ahead for canoes meant many hours of reed cutting. There was nothing for it but to accept a day's delay, and send men back for the ones they had seen. At least, they would be able to return by the river, rather than carry them overland. He also ordered that their position should be fortified against any attack from the river.

Next morning, they had barely stirred when Chitaonga's men began attacking from the land. It was a horrible battle that lasted until late afternoon. The Kololo did the same as when they had ambushed the rear of *Muzungo Nkulu's* column. They attacked swiftly from the reeds, in a marsh they knew thoroughly, and withdrew with equal swiftness when the Portuguese tried to counter-attack. They had another tactic that frustrated resistance. When they fired a shot, they immediately changed their position, so that any return fire was wasted. They had time on their sides. It was no matter to them if the battle lasted a week.

Muzungo Nkulu still had some four hundred men to deploy, including the experienced elephant hunters from across the Zambezi and men from the prazos. The remaining seven Portuguese were well armed with Martini-Henries. He ordered Afonso to turn the Armstrong to face inland—a complicated operation since the wheels had sunk in the riverside mud, so it had to be dismantled and re-erected. Finally, with Captain Brito's help, this was managed and a single shot was fired, not at any target that was visible. The gunners simply pointed the gun at the endless sea of reeds, and fired.

I'd heard it before at Mpassu, so the noise didn't take me so much by surprise and didn't stop my current. It was much less frightening than the two guns at Chiromo, but, for the moment at least, the cannon halted the Kololo attack. I told you the wars I was used to were mainly about who could make most noise, and this gun was loud. It forced the Kololo to pause. It hardly killed any of them, and I never heard the shell explode. In Dambinyi, it probably buried itself in the mud, but it gave the Portuguese some breathing space.

The attackers quickly realised the gun's limitations, mapped by the corridor of flattened reeds. To the right and left of that they were safe, until the gun was re-positioned, and shifting and re-loading it took time. So they resumed in the original manner, attacking from the reeds, killing and wounding a few men, and withdrawing quickly. *Muzungo Nkulu* responded by ordering Captain Brito to get his men to fix knives to the muzzles of their rifles. I'd never seen this before. When the Armstrong was fired for the second time, the men followed it up by charging the reeds. There was fighting, horrible fighting, hand to hand, knife to spear, red eye to red eye, right there in my swamp, and who knows to this day how many died and for what? It didn't resolve anything. The Kololo retreated, and the survivors of *Muzungo Nkulu's* army returned to the river bank. After all, the Kololo had all week. All month, if necessary.

I lost count of how often this happened. Chitaonga's men attacked, the Armstrong boomed, and men with knives ran into the reeds to repel the enemy. Each time the gun was fired, a few more reeds were flattened, so that the area Countinho's men were protecting grew steadily wider. But, increasingly exposed by their own fire, they were still well within range of the Kololo arrows and muskets, and still unable to see their targets. It was hard to tell how many had been killed or wounded in the reeds, but their numbers were certainly diminishing. Even firing the gun was dangerous. The Kololo had worked out how long it took to re-load, and for those minutes the gunners were fair game. Afonso was still running backwards and forwards between blasts, but two of his gunners were wounded and another was lying in the mud, probably dead.

Then I heard the beat of a rear-wheeled steamer approaching. It wasn't one I recognised, not one of the Company steamers, but it resembled *Muzungo Nkulu's* own ship, the *Chirem*, which I knew was still at Chiromo. Before its name was reflected in my surface, it gave three whoops on its whistle, and *Muzungo Nkulu's* men started cheering. It was the *Maravi*, arriving in the nick of time. Of course, the very sight of the steamer made the Kololo retreat from the reeds and creeks where they had been hidden.

'Where in the name of God have you been?', shouted *Muzungo Nkulu*. 'Fire at once to the port side.'

'Sir', said de Sousa. 'I am captain of this vessel. You do not give me orders.'

'*Por amor do Deus*, I am in command of this expedition. Fire immediately on the right bank.'

De Sousa hesitated, then complied, raking the reed plumes with a horizontal hail of lead bullets, continuing without pausing to re-load for a whole minute.

'Now starboard,' ordered Muzungo Nkulu.

The twelve barrel gun was trained on Mitengo, and another storm of hail burst on Chitaonga's village, from which all but the elderly and the previously wounded had fled. The battle was over.

'I have been four days on the river,' said Captain Salter de Sousa. '*Foi difícil.*'

Nine days by land, four days by river!

'It began with that scoundrel of a pilot,' said de Sousa. 'They told me he was the best on the whole river. He didn't want to work for me, so I forced him at gunpoint. Then deliberately, he ran me aground just where the marsh begins. Before my man could react, he had jumped overboard and vanished in the reeds. I used the Nordenfelt to rake the reeds, but I don't know whether or not I killed him.'

The Nordenfelt was the gun with twelve rifle-like barrels arranged in a line, mounted on a capstan before the bridge.

'We were aground for twenty-eight hours before we managed to pull free. I have spent the rest of the time trying to find the channel.'

This was Mbewe, of course, and he wasn't killed, though he would have to be careful now the Portuguese were in control.

Not only the battle, but the whole campaign was decided.

39 Shire

Exactly one month later, all the Kololo chiefs travelled to Chiromo to sign a treaty pledging their allegiance to Portugal. Chitaonga was there, along with his brother Chikusi. Mlauri was there, along with Mulilima, Masea and Katunga, whom he regarded as his own subjects, but who were now even less inclined to accept his authority. Even Mwita, who lived close to my first cataracts and who had never joined the war, made his mark. Despite his youth, *Muzungo Nkulu* received them graciously. Captain Brito and Engineer Álvaro, now fully recovered from his fever, acted as witnesses.

Meanwhile, *Muzungo Nkulu* celebrated his second victory, opening the last two tins of *Sutherland Brand J & A Carpenter* corned beef, and drinking bottles of Kopke port, as I saw from the labels when the *azungu* threw the empty cans and bottles in my river. He named his victory after something he called the Feast of the Immaculate Conception.

The missionaries always bewildered me. Their god was sometimes a book, sometimes a person beyond the book, sometimes three persons in one and one in three. Having myself been a god, or revered as a god, I thought their god was too complicated to be of any use, a bit like the riddle of the treaties, signing a paper saying they would not sign any paper. Gods should do useful things, like Mbona bringing the rains or forcing invaders to respect the ancestors. This Immaculate Conception was another mystery. God was a father who had a mother who had been impregnated without a husband. She was impregnated by god before god was born. Why had they come from Europe to tell us these things? Anyway, that's what the Portuguese celebrated with their Sutherland Brand beef and Kopke wine, which was much sweeter than the Courvoissier that had burned my stream.

Next morning, fifty wounded men were sent in the *Maravi* back to Chiromo, along with Captain Brito, whose heart was troubling him. Engineer Álvaro was ordered to fortify Mitengo, while *Muzungo Nkulu* led the Landeens in a raiding party to Mount Thyolo, where Mlauri had taken refuge after his defeat at Mpassu. The villages there were deserted, but he burned them anyway, and then headed back to my river, north of Dambinyi. Here, in quick succession, he defeated Masea, Mulilima and Katunga, crossing the river several times using large canoes the fleeing fishermen had abandoned. Masea presented him with an ivory tusk as a sign of vassalage. The land was his. The Portuguese flag was hoisted at Katunga's, and the *Maravi* brought up Lieutenant Afonso, along with the Armstrong and twenty of the Sena men, to establish a small fort on a bluff on my right bank. *Muzungo Nkulu* himself returned in the *Maravi* to Chiromo, to compile his reports on the campaign and celebrate Christmas.

Meanwhile, the Kololo chiefs had retreated past my first cataracts to a wide gorge where my river formed three large islands at a place called Mpatamanga. Chitaonga arrived there, along with Katunga, Masea and Mulilima, their elders and warriors. There they were well beyond the reach of the steamers with their terrible guns, and they were confident they could ambush any Portuguese advance on foot. Mlauri joined them, having been expelled from Thyolo Mountain, and having effectively nowhere else to go. His doing so was recognised as a renunciation of any claim to be Paramount. There, on the second of the islands, they held another *mirandu* to discuss their options.

Except for the high waterfall at Matope, there is nowhere in my whole course where my stream runs faster than when it past those islands at Mpatamanga. It wasn't easy for me to reflect what the chiefs were saying. This time, no outsiders were present, no Mr Consul or Mr Acting-Consul, so no need for interpreters. Mphetomwanyama was present as Ramakukan's former messenger. Even after the paramount chief's death, he had retained much of his influence. Mbewe was still in hiding after his adventure with the *Maravi*. In any case, if the chiefs were planning to follow Masea's example, he didn't want to be handed over as a token of their good will. In their eyes, and his own, he was still a slave.

Chitaonga was conciliatory. It no longer mattered who was paramount, neither he nor Mlauri nor Kasisi. The land had new rulers. What mattered was to be allowed to return to their villages.

'Do I speak truly?', he asked, following the custom.

'You speak truly,' the chiefs agreed.

But it was not so simple.

Kasisi raised the first problem.

'Mr Acting Consul said the English would protect them. But he also said he would have to ask the Queen if she wanted the country. Was she drunk this time with whisky? Or was she too far away to give her answer quickly?'

Mphetomwanyama grunted in agreement, but made no comment. It was obvious what he was thinking. There were those papers everyone had signed. Even Masea, whose ancestors would not let him hold a pen, had allowed Mr Acting Consul to make his mark and afterwards sign that it was his mark.

They had all signed that they would not sign any other paper. It had seemed like a riddle, but now the riddle had come to life. This was a matter of words on paper. Words spoken can be withdrawn, but words on paper are for ever. If they signed the Portuguese papers, would happen to their first words? Would the English be angry? Would they end up with two enemies, Portuguese and English?

Again, Mphetomwanyama grunted. As Paramount Chief Ramakukan's messenger, he had spoken with the Queen's messenger. He understood all the diplomacy. But he also understood the real problem lay elsewhere.

Mulilima put it into words.

'Who will keep the people down?'

The Kololo had settled in the valley and made themselves chiefs by the power of their guns. Now they had been defeated, there were bigger guns in the land. Would the Manganja continue to respect them as chiefs? Or would the people laugh, pointing to the Portuguese as their new rulers?

The English had respected them. When they signed the papers, they had done so as chiefs recognised by the English. But the papers had not protected them. All of them understood that Masea's action in offering ivory had been an act of submission. But it had also secured his own position, because in accepting the ivory *Muzungu Nkulu* had recognised him as chief. Could the rest do the same? Even Mlauri, who had launched the attack on Mpassu? Or Chitaonga, who had attacked *Muzungu Nkulu* in Dambinyi and almost defeated him?

If they signed the Portuguese papers, would they be safe? From the Portuguese? From the English? From the Manganja?

'Yes,' said Mphetomwanyama firmly.

He had their attention.

'The *azungu* have a strange proverb, *the pen is mightier than the sword*. We know it is not true. We tried signing papers and it didn't stop the big guns coming. But for the Portuguese fighting the English, it may be true. They need your marks on their papers to help them win their own war. When you sign, it will mean they recognise you.'

So the chiefs and elders and warriors travelled back to Chiromo to pledge their allegiance to Portugal. They said they had always considered themselves Portuguese. It was the Governor of Tete who first allowed them to settle along my banks, after Living Stone failed in his promise to return them to their home country. Serpa Pinto was still absent at the coast, but *Muzungo Nkulu* received them graciously. He was their father, and he would always treat them as a father should.

After the ceremony, Álvaro wandered to my bank and among the reeds I heard him chanting:

> I salute you, broad and deep river
> reflecting the profound blue of the sky
> in your bosom of limpid silver.
> You have been for us the road of discovery.
> I hail you, conquered frontier,
>   O most Portuguese Shire.

40 Shire

Then suddenly, the English Queen awoke from her drunken sleep. Álvaro was the first to hear of it, when an open telegram was delivered to *Muzungu Nkulu* at Mpassu. Álvaro assumed that a telegram sent uncoded would contain congratulations, perhaps even a promotion, and couldn't believe what he was reading.

'Withdraw immediately from all positions north of the confluence of the River Shire and the River Ruo. Signed, Major Serpa Pinto.'

Muzungu Nkulu couldn't believe it either.

'Has the Major gone mad? Is he out of magnesia?'

He sent a reply asking for clarification of his instructions, signing himself as Military Governor of Chire.

While he was waiting for an answer, Lieutenant Afonso was visited by Mr Acting Consul in the fort at Katunga's. He couldn't believe his ears. The English Queen had issued an ultimatum. Unless he withdrew his platoon, there would be war. Not on the banks of the Shire, but in Europe.

Convinced this was a bluff, Afonso took the precaution of sending a messenger to Mpassu.

'You have little time,' warned Mr Acting Consul.

'I will await orders.'

While he did so, incredible rumours were reaching him. Traders were still passing up and down the Shire, unloading their goods at Katunga's to be carried up the escarpment to Mandala. Indians, Jews and the odd German all told the same story. Ships from the English anti-slavery patrol in the Indian Ocean had been ordered to stand off Mozambique Island, Quelimane and Lourenço Marques. Battleships from the Mediterranean fleet had been dispatched to Gibraltar, ready to sail for Lisbon. The rumours were so wild, they began to impress him, yet when he left his desk and walked down to the bluff overlooking the river, they seemed absurd.

I'm a river. I mirror what's happening around me. I can't say what people are thinking. Sometimes, I can understand. When a girl pauses on my beach as she fills her water pot to admire her reflection, I think I know what is going through her mind, even when I want to warn her, be careful, there are crocodiles. When a fishermen is standing in his canoe, spear in hand, waiting as patiently as a heron for the moment to stab, I can read his thoughts. But most times, especially when it concerns the *azungu*, I'm out of my depth. Even when they're speaking, I find what they say hard to understand, though I've come to share their languages. Álvaro's chants, for example, addressed directly to me. What was he saying, beyond the fact that I belonged to him?

So when young Afonso was standing on the bluff that morning, after hearing the rumours of war, I could only guess at his thoughts. Something about his pensiveness reminded of the lady I told you about, reading from her diary about the heat and stillness, about the dugout canoes on the sandy beach and the baobabs looking as though they had been planted upside down. She described the purple water hyacinths, and the red-legged waders splashing from one leaf-palette to the next. Her voice was gentle and melodious and made me see myself differently.

Afonso was staring at a point where my banks are far apart and my current deep and swift, but my surface is so smooth and radiant that only the odd bit of debris reveals how fast I'm moving. On the beach below him, some women were washing flour they had just pounded, to separate out the chaff. Others on both banks were weeding the sorghum, millet and pumpkins they had planted the month before. In Katunga's, the little girls were playing at *matenje*, or home-making, some already carrying their infant brothers or sisters on their backs, tending fires with pots of beans and *nsima* they would shortly carry to their mothers in their allotments. Did he wonder whether all this was worth fighting over, with English gunboats threatening to bombard Lisbon?

I saw him lift his gaze to stare further down my stream. There were the usual fishermen, some twirling nets weighted with stones from their canoes, others wading in inlets to check their *mamono*, or fish traps. There were baobabs and acacia trees and tall borrasus palms and, in the distance, indicated by the vast sky over a wasteland, the beginnings of Dambinyi marsh. Was he thinking of the terrible battle in the reeds? Or the accident with the wheel of the Armstrong that killed his friend Zé Miguel? Once again, had that been worth it? I can only reflect what he did. I can't guess at his thoughts.

He was interrupted by one of the Sena men bringing a sealed order. It was from *Muzungu Nkulu*. He was to vacate Katunga's immediately, travelling with his men by canoe if no steamer was available, and abandoning the Armstrong. The evacuation was that urgent.

He couldn't just leave the gun behind. He had it dismantled and, helped by six men, carried the separate parts one by one to the bluff overlooking my stream. First the carriage was tipped into my depths, then the barrel, then the innocent wheel, and finally the wheel that had killed Zé Miguel. Their weight made them sink immediately, and within half an hour my silt had covered them.

Embarking his men in three hired canoes, he returned to the fort, lowered the Portuguese flag and personally axed the flagpole. No English flag was going to fly on that mast. Wrapping the flag round his shoulders, and taking with him only his rifle and revolver, he commandeered one of the smaller fishing canoes and let my current bear him along, with the merest touch of a paddle

The first few miles were straightforward, but as he entered Dambinyi he was very quickly lost. It seemed he intended to pass Mitengo and stop at the creek where Zé Miguel had died. But he could recognise nothing about the banks of reeds and papyrus. Once, he thought he had located the place where the tragedy occurred, and pulled up to the mudflat, scrambling ashore. But he couldn't locate his friend's grave. Either the place was wrong, or the grave with the simple cross had been washed away or trampled by hippos.

Returning to the canoe, he allowed it to drift into the stream and, crossing himself, adjusted the Portuguese flag round his shoulders. Then he placed his revolver in his mouth, and pulled the trigger. A hundred yards downstream, swirling without control in my current, the canoe hit a submerged log, tipping Afonso's body into the marsh he so much detested.

I covered him quickly, to protect him from the crocodiles.

Afterword

Now he was no longer a slave, Mbewe's options had narrowed. The British had taken over, so being the son of Chipatula's slave wife no longer mattered. What he knew best was the River Shire, especially the difficult parts like Ndindi and Dambinyi. But, precisely because of those difficulties, the British were already talking about building something called a railway. There was a sort of steamer than ran on land, on iron rails laid on the earth. If they managed to make this happen, the river steamers would become obsolete, and he along with them. Pilots would still be needed on the Zambezi, but after his adventure with the *Maravi*, Mbewe was wary of dealing with the Portuguese. Someone might recognise him.

He had learned to read and write at the Blantyre Mission. But so had dozens like himself, and there were not enough jobs as clerks to go around. He could have become a teacher, or even a *catequist*. But that involved believing the strange things the missionaries believed—a god who was three gods and at the same time one, a god who had fathered himself with the help of a woman who was intact. Worse still, he would be drinking god's blood at their services. No, he couldn't tell Masamanga he had come to do such things.

Lorenzo was released from the jail in Quelimane just three months after the Ultimatum. The Portuguese called it a gesture of good will, but Dr Rato, his lawyer, was confident the case wouldn't have stood up anyway.

It impressed him that Lorenzo, who was old enough to be his father, had fallen on his feet. He had become field manager for the *Zé Miguel Sugar Company*, based in Prazo Maindo.

'Exporting arms from the country?' he said. 'Where's the law against that?'

He had returned to the small estate where he was already growing sugar. Under his wife Luiza's supervision, the labourers had planted another field of cane, together with crops of maize and sesame. But he had lost two years, and had

257

also lost the chance of getting a good deal on the *John Bowie's* engine. Learning from Dr Rato that Lorenzo had been freed, Tony St Claire got in touch. It was his late father-in-law, *Senhor* Augusto, who'd given Lorenzo his first cane for planting. Now Mr St Claire offered him a job in the new sugar company he was starting. He would also pay him for the cane he was growing on his own account.

'Mr St Claire?' said Mbewe.

He racked his brains. Then he remembered the young man who had had laughed when Mphetomwanyama insisted on speaking directly with Mr Consul..

'This is worse than the Portuguese,' Mr St Claire had said.

'I didn't realise he was such a rich man.'

'That the cleverest part,' said Lorenzo. 'He turn Catholic to marry the madam, and he mek the Portuguese pay for everything. After the war finish, he sailed to Lisbon and get the *Companhia de Açucar Zé Miguel* on the stock market. He appeal to they patriotism and raise thousands of *reis*. The Portuguese feel so bad about what the English do to them, they flock to finance this 'colonial venture'. Small investors, but hundreds. You ain't reckon that' smart?'

'Didn't they know he was English?'

Lorenzo laughed appreciatively.

'He meet up with a old friend of Zé Miguel's. A big man in the Republican Party. You know they against the monarchy? They already try to kill King Carlos. Anyway, this Alfredo de Sá Costa is a college friend of Zé Miguel and he agree to chair the Lisbon board and put he name to the prospectus. For the Portuguese, is a matter of national pride.'

'But who is this Zé Miguel?'

'Ah, that the sad part. Zé is the brother-in-law. He get killed with the Portuguese on the Shire. Actually, he drown when the self-same gun they jail me for smuggling fall on him in the swamp.'

'Where was this?'

'I ain't know exactly. Somewhere near Mitengo. One of the wheels slip into a creek. He drown underneath before they could lift it.'

Lorenzo sighed.

'I still ain't tell the madam this. It go have to stay secret.'

There were in Lorenzo's office, which was a bit like Chemandala's office and, indeed, Lorenzo was sitting behind a desk, his brightly polished boots protruding. Maps of the cane fields were pinned to the walls, with charts showing planting schedules.

'Is this all your work?'

'No, no, I only take over four months back. I just bring a little order to the place.'

Suddenly, Mbewe was startled by a shrill ringing. It came from a black box on the wall, that looked at first like some kind of skull, with two eyes, a round nose, and a huge knob by way of mouth. It was the eyes that were ringing, and he watched in wonder as Lorenzo picked up a pestle dangling to the left, and wound a handle on the right several times.

Then he held the pestle to his mouth, said 'Yes, boss?', and put it to his ear. Mbewe could hear a tinny kind of speech.

'It already in hand, boss,' said Lorenzo once again to the pestle. 'It go be finish by this evening.'

He listened a second time, then repeated 'Yes, boss,' and hung the pestle on the side of the box.

'You ain't see one of these?', he grinned. 'Is a new kind of telegraph. But with real talk.'

'You were speaking with a real person?'

'That Mr St Claire. He want some planting schedules for a meeting tomorrow.'

Mbewe was astounded.

'But where is he?'

'He calling from he house. Next the coconut plantation.'

In his dealings with the *azungu*, Mbewe had always assumed they were not particularly intelligent. Perhaps clever in their own world, but not in his. Their religion of the book was very strange, not something the ancestors recognised, and they didn't know how to make rain. They didn't understand much about trade, about the need to deal in what the customers wanted. Their river steamers made a lot of noise but, for carrying goods and people on the Shire, canoes were far more efficient. How many hours had he waited for firewood to be cut, while traders like Sacur and Selemane paddled half a day faster than the *Lady Nyassa*? Their attempts at agriculture took no account of the need to protect the soil. Ploughing, for example, turning the soil a foot deep. Didn't they know the November winds would dry it out and blow away the topsoil?

He had to admit the *azungu's* guns were frightening. That they could impose themselves was a new fact of life. But his people had accepted new rulers before, who eventually had to come to terms with the real owners of the land. It was true he had learned reading and writing, but that hadn't benefitted him much. He could have gone on to do something like Lorenzo's job, or at least become one of the clerks. But there weren't many such jobs, and all the best ones seemed to be Portuguese side, where he wasn't safe.

But this talking machine was something beyond knowledge. If the *azungu* could throw their voices down a wire, what else might be in store? It impressed him Lorenzo had already got used to using it. He remembered that his friend had already studied the *azungu* at home in England. He had travelled on this railway. It was not something they had ever talked about.

'I've been wondering what to do when this railway comes,' said Mbewe, as though he was fully on top of the subject.

They were walking back to the river that marked the *prazo's* boundary, where Mbewe had left his canoe. It was late afternoon and the sun was low as they left the office, crossing a wide garden surrounded by eight houses, with candle flies beginning to signal from the bushes. Lorenzo pointed out one of them as his new home. But Mbewe was preoccupied. He paid little attention as Lorenzo showed him the site for the new sugar factory, and the foundations of the future engine shed with its railway lines already pointing to the cane fields. Everything looked very new, except for a large brick house with a thatched roof.

'This Sr Augusto's experimental farm. Is where I come to collect the sugar cane he give me for planting.'

They passed between small fields divided by irrigation ditches, with small patches of tea, cotton and coffee.

'You go get a work here easy,' said Lorenzo. 'You know Mr St Claire from longtime.'

Mbewe didn't hesitate.

'I don't want to call him boss. I want to go on being as free as when I was a slave.'

Lorenzo turned to him, laughing.

'Don't worry, he ain't my boss. He need me more than I need him. But you need to learn some Jamaican sweet-talk. It go keep you on top when they think you down.'

'But tell me,' he continued, walking ahead, 'when you first start being paid, that money you get from piloting on the river. What you do with it?'

Mbewe counted on his fingers.

'First, I paid bridewealth for Masamanga. Not a slave wife, a proper marriage. Then I bought three hoes from the Indians, strong iron hoes made in Sheffield. Then I bought a canoe for fishing. Finally, I bought a slave.'

'You have a slave?'

'I am responsible for his life. I protect him, I feed him, I give him a wife. He helps Masamanga in the fields, and he catches fish for me. He was an orphan and now I am his family.'

Lorenzo nodded and sighed deeply.

'Is exactly what Mr St Claire say. I tell him I don't like our labourers not getting pay.'

He had no need to explain. Mbewe knew the arrangement. The Portuguese had imposed a poll tax on everyone, men and women, in their new colony and, since nobody had any money, they had to find an employer who would pay the tax on their behalf. Mr St Claire's field workers did a month's clearing and hoeing and ditch digging, and he paid the poll tax for them and their wives.

'Is a beginning,' he tell me. 'If I pay extra, they only go use the money to buy slaves. Better will come.'

'Do you believe him?'

'Everything he done say so far prove true. But, no, I ain't believe him. This a colony, and it go be another Jamaica. Is the logic of colonies. He ain't able to stop it.'

Following the stream which was no more than two yards wide they passed a compound built along a wide curve, ending in a swamp where the labourers could plant their own gardens with maize, pigeon pea, sweet potato and casava—that is, Lorenzo explained, if they chose to work for longer than a month. Beside the track, some women were selling baskets of fish that had been trapped in the stream or captured in the wetter parts of the swamp.

'Dr Laws have the colony he want,' said Lorenzo. 'It ain't never my intention to play any part in that, but I find is so. Helping him stamp the Union Jack in the sand!'

'Maybe he was just homesick,' said Mbewe. 'All the Scotsmen, even Chemandala, were forever talking about Scotland.'

'No, right from the start he have plans. And my plans, about abolishing slavery and the slave trade, ain't fit with his. Slavery always my cause. That why I join the Bishop, that why I join Captain Young, that why I come back to work for the Company.'

'It seems to me,' said Mbewe gently, 'that you had plans for us, just like the rest.'

'So you mek me understand,' admitted Lorenzo, 'that day you show me to play the *mbira*. The day we become friends. I explain all that in the book I done write. But these colonies go be new Jamaicas. Portuguese Jamaica this side, English Jamaica that side. In fact, better than Jamaica. The slaves already here. It not necessary to pack them like sardines across the Atlantic.'

Mbewe was reminded of Selemane's prediction.

'You know what they already calling your country? British Central Africa! British Africa! How could there be such a place? Down here is Portuguese East! There is a Portuguese West the other side. Between them is Southern Zambezia, under Cecil Rhodes. What the British done with their machine guns even worse than the Portuguese do at Chiromo. It mek my heart sick.'

Lorenzo had travelled, Mbewe reflected, and he knew more about these colonies that were coming. The English hadn't yet imposed any taxes. But what was the point of ruling if you didn't collect tribute? The thousands of people running away from Portuguese East, as Lorenzo called it, to avoid paying the poll tax, would not be safe for very long. The English planters were already making them work for the right to settle on their new estates. To build a hut on the master's land, you had to work for him for free.

'That is the English through and through,' Lorenzo scoffed, when Mbewe told him of this. 'They abolish slavery, so they could mek us serfs.'

Mbwew stopped by one of the women's baskets.

'I don't know this fish,' he said.

It was a long pink fish with bulging eyes and a serrated mouth.

'Is sweet-sweet,' said Lorenzo. 'Only with too many bones. It call *ncheni*. You only find it down here near the delta. They catch it in they bamboo traps.'

They both paused and stared at each other. It wasn't clear which of them had the idea first, but it was Lorenzo who spoke.

'The English eat fish,' he said. 'They cook it with them potato fries.'

'There are so many fish in Dambanyi,' said Mbewe. '*Chambo, mlamba, dowe, ncheni, usipa, kapenta*, so many types of *nsomba*. I know where to lay the traps, I know how to spin the nets, I can fish with spears, and I know how to dry them with salt or smoke them.'

'No, no,' said Lorenzo, 'the *azungu* need they fish fresh. But if the railway come, that no problem.'

'They are building a new *boma* next to Mandala, including a market for vegetables. Masamanga could have a stall there.'

'Is as Selemane tell us,' concluded Lorenzo. 'You go be doing what in you blood. Is the only way we go best them.'

www.ingramcontent.com/pod-product-compliance
Lightning Source LLC
Chambersburg PA
CBHW061955170626
46813CB00006B/2645